# SLOW TANGO IN TAOS

## A Journey of Self-Discovery

By

**PHIL CLINE**

# Phil Cline

Published in the USA by Amazon Digital Services, LLC - KDP.

410 Terry Avenue

North Seattle, WA 98109-5210

Library of Congress Control Number: 2022901623

Soft Cover - ISBN: 9798771787954

Hard Cover - ISBN: 9798771919607

Note: *Any similarity in this novel to real persons living or dead is purely coincidental.*

Copyright © 2021 Phillip A. Cline

All rights reserved. No part of this book or any portion thereof may be reproduced or used in any manner whatsoever without the express written permission of the author, except for the use of brief quotations in a book review or scholarly journal. [*For more information, contact*: *Phil Cline,* pac@pacline.net; (918) 254-6614.]

## Acknowledgements

This book is dedicated to my parents. My dad often used an expression which I incorporated in this book: *Everyone has a story to tell and you can learn if you'll only listen.*

I want to thank Jean-luc for his insights and editorial help; to Steve and his writers' group for their useful suggestions, to Véronique, Richard, Eric and many others for their helpful comments. Creating a book truly does take a village.

Phil Cline

# SLOW TANGO IN TAOS

# CHAPTER ONE

JOHN TOLLIFSON tried to forget the tragic day the Guillotine ended his walk of life. Sitting on a granite ledge high on Taos Mountain, he took a deep breath of crisp morning air, leaned forward, and studied the Sangre de Cristo Mountains that stretched into the distance as far as his eyes could see.

An athletic middle-aged man with salt and pepper hair, he attempted to capture on paper the majesty of the mountains. As he sketched, a low hum vibrated the ground under him that legend says comes from a powerful spirit located in the heart of Taos Mountain. People from the Taos Pueblo say the spirit protects the mountain and Blue Lake in the sacred valley below. John didn't mind the tremor. To him, it was the presence of just another spirit.

He examined his sketch with light from the morning sun as it peeked over a distant range. His brow wrinkled. The beauty and spirituality of the mountains had once more evaded him. He tore the paper from his sketchpad, folded it, and stuck it into an upper pocket of his tattered jacket.

A tinge of excitement ran through him as he absorbed the natural beauty of his surroundings. With his senses fully alive, he took another deep breath of fresh morning air, and slowly exhaled. He smiled and his eyes sparkled with knowledge that he had found peace within himself and the new world he had grown to love. Then, his thoughts flew to a former time when his life had been very different.

* * *

A typical Chicago morning awaited John as he kissed his wife, Wilma, goodbye and tossed the morning newspaper into the passenger seat of his sleek new metallic red 450SL Mercedes. A streak of excitement ran through him as he slid his slender six-foot two-inch frame under the steering wheel. He delighted in the smell of new leather. The interior smacked of success. He glanced at the headline of the newspaper lying on the seat: *Nixon Resigns!*

"Damn!" He said in a muffled voice.

He adjusted the mirror, and pushed his prematurely grey hair to one side. A quick glance in the mirror showed a man much younger than his thirty-some years owing to his high cheekbones and boyish good looks. John left his large Tudor-style lake front home that morning and drove past other large imposing mansions with massive ornate gates, long tree-lined driveways and manicured lawns.

*Only successful people live in my neighborhood*, he thought, as he took a deep breath of fresh morning air and

## SLOW TANGO IN TAOS

savored his accomplishments: An MBA at University of Chicago's Business School, a short stint as a trainee at Continental Illinois, then on to Cyrox. A fast move up. Marketing Analyst, then Manager and now the executive-suite.

As he waited at a stoplight, a man with a sign asking for money stood by the side of the road. John glared at him, and lowered his passenger window. "Get a job, you bum!" he sneered, and drove off. *I can't stand losers*, he mumbled.

He smiled with deep satisfaction as he pulled into the parking-lot of the Cyrox Corporation, and stopped in front of a sign symbolizing his status: *Vice President*. He took one last whiff of new leather in his Mercedes, entered the building, and pushed the button for the twelfth floor. The smell of coffee from a cup on his secretary's desk wafted across the room as he entered. She greeted him with a smile.

"Mister Stevens wants to see you."

"Oh? When did he come by?" John asked.

"A few minutes ago. He left a message on your desk."

"Thanks." John set his briefcase next to an imposing dark oak desk, picked up a yellow slip of paper near his telephone, and read: *John, I'd like to talk to you at your convenience. T.S.*

Art objects in the room offered a statement of status to anyone entering his office. A Persian rug lay on the floor in front of his desk. Art by well-known artists hung on the walls. A Salvador Dali lithograph from the Historical Origin Series, and a serigraph by LeRoy Neiman entitled Bass Man.

## Phil Cline

Behind his desk hung John's favorite painting by Neiman, an oil titled A Day at The Races, A Night at The Opera. The art gave his office an ambience of culture, if only of a popular sort. He enjoyed art and the thrill of being around artists. He checked his schedule before leaving his office, then walked to the bank of elevators.

A quick ride up the executive elevator and John stepped out into the Board Room on the top floor. He went to the Chairman's large glass-lined office, and paused at the entrance before tapping on the glass.

"Come in," Stevens waved. "Have a chair."

Stevens, a short balding man with his remaining grey hair combed back over the top of his head to hide his shinny scalp, possessed a ruddy smile and shifty eyes. Behind him rested a gold framed picture of himself from his football days at Notre Dame where he had developed a successful play known as Quickie 44. It became an efficient play still used to this day and was one reason for his being hired by the sports loving board at Cyrox.

Brenda Walker, a tall brunette in a tight beige dress and a stand of grey pearls around her neck with matching earrings, sat to the left of Stevens. That morning, she was stone-faced.

John sat down in a leather chair in front of Steven's desk and straightened his tie.

"You know Brenda, head of Personnel"

"Yes. Of course." John's brow wrinkled. *Why is she in our meeting?*

# SLOW TANGO IN TAOS

John glanced at Brenda and smiled, but she seemed restrained.

"John, we have bad news," Stevens said.

John stiffened in his chair, his pulse quickened.

"The Board reviewed our projected revenues over the next couple of years. In light of what is going on..." Stevens paused and looked at Brenda.

"Like what's going on?" John's eyes shifted to Stevens.

"You know...the oil embargo...the economy." Stevens and Brenda exchanged sharp glances.

"The Board has recommended that we cut staff."

Blood seemed to drain from John's head. "What does that mean?" John asked.

"We're eliminating your division," Stevens said.

"My division!" John exclaimed. "What the f---?"

"John, we have to let you go...for the survival of the company."

"What?" Blood raced to his head, his face flushed. Panic raced through his body. "You can't do that!" His heart pounded.

"John, your division sales are down...revenue has fallen off a cliff. The Saudi oil embargo is sending the economy into a recession. Analysts are predicting the worst depression since the nineteen thirties. Our analysts say the consumer electronics division will be a drain on our resources for the foreseeable future."

"But-" John protested.

"I'm sorry, but a business can't be run in the red. The Board voted and that's the way it is!"

"I've been a loyal employee; doesn't that mean anything?" John's pulse raced.

"John, until recently, your division did very well…but that no longer matters. That's all in the past. The Chinese are killing us. The Saudi's are killing us. Electronics manufacturing is not coming back to this country."

"I turned around a losing division and made it profitable. I can do it again! Put me in charge of another division."

"There's no place we can use you. Maybe in the future…"

*That's not helping me now!* Came a deep resonate cry from the depths of his being.

"Look, if it were up to me, I'd keep you, but….well, the Board empowered me to carry out their recommendation. There isn't any more I can do."

John's head throbbed. His face flushed. Anger ran through his brain like a raging bull. Shock bludgeoned him with disbelief. After a moment of reflection and terror, he spoke.

"What about, my family? I have mortgage payments on my house, on my cars, club dues. My daughter Jennie is going to Smith next year!" John's eyes narrowed to a slit as anger shot through him. He stood and pounded the desk. "This is crazy! You can't do this to me! I'm too valuable! What the hell! You're letting me go – just like that? After all

## SLOW TANGO IN TAOS

I've done for this company!" John shouted.

"Calm down! You're still a young man. You'll land on your feet." Steven said, undisturbed.

*I Can't believe this is happening!* John glared, but restrained himself from grabbing Stevens by his tie and choking him.

"Settle down!" Brenda said. Her deep husky voice echoed in John's head. "We have an outplacement clinic you can use, and we're giving you three months of severance pay. That should help until you locate a suitable position."

John glanced at Brenda. She had a wide mouth that curled into the same self-satisfied smirk he had seen just a week earlier when he dropped by her office.

"Anyway," Stevens said, extending his hand.

John stared at the hand looming in front of him as though it were a snake ready to strike. Stevens withdrew his hand. "It's been a pleasure having you on my staff. Brenda will accompany you to your office. Keep in touch."

"That's it! Just like that, I'm fired? After all the years I've put into this company!" John said, his eyes glaring at Stevens as he fought to control his impulse to attack and destroy the person in front of him.

"Yes! Sorry, but that's the way it has to be. Brenda will show you out."

A wave of panic seized John as he left with Brenda. It all seemed so unreal. He had been loyal and hard working. All the hours of work he had put into increasing sales, increasing revenues, creating excellent marketing teams.

# Phil Cline

And for what! To be laid off? Blood pounded in his head as though it would burst through his skull. Nothing seemed normal, not the room, not the people, nothing. Anger welled up in him at the thought of being let go.

"You can put your things in this." Brenda handed John a large cardboard box.

He sat down in his leather chair. His heart raced. Shock and panic attacked him like a savage beast. *Why!* came an unspoken scream from the depths of his being. Why was this happening?

A buzzer sounded and a light at the base of the telephone lit up. He pushed the intercom button. The voice of his secretary came through the speaker.

"Mister Jennings is on the line. Do you want to speak with him?" she asked.

"No," Brenda interrupted. "Refer all future calls for Mr. Tollifson to my office."

John glanced up. Brenda's smirk widened into a cruel sadistic smile like that of a predator toying with its prey.

"Mister Tollifson is not taking any more calls?" the secretary asked.

"I'm taking the day off," John replied, a crack in his voice.

"Also," his secretary said, "your wife called. Said she has a beauty appointment, and will be home later."

"If she calls again, tell her… tell her I'll see her tonight." John flipped off the intercom, crumpled the piece of paper containing Steven's message, and threw it into the

## SLOW TANGO IN TAOS

trash. The Chairman's words rang in his head like an echo chamber: *I'm sorry, but a business can't be run in the red.*

John placed the contents of his desk into the box. He picked up an at-a-boy coin he had received when he first started at the company. He placed it in the box along with a birthday card he received from a friend, a gold fountain pen he had received for a profitable year, and other items from his years with the company. He paused to examine each item. John glanced up at Brenda. She perched over him like a vulture scrutinizing everything he put into the box.

"I can't carry my paintings, the rug, or the other items home today," John said.

"We'll box them up. They'll be waiting for you tomorrow downstairs behind the security guard's desk."

He finished cleaning out his desk and putting the items into the box. Then, he closed his briefcase and cast a final glance around his office before leaving. He headed for the executive elevator, but Brenda stopped him.

"We'll take the delivery elevator down to the parking lot," Brenda instructed.

*Fine! What next? The freight elevator?*

The elevator ride down to the parking lot was quiet and efficient.

"Have a nice day," Brenda said when they reached the ground floor. John grimaced and stepped out onto the loading dock. As he walked down a metal stairway leading to the parking lot, he paused to look back at Brenda, but caught only a glimpse as she disappeared behind the closing elevator doors. He put the box in the trunk of his car and drove away.

John's head throbbed as he drove into the parking lot of the Oakdale Country Club. He got out of his Mercedes and walked past a colonial style portico at the entrance. Inside was a long leather bar and a much-needed drink. John sat down on a stool at the ornate brass and quartz bar. He took a deep breath and looked around at the mostly empty room before turning to the bartender.

"Scotch," John ordered. "On the rocks."

"What's your number?" asked the bartender.

"C-47," John replied.

The bartender scrolled through a rolodex before stopping at one of the cards.

"John Tollifson?" the bartender asked.

"That's right."

"Your number is no longer valid. I got a call from Brenda in Personnel. Says you no longer work for Cyrox. I'm sorry, but I can't serve you a drink."

"What?" John exclaimed with disbelief, "I always have a drink here!"

"This club is for employees only."

"I can't even have a drink?"

"Sorry. I would make you a drink if I could, but I didn't make the rules. You should leave."

John shook his head in disbelief as he left.

*A dog would get better treatment than this!*

Later, when John returned home, he entered to find

## SLOW TANGO IN TAOS

his wife handing a check to a maid. "Thank you," the maid said as she left by the side door.

"Is that you, John?" Wilma stood in the wide arched kitchen doorway. Behind her in the kitchen was an arrangement of oak cabinets and quartz counter tops of a very upscale kitchen.

"Yes, dear." John tossed his briefcase onto a chair.

A red silk dress clung to Wilma's tall slender frame. A long strand of cultured pearls hung around her neck. She flipped her long blond hair to one side. She appeared to be the perfect trophy wife for a successful executive.

"Are you ready?" She asked.

"For what?"

"Honestly! We're going to the McFarlin party!"

"Sorry, I forgot," John replied. "I've had other things on my mind."

"Really! I don't know what I'm going to do with you. You're getting more absentminded every day!"

John struggled to force the words out of his mouth, to tell her what had happened: "Wilma, there's something I need to tell you--"

"What?"

John took a deep breath and rubbed the back of his neck. He looked at Wilma who stood with arms akimbo, frowning.

"I'd rather not go, dear," he said. "I'm not in the mood."

"We're supposed to be there in an hour. Now get

ready!" She snapped. Reluctantly, he turned and trudged up the staircase, but paused midway.

"Suit or Tuxedo?" he asked.

"Honestly!" She yelled, "sometimes I wonder about your upbringing. You know this is a formal affair. Wear a tux and that light pink ruffled shirt, the one I bought you last week."

John undressed and showered. The warm refreshing water seemed to wash away some of the Chairman's haunting words.

"Hurry up, haven't got all day!" Wilma pounded on the door.

John wrapped a towel around himself. He picked out a tuxedo, dressed and walked down the dark oak staircase. Wilma met him in the foyer.

"Look what I bought!" she exclaimed with a broad smile.

John's stomach tightened as he saw what she had purchased.

"Saks had a special today. This is what I've always wanted? Well, voila!"

"You didn't! A sable coat?"

"That's right!" She lovingly stroked the titanium colored fur as she turned to display the full-length coat. "It has a bateau neckline, elbow-length sleeves, side seam pockets, and silk lining. And, it's from Russia."

"How much?" John's whole body grew limp.

"Isn't it beautiful?"

## SLOW TANGO IN TAOS

"We can't afford the coat," John choked. "You need to take it back."

"Not on your life, buster! I'm wearing it to the party! Now move!"

Later that evening, they drove down a long tree-lined driveway that emptied into the parking lot of a large French-style home with stone turrets at both ends of the house. Two marble statues of ancient Greek athletes stood alongside a well-manicured lawn. He parked near a white marble fountain of a nymph with water pouring its mouth. They left the car and entered a house overflowing with guests. Music drifted from the main ballroom as John and Wilma navigated past a throng of people. John's attention shifted to a voice calling him from behind.

"Tollifson!"

John turned to see a rather athletic business associate approaching from the base of an ornately carved teak staircase. Recognizing the man, John extended his hand in friendship.

"Marc Newhouse!" John said.

"John, I've been wanting to speak with you. Heard some rumors." His words rang out as though he had shouted them through a megaphone.

"Wilma, go join the guests," John said. "I'll catch up with you later."

"Don't be long," She instructed.

Marc motioned for John to follow him outside. Once they were in the courtyard away from the hearing range of others, he stopped and turned.

"I heard what happened."

"What did you hear?" John asked defensively.

"News travels fast in our company. They don't call Stevens the Guillotine for nothing. He enjoys lopping off heads. Look, you and I have had our ups and downs. We've been in competition for jobs before. But, I have a soft spot for people who have been mistreated. What they did to you was unfair. If I can, I'd like to help."

"How could you help? The Guillotine fired me!"

"There are rumors that Stevens may retire soon. If he leaves, I should be on the short list. If I get the job and there's an opening, I'll let you know."

"I appreciate that," John said, relieved that he had at least one friend left in the company.

"This economy will eventually turn around and we'll be off and running again. Keep your chin up. Things will improve."

"Sure thing," John replied.

"Well, gotta go mix with the people," Marc said. "You know how important networking is. Keep in touch."

John walked to the far end of the courtyard where a marble fountain with three fish spewing water from their mouths stood near the entrance to a topiary garden. Inside the garden was a labyrinth of shrubs in a pattern that reminded him of Alice's garden in her wonderland adventures.

The shrubs were sculpted as a deck of cards: At the

## SLOW TANGO IN TAOS

four corners of the garden were the hearts, in the middle the spades, and at the edges the clubs. Circling the spades were a series of shrubs shaped as diamonds.

"Enjoying your evening?" Came a voice. John turned to see a tall silver-haired man of distinguished good looks.

"Mister McFarlin."

"Call me Sam," McFarlin replied, extending his hand.

"Congratulations on your son's appointment." John said.

"Thank you. He clerked at the Supreme Court up until last month when this offer came through."

"White-Weld-Smith is a fine law firm. He'll do well there," John replied.

"So," McFarlin said as he sipped from his drink, "how are things with you?"

A sudden lump came into John's throat. Those words seemed to have developed an emotion of their own. He coughed before answering. His words were labored.

"I'm fine, things are great," John replied, but wanted to change the conversation. "I noticed the unusual designs in your garden."

"Oh, that." he replied with a self-deprecating laugh.

"I'm in a somewhat dubious profession."

"Which is?"

"I prefer to say…I'm in the actuarial business."

"Insurance?"

"Not exactly. I'm a player of odds."

John snapped his fingers, "The four suits...I should have guessed. Poker!"

"Five card stud. I play no other game. I can make more in a single evening than most professionals in a year."

"Impressive," John replied. "Where do you play?"

McFarlin laughed, "You know the law, we play on yachts out on the lake away from the law. Other times in a private residence, usually I play with politically influential people. They love to gamble. Occasionally, I go out to Vegas, and--"

"You-hoo!" Came a voice.

McFarlin turned to see his wife waving to him. She was an attractive well-dressed middle-aged woman standing in an open doorway.

"Ops, my wife is signaling for me. Been pleasant. Enjoy your evening," McFarlin said as he walked away.

John sat on a wooden bench. He listened to crickets and the croaking of frogs from a nearby pond. He liked the cool refreshing air, but he wished he could be elsewhere.

A multitude of conversations drifted into the courtyard from the open doors of the house. Wilma's sultry voice would occasionally drift out to where John could hear her talking about that damn sable coat! How could he afford a sable coat when he was no longer employed? There was one piece of conversation he heard clearly: "Wilma, dear, you're so fortunate to have a husband like John. Why, my husband is so…" then, her voice was drowned out by the

## SLOW TANGO IN TAOS

clinking of glasses in a toast to honor the host's son.

John finished his drink and headed back into the party. He meandered through the guests until he found Wilma. He pointed to his watch, but she ignored him. Finally, John pulled her away from two admiring women fixated on Wilma's coat.

"Let's go," John demanded.

As they drove, Wilma shook her finger at John, "I hope you realize you embarrassed me! Those women were complimenting me on my wonderful husband. Little do they know what a complete…well I won't go there. I will say you created a very poor impression."

"I'm not worried about impressions," he replied.

"Well it's about time you did!"

John said nothing for a long time as they drove. Wilma sat silent with her arms crossed. Finally, John mustered his courage. "Wilma, there's something I need to tell you."

"What! That you ruined my evening?"

"No! Listen!" he commanded. "You remember when we talked about what would happen if I ever lost my job?"

Wilma's eyes widened before narrowing to slits.

"What are you saying?"

"I've been fired!"

"You lost your job?" she sneered.

"Yes," he said. "We can't afford that coat. It's got to go back."

"Oh, I beg your pardon! Did you see the way the

ladies complimented me? What do you think they'd say behind my back if I took it back? Why I'd be a laughing stock!"

"Wilma, we can't afford the coat!"

"You listen to me, mister," she scoffed, "if you want to economize, you can start by selling this car. I'm not about to part with this coat, and that's final!"

# CHAPTER 2

John sat at the kitchen table with a cup of coffee while perusing a newspaper. Next to him lay a page of want ads that he would eventually get to, but first, he wanted to enjoy the news of the day. Wilma sat across the table nursing a long icy silence. Then she spoke. "I can't take any more of this!"

He glanced up. Her piercing glare startled him.

"What do you mean?"

"You've been out of work more than ten months! People are starting to talk."

"Let them talk. Look, every day I study the want ads looking for work. I've called hundreds of companies, but they're not hiring right now. I've registered with seven different employment agencies. What more do you want?"

"Well, dear! You sold both our Mercedes. Now, that money is gone! It went into our mortgage payments, and your futile attempts to find work. We can't even afford to

## Phil Cline

take a cab. Am I supposed to take a bus? Do you have any idea how low my reputation has fallen? When my friends planned a party, I was always the first one they contacted. They always came to me for guidance. Now, they never call. I call them, and they politely put me off. And what have you been doing to help? I've got a failure for a husband!"

"I've been a winner all my life!" John retorted in defense. "Doesn't that mean anything?"

"That's all in the past," she said. "The only thing that matters is the here and now. When I married you, I thought you would make something of yourself. I never thought for one moment that you would turn into…into a bum!"

John's eyes were fixed on the top of the table. With each intonation of her voice, a great weight seemed to descend on him.

"But...I'm trying," John pleaded.

"It's no use, John. I fail to see that my supporting you as a wife has amounted to anything."

"Do you know how many interviews I've tried to get? No one is hiring!"

Wilma diverted her eyes, shook her head, then started to leave, but stopped and turned.

"I've decided to take Jennie to my mother's house in California. We're going to remain there. When you begin acting like a husband and a father…" Tears welled in her eyes as she turned to leave.

"You can't do that! You can't leave me!" John protested.

# SLOW TANGO IN TAOS

"Do you know the hell I've been going through trying to keep this house clean without a maid? I've been working myself to death trying to make ends meet. I can't even meet the girls at Bloomies for lunch anymore, and I'm embarrassed about buying anything. Is that any way to live? Do you know what happened to the last two dresses I bought?" she demanded.

John stared at the floor. *What next?*

"I'll tell you, John Tollifson! I only wore them one time. I felt so guilty, I..." she burst into tears and ran up the stairs, but paused at the top. "So ashamed, I gave them to the Salvation Army! Don't you care what you're doing to your daughter and me? We're leaving tomorrow morning! You're a loser, John! I never want to see you again!"

She rushed into a bedroom and slammed the door. John remained sitting at the table staring into his cup of coffee. His arms became strangely limp as he sat motionless. His whole world seemed to disintegrate. The room became quiet, totally devoid of sounds, except for the steady drip of a faucet.

*Drip, drip, drip. Funny, how a drop of water can be so loud.*

Weeks later, John sat alone in the kitchen reading the morning newspaper, searching the want ads. He opened an envelope from his bank that sat on the table unopened for more than a week. As he viewed the statement, a surge of panic made his heart race. He could no longer concentrate. His vision blurred as he tried to understand the meaning of the bank's financial statement. He stared at the numbers for a long time feeling that he had been tossed into an alien world with his financial security gone. *Nearly broke.* He tossed the statement aside and buried his head in his hands. *What am I going to do?*

Once more he slipped into the deep abyss of depression that often came as a wolf stalking the edges of his consciousness; always, it would lay in the dark recesses waiting for John to weaken, then it would savagely attack, shredding his self-respect. In time, other wolves emerged from the shadows and joined in the attack, ripping apart his mental health and throwing him into hopeless depression.

In the days that followed, he took walks through the neighborhood and exercised in the house trying to stave off the dark thoughts that often lead to suicide. Day after day turned into the same routine with morning coffee, perusal of the newspaper adds, then a quick walk around the block, hoping he would not see any of his neighbors who hopefully were at work.

One day, as he read the newspaper, an advertisement jumped out at him. R.L. Securities is looking for an account executive. John dialed the number. A pleasant-sounding woman answered, "Ratland Securities."

"Yes," John cleared his throat. "I'm calling in response to the advertisement appearing in the Chicago Sun."

"One minute, please." A short pause and a man's voice came over the phone.

# SLOW TANGO IN TAOS

"Hello, may I help you?"

"Yes, I'm calling about your ad in the paper...for an account executive."

"Could I have your name?" the man asked.

"John Tollifson."

"Well, I'll tell you John, we're pretty selective here at Ratland Securities. We hire only the best. Do you know anything about Ratland?"

"No, I don't," John confessed.

"Well, we're a major company listed on the New York Stock Exchange. Tell you what, you sound like a good candidate. Come in and we'll talk. I hate discussing employment over the telephone."

"Sure," John replied.

"Say, Ten O'clock this morning. We're at 244 State Street."

"Great! I'll be there," he smiled with satisfaction.

For the first time in many weeks, John's confidence soared. His first job interview in months. His spirit lifted and the depressive weight of unemployment disappeared. John walked to the nearest bus stop and got onto a bus destined for downtown. He got off in front of an old bank building that had long since lost its beauty. Inside, John examined an antiquated directory in the once opulent lobby. Under "R" he found Ratland Securities scribbled in ink on a slip of paper taped to the glass. John took an elevator to the fifth floor and stepped out onto a hallway missing several white squares of linoleum that exposed dark squares of dried adhesive.

# Phil Cline

A piece of paper taped to the wall opposite the elevator said *Ratland Securities*. A series of papers with arrows pointed the way to a door with flaking white paint. He entered and meandered around a bewildering array of boxes and dusty filing cabinets.

"Hello, anyone here?" John called out.

"In here," came a deep voice from a backroom.

John navigated his way through a warren of stacked boxes. When he finally found the room, two men were removing contents from boxes and placing them into grey metal filing cabinets. Another man in his forties with slicked back dark hair sat with his feet resting on the top of an old desk. Deep lines in his face showed a life of hard times.

"And you are…" the man asked.

"John Tollifson. I called earlier—"

"Yes, yes." He replied. He motioned for the workmen to leave. "I'm Tepper Smith. You'll have to excuse the looks of the place." He took his feet off the desk. "We're just getting set up. Have a seat." He removed a box from a chair and pulled it up for John.

"Sit down," he pushed a chair toward John. "Care for a cigarette?"

"No, I don't smoke."

Tepper lit a cigarette, leaned back in his chair, and placed his feet on top of the dusty desk. He took a deep drag from his cigarette as he studied John, and blew a smoke ring.

"Tell me about yourself." Tepper took another deep drag.

## SLOW TANGO IN TAOS

"I have an MBA from the University of Chi--"

"Yes, yes I know you've got degrees," he interrupted.

"What kind of sales experience do you have?"

"Well, I've worked in sales,"

"What have you sold?" Tepper asked.

"Electronics, mainly appliances."

"How about securities? Sold any securities?" he asked, puffing on his cigarette and looking at the ceiling.

"No, I haven't," John confessed.

"Good." He took a small pin knife from his pocket.

"John? That right?"

"Yes, that's correct."

"Tell you, John," he said as he cleaned dirt from under his fingernails. "We're pretty selective here at Ratland. We want men who know the securities field. Men who are strong closers. Our salesmen here at Ratland can make five, six thousand a week. When's the last time you make that kind of money?"

"Well, I—"

Tepper leaned forward and looked directly at John.

"What do you know about Ratland Securities?"

"Just what I saw in your advertisement."

"We're a major company listed on a regional exchange." Tepper continued cleaning his fingernails.

"When I called, I was told Ratland is listed on the New York exchange."

"Whoever told you that was mistaken." He finished

cleaning his nails and put the knife aside. He retrieved his smoldering cigarette and took a drag, then extinguished it in an ashtray while blowing another circle of smoke. His expensive suit and shoes seemed out of place in such an office. He ran his fingers through his black oily hair, then continued with the interview.

"Tell me something, Tollifson, are you a strong closer?"

"Sure," John replied in anticipation of being offered a job. "I'm a strong closer."

"Are you a high-pressure salesman? We need someone who is good at hard sales pitches. A good closer. Can you do that?" Tepper looked John straight in the eye for a moment, then picked up the knife and resumed cleaning his nails.

"You mean can I be persuasive?"

"Have you ever seduced anyone for money?" he asked.

"Seduced?" John was shaken. "What do you mean?"

"I don't mean seduce in the sexual sense." His eyes narrowed as he studied John. "I'll tell you what, we've got a series of profitable situations, and we need salesmen who are good at working people."

John shifted in his chair. "What do you have in mind?"

Tepper smiled and reached for another cigarette. He lit it and took a puff. "Tell you something, Tollifson," he said. He took a deep drag on the cigarette, blew a small

## SLOW TANGO IN TAOS

smoke ring and tapped ash onto the floor. "There's an old man here in town who's got over five hundred thousand dollars sitting in his bank account. We want a salesman who will go out and convince him to let us handle his money. After all, it doesn't make much sense to let money sit idle in a bank account when we could guarantee thirty, forty percent. Don't you agree?"

"Forty-percent?" John winced at Tepper's words.

"How can you guarantee that kind of percentage."

"We'll put him into Dealer Options – it's a new trend."

"Dealer Options?"

"Yeah. They're Ratland's options."

John leaned back in his chair and fingered his briefcase.

"Tepper gave John an icy stare. "We want someone…say, you…to talk the old man into giving us his money, so we can put it into our Dealer Options."

"I don't understand."

"Okay, look, I'll spell it out for you. Here's the deal. We put his five hundred thousand into dealer options. So, let's say we sell them to him at five hundred bucks each. Then say, an hour later, he wants to sell and get his money back. Since we create the market, we tell him the market has changed, the price has dropped and his options are now only worth twenty bucks. Now, do you understand what we're doing?"

"What would you do with the money?"

Tepper closed the pin knife and tossed it onto the desk. "That's no concern of yours. We'll cut you in. Say, you bring in five hundred thousand, we'll give you…say, fifteen percent."

"Fifteen percent?"

"Yep."

Conflicting thoughts raced through John's head as he envisioned an end to his financial problems. The thought of having a source of income was compelling. If this worked out, he would once again have money to coax Wilma back to Chicago. Then, John thought of the old man and the pain it would cause him from being swindled. At his age, John thought, the old man might not be able to recover and could end up sleeping on the streets. John sighed.

"I'm going to have to turn down your offer."

"What's the matter? Cold feet?"

"Not interested!" John said.

"You were interested enough to come in for an interview!"

"You're asking me to commit a criminal act!" John said.

"Suit yourself, but you must need money, or you wouldn't have stayed this long!"

The longer John remained in the interview, the more power Tepper seemed to acquire over him. The thought of having an income tempted him, but at the same time, his conscience and all the morals he had been taught weighed on him. Resolved, he stood up and forced himself to walk out of the room.

As John returned through the room of empty boxes, Tepper shouted, "You'll be sorry you didn't hire on with Ratland. Our salesmen make several thousand a week. Probably been a while since you've seen that kind of money!"

"I don't need it!" John shouted back.

He pressed the elevator button. It seemed a long time before the doors opened. Once on the ground level, he stepped out onto the street, and ambled to the bus stop for the trip home.

Later that day, as John walked up the driveway of his home, a well-dressed middle-aged man in a dark tailored suit walked up to him.

"John Tollifson?" The man asked. John nodded. The man reached into his suit coat, retrieved folded papers and handed them to John.

"I'm serving you with court papers." The man placed the papers in John's hand.

"Who are you?" John asked.

"My name is Eric Dusseldorf, attorney-at-law. I'm your wife's attorney."

"What is this?" he asked holding up the papers.

"It's a court order. Your wife has legal possession of the house, and she wants you to vacate the premises. She exercised her right to sell the house in lieu of alimony and child support."

## Phil Cline

"Why wasn't I notified?"

"You were. First by a process server who testified he couldn't locate you. When good service couldn't be made, we went to publication. You didn't show up in court, and so my client received a default judgement."

"No. no. no. This isn't happening! There must be a mistake!" John's mouth turned to cotton, his heart raced and his legs threatened to give out from under him.

"No mistake. Your wife asked me to personally serve you with the court order." The attorney got back into his car.

"Bastard!" John clinched his fist and shouted at the sleek jaguar as it drove past. The attorney stopped momentarily.

"You've got twenty-one days to vacate," the attorney shot back.

*Twenty-one days to vacate my own house! What next?*

John went inside the house, poured himself a double scotch and sat down on the sofa. His head spun and his breathing was shallow. He picked up the telephone and dialed his attorney.

" Hello, Ted?"

"Yes" came the voice at the other end.

"John Tollifson here."

"John, been a while."

"Sorry to bother you, but I need your advice."

"Shoot. What's bothering you."

"I received…a court order…delivered by…Wilma's

attorney. I've been given...three weeks to...vacate my house," John said between short terrified breaths.

"John, I vaguely recall you telling me years ago to transfer the title to your home into your wife's name. I believe we discussed the legalities of such an act at that time. I advised you against transferring title. I advised you about the potential legal problems."

"Yes...but...what can...I do now?"

"With the title in her name, it's her house to do as she wishes."

"I can be...evicted...from my own house?" His head spun as though he had fallen into a vortex of disbelief.

"If it's a court order, believe me, John you'll have to be out on that date. I'm sorry, I tried to explain what might happen when you transferred title."

"I know...I know. Totally foolish! I don't know...what...to do. My bank account... is low. I have...no place...to go. No job!"

"Do you still belong to those clubs you joined? Ted asked.

"No, I stopped...paying dues...months ago," John said between breaths.

"A smart move, John. Let's face the facts. You've got to watch out for yourself and learn how to survive until you can get back on your feet."

"What... should I do? Where should...I go?"

"I know it's not pleasant, but you've got to learn to survive during lean times. I don't know what other advice I can give."

John fought to catch his breath.

"Thanks…for…your help. I'll figure…something out."

"Take care of yourself, John. Good Luck."

"Thanks," John replied as he put the phone on the hook. *After all this time, after all that work, all the plans and dreams. It's come to this.* He collapsed on the couch sobbing uncontrollably. *It's not fair, it isn't fair!*

Over the next few days John collected everything he could claim and took them downtown to a storage unit that Wilma had rented near the harbor. After several trips, all his things were out of the house and in storage. On the twenty-first day, John stood outside looking at the house that had been a source of so much pride and satisfaction. His bottom lip quivered. He took a deep breath, turned away and walked down the driveway for the last time. As he walked to the bus stop several blocks away, his body seemed heavier than normal. He could sense neighbors looking at him carrying his suitcase, like a vagabond. His cheeks flushed as a wave of shame swept over him like a tidal wave.

Later that day, he took a bus to a residence hotel in Evanston. He got off the bus and stood looking at a large grey gothic building. A deep sense of loss and humiliation haunted him. After a long pause, he picked up his bag and walked inside. A large crystal chandelier hung from the high ceiling. Inside, residents sat watching television and playing chess in a large room near a fireplace. A motto inscribed on

## SLOW TANGO IN TAOS

the mantel read: *Raise thyself from the surging earth and make thyself a master.*

John sat his bag down in front of a matronly woman with grey hair and black glasses setting behind an ornate oak reception desk. She looked up and smiled.

"I called about a room," John said.

"What's the name?" she asked.

"Tollifson, John Tollifson."

She shuffled through a few slips of paper on her desk and picked out one.
"Here it is. How long do you think you'll be staying?"

"A week, maybe two," he replied.

"Fill this out. We'll need the signature of your supervisor to verify employment." She pushed a form in front of John.

"Supervisor?"

"Yes, your supervisor. You are working, aren't you?" She asked.

"No, I'm not...working. Laid off!" John stammered.

"Mister Tollifson, this is strictly a residence hotel. You cannot stay here if you're not employed."

"For Christ's sake! If I had a job, I wouldn't be here. I need a place to stay until I can find employment. I lost a million-dollar home, my wife divorced me. Please, can't you give me a room?" His breaths became labored and quick. His ears flushed bright red.

"I'm sorry," she said. "I didn't make the rules. If you

need a place to stay, there's an inexpensive hotel downtown that should have a room." She wrote the address on a piece of paper. "I'm sure they can put you up for the night."

John took the slip of paper, folded it, and left.

Later, John stepped off a bus in front of an old dilapidated red brick building with the fading letters RH painted on a sign above the entrance. He picked up his bags and walked up the worn marble stairs. A security guard stood behind a desk near the entrance.

"Where is the reception desk?"

"On the second floor, Sir." He pointed to a flight of stairs. Tired, John trudged up the steps. On the second floor he found a white-haired man behind a registration desk whose newness had long since disappeared. The man smiled as John approached. "Can I help you?"

"Yes." John dropped his bags onto the floor. "I'd like a room."

"Temporary or permanent?"

"What's the difference?" John asked

"Permanent status candidates must be approved by the staff, and you must have a job."

The word *job* grated on John's nerves. He cringed at the word.

"Are you employed?" the man asked.

"No," John replied with a sense of bewilderment. "I'm not employed."

"In that case, I can only offer you one of our temporary rooms."

# SLOW TANGO IN TAOS

"I'll take it," John sighed.

"Fill out this here form." The man handed John a form. John filled in the blanks and handed it back to the man.

"How long you planning on staying?"

"Don't know. Maybe a week or two."

"I'll put you in room three thirty-two."

John picked up his bags and walked to the elevator. When it stopped on the third floor, he stepped out into a dingy hallway. He stopped in front of a door with the numbers 332 hastily painted on the front. The wooden door had a crack in the center, and a six-inch strip of wood missing from the edge.

*Looks like someone has broken into this room.*

John inserted his key and entered. A simple bed with a torn terry cloth cover stood under a metal window that opened out onto a noisy street below. On one side of the room was a desk and a mirror. On the ceiling, a small piece of plaster dangled near a naked bulb that hung by a single strand of electrical wire. All the furnishings in the room were old and of poor original quality. The room smelled of urine and decay.

He stood looking at his new surroundings with disdain. Disbelief dominated his thoughts at the realization that he was no longer a valuable member of society.

*Damn! This is not me. I'm not a bum!*

He sat down on a rickety chair next to the dresser, placed his head in his hands and starting crying uncontrollably. After a while, he dried his tears and stood.

# Phil Cline

*I can't let this destroy me! I'm better than this! Okay, John, take a deep breath and get back in the game! You can do it!*

Resolved to make the best of a bad situation, he unpacked his suitcase and hung his suit in the small musty closet. He opened the window and stuck his head outside. An array of vehicles paraded below in the darkness. Then the thought occurred to him that people he knew might recognize him with his head stuck out the window of this fleabag hotel. He withdrew into the room and closed the window. He pushed down on the mattress with his hand. As he did so, the springs squeaked. John noticed a small black knob on the wall above the bed. He turned the knob. To his delight, Pachelbel's *Canon in D* played through the speaker. Exhausted, he lay down on the bed, closed his eyes, and fell asleep.

**SLOW TANGO IN TAOS**

# CHAPTER 3

John got out of bed promptly at six o'clock. He picked up a towel and walked to the public showers located midway down the hallway. The shower stalls of once new white porcelain had small cracks throughout from the passage of time. He turned a corroded handle that released warm water, lathered and took a leisurely shower. The warm water provided a welcome relief from his worries. A huge sigh parted his lips as he stood under the warm shower.

John sensed other men taking showers were also down on their luck. Most were young, but some were older. John found the sordidness of the place repulsive. After showering, he returned to his room. He put on a gray suit, a pair of black leather shoes, and arranged his tie. After leaving the building, he walked to a nearby bus stop where he waited. Soon a bright blue bus stopped.

The express bus made only limited stops. He got off

on South Clarke Street. Hungry and in need of a meal, he walked to a nearby restaurant. As he entered, he noticed a man with thinning sandy hair sitting at the back of the restaurant. Something about the man seemed vaguely familiar. John made his way to the back of the restaurant and paused in front of his table.

"Excuse me," John said.

The balding slightly rotund man looked up. His brow ruffled slightly.

"You look familiar, don't I know you?"

The man's frown turned to a smile. "Don't tell me," he said. "John Tollifson! My old roommate!"

"George Proctor! I haven't seen you in--"

"A long time!" He shook John's hand. "Please, join me. Care for coffee?"

John nodded and sat down. George signaled to the waitress.

"Tell me, the last time we saw each other was…"

"Senior year at UC. We roomed together, remember?"

"How could I forget?" George replied. "Let's see, you took over Olivier's room when he returned to France." A pretty dark-haired woman in a blue apron brought two cups of coffee and set them on their table.

"What did you do after graduation?" John asked.

"Well, as you may remember, I was never keen on the nine-to-five routine. I suppose I got that trait from my parents, they were travelling actors, you know. They

## SLOW TANGO IN TAOS

eventually landed some nice contracts in Hollywood."

"Did you join them?" John asked.

"Heaven's no! Too independent for that. I bought a one-way ticket to Europe. I bummed around Paris for a while. Then one day I was having coffee at one of those little al fresco restaurants on Boulevard Saint-Germain, one called Café de Flore. While there, I overheard a young man talking to a friend about Tibet. Said he wanted to go there to learn about Tantric Mysticism. Well, that got my interest, so I introduced myself. I told him I was also very interested in Tibet. We became friends and met often at various coffee shops, and had many long interesting conversations. When he learned about my dire financial situation, he offered to pay for my ticket if I would join him on his next trip to Tibet. I learned he had grown up in a wealthy well-connected family, so money was not a problem for him."

"Sounds fascinating," John said, leaning forward.

"So, what happened?"

"Well, when we arrived in Tibet, he introduced me to the Dalai Lama, whom his parents knew quite well. Later, my friend needed to fly back, so he didn't stay with me very long. A family emergency. Being that Tantrism fascinated me, I decided to remain in Tibet, which was rather fortunate."

"Why is that?" John asked.

"Fate works in mysterious ways. My friend's plane crashed into a mountain not far from the airport. He was killed."

"I'm sorry."

"I remained in Tibet for several years. During that time, I learned a great deal about metaphysics. Then, I left Tibet and began travelling and writing."

"I'm envious."

George smiled and leaned back in his chair. "I've been doing all the talking. Tell me about yourself. What have you been doing?"

"There's really not much to talk about." John grimaced and shifted in his chair.

"Oh, come now," George said. "I remember at one time you talked about becoming an artist. Did you study art after graduating?"

John took another drink of coffee and swallowed hard. "No, I went to graduate school in business and got an MBA. I worked for a bank a short time, and then for a large corporation. I received regular promotions and ended up Vice President."

"Impressive, but I never thought of you as a businessman."

"There isn't much else to tell, except," John groped for a way to change the subject.

"Except what?"

"I'm…" John hesitated. The words did not come easily. George studied him with an intensity born of understanding.

"I was fired. I'm out of work," John said, his face flushing.

## SLOW TANGO IN TAOS

"Oh," George replied with a smile. "I'm relieved that your predicament isn't more serious."

Surprised by George's comment, John cocked his head and wrinkled his brow. After taking a deep breath, he continued. "Headquarters cut my division. Me and several hundred others."

"I see." George leaned back in his chair. "How long have you been out of work?"

"Over a year."

"And your finances?"

"Not good. I don't even have a bank account. My funds dropped below the minimum and they closed my account." John struggled to hide his discomfort. "Tell me about yourself. I've seen your books. You had one on the best seller list. You must be pleased."

"Well, I wrote the Snow Birds while in Tibet. It's selling well."

"Fate is ironic isn't it," John said. "I went after money and status, and look at me, I'm nearly broke and homeless. You didn't seek money, but, you're well-off and famous."

"Not exactly, this is the first book that made it to the bestseller list. I'm here in Chicago for a book tour." George sipped his coffee and studied John.

"I don't know what to do" John said. "I'm at my wit's end. Yesterday, I moved into a cheap hotel. That's all I can afford. I'm terrified of running into people I know. Afraid of what they might think of me. Sometimes I walk past people I knew socially, but they divert their eyes. It hurts."

"I see," George said. "One thing I learned in Tibet is to be aware of the destructive effects of consensus reality."

"What?"

"Don't get too involved with what other people think. People tend to define their reality by how others around them view theirs. You need to understand that you're unique. You can see the world as you wish. It's a personal choice of how you choose to see your world and your place in it. I learned while in Tibet the value of rejecting herd mentality."

John nodded that he understood, but his lips tightened and skin on his forehead wrinkled. "I used to think unemployed people were lazy bums who didn't want to work. Now, I'm one of those lazy bums. The damn part about it is…everything I worked to achieve has evaporated." John choked back tears.

"John, have you ever thought about doing things differently?"

"Like what?"

"I learned many things in Tibet. I think the most valuable lesson is that the human spirit is only as free as the mind wishes it to be. You have control of your destiny. Perhaps you might concentrate more on listening to that little inner voice inside your head," George said tapping his skull with his finger. "It's your guide."

"I hadn't thought of that," John confessed.

"Tell you what, I have friends out in Taos, New Mexico. I can arrange for you to stay with Tina, a good

## SLOW TANGO IN TAOS

friend of mine. Go out there and stay with her until you get back on your feet."

"I'm not a kid anymore. I can't hop around the country staying with people I don't know."

George smiled and wrote on a slip of paper, then handed it to John, "This is Tina's address. I'll let her know you're coming."

"But--"

"Think about it."

John took the paper and looked at it. "Who is Tina?"

"We go back a long way. Been friends many years."

"Would I be interfering if I stayed with her?" John stared at the paper.

"Not at all. Tina would love to have you. Besides, she has a guest house. Taos is in the Sangre de Cristo mountains, the air is clean, and the area is beautiful. It'd do you good to get away."

"How would I get out there?"

"A bus ticket doesn't cost much," George said. "Here," he said opening his wallet, "I'll give you some money."

"No! I have enough for a bus ticket."

"Okay," George said. "Another lesson I learned in Tibet…always do what seems most difficult…those things that are outside your comfort zone. That's where your most important lessons lie."

As George talked, a spark of excitement shot through John as if a new phase of his life had opened. A vista of open spaces, clean air, and beautiful mountains.

George checked his watch, "I'm scheduled to meet with my editor in a few minutes. I need to leave." He finished his coffee and stood up.

"George, I really enjoyed seeing you again." John said.

"Promise me," George said, "that you'll go out and spend some time in Taos. Explore new territory. View your life differently."

"I'll think about it."

"Promise me, or I'll never forgive you."

"I promise." John said.

George put a few dollars on the table. "This will pay for the coffee and a little tip." George put on his coat, picked up his leather portfolio and headed for the exit. He paused at the door, waved and left.

After his friend left, John ordered breakfast. After eating, John stepped back out on the street and walked into the lobby of a nearby building with a revived spirit of optimism. He looked at the directory and found an employment agency listed on the fifth floor. Once of the floor, he came to a door with painted letters that said *Ace Employment.* Inside the agency, an assortment of young and older job seekers sat in chairs awaiting counseling. John walked up to the reception desk.

"I'd like to register," John said to the receptionist, a young blonde wearing a smartly tailored navy-blue suit and a yellow silk scarf around her neck.

## SLOW TANGO IN TAOS

"Fill this out and return it to me." She handed John a form.

*Another form!* He filled in the required information and returned it. "Here is the form," he said.

"Take a seat and someone will be with you shortly."

About fifteen minutes later, a tall slender blond-haired man with gold-rimmed glasses walked into the lobby area and called out, "*Tollifson!*"

"Right Here," John said. He stood up.

"Let me tell you something... John, is that your name?"

"Yes, John Tollifson."

"This is my agency, and I choose who I take on as a client."

"Is something wrong?" John took a step backward.

"You stated here on the form that you're staying at a fleabag residence hotel. I'm not going to tell any prospective business client that I'm sending them someone who is staying at a place like that!"

John's face flushed as he stood in front of other job seekers. "I only recently…moved in there," John stammered, trying to conceal his discomfort.

"There are a lot of upscale motels in the downtown area. You can afford one, can't you?"

"Yes, I think so," John grimaced.
*And pay for it with what? I have no money!*

"Tell you what, you go check into a respectable hotel. Then, you come back here and I'll see what I can do," he said, then abruptly returned to his office.

For a long moment, John stood aghast. Then, he left the agency, carrying his embarrassment with him. He stepped back onto the street with a hollowness in his chest and legs that seemed unusually heavy. His breathing was shallow and his body ached, but he was glad to be away from the agency owner whose stinging words still echoed in his head.

Dispirited and disheartened, he returned to the hotel and spent the rest of the day reading a novel, trying to escape into a friendlier world. After dark, he undressed and got into bed.

Next morning, John left for another day of job hunting. As he walked along State Street, he came upon a thrift store with camping equipment displayed in the window. George's description of Taos prompted him to go into the store to inquire about the price. His interest shot up when he saw a sign on the wall: Today Only, 50% off everything. He went inside and examined the equipment. On one shelf he found a used sleeping bag that looked almost new. Near it rested a backpack that showed a bit of wear but still in good condition and a half gallon canteen. Then he found a pair of nearly-new hiking boots.

As he waited to pay for the items, he started thinking about what he wanted to do.

*George is right, I need to do things differently! I'll buy a bus ticket to Taos! I Can't wait to get the hell out of this damn city! I'll go back to the hotel, pack and go to the*

# SLOW TANGO IN TAOS

*Greyhound Station.*

As he checked out at the thrift store, he noticed some dried food near the cash register.

"I'll take seven packets of the beef jerky," John said. He handed money to the young woman tending the cash register. Then he walked from the shop with the backpack slung over one shoulder, the canteen over the other and the sleeping bag under one arm. As he returned to the hotel, a new wave of optimism flowed over him as though walking into a field of fresh air and bliss.

In the hotel room, he opened his suitcase. He removed two pairs of jeans, t-shirts, underwear and a jacket. He folded them and placed them into his backpack. Then, he tied the sleeping bag to the bottom of his backpack and filled the canteen with water. He took off his suit and tossed it onto the bed, then slipped on a t-shirt, a pair of jeans and hiking boots. Ready to leave, he reached under the mattress where he had hidden his money, but it was not there. Someone had gotten into his room and stolen his money.

*Damn the luck! No money for a bus ticket! What am I going to do?*

Gathering all his courage, he departed the hotel with whatever he could carry, but left everything else in the room. As he walked, a sense of terror gripped him. All that he had known in the past was now behind him. What lay ahead was a new and uncertain world.

# Phil Cline

# CHAPTER 4

The interstate highway stretched out in front of John like a ribbon of concrete as far as he could see. Many cars sped past as he hiked. Now, Chicago loomed behind him like an unwanted pestilence. For the first time, he was free from the pressures of job seeking. Each step put him farther away from his troubles. After hours of walking, he was tired and sweaty. A fresh breeze blowing out of nowhere cooled John's sweaty cheeks and provided momentary relief from the heat. Songs from Meadow larks in a nearby field provided him with natural music that he had never appreciated before. Now the birdsongs were a source of great enjoyment that helped fill the void in his day.

At times, he was full of optimism about his future life and the freedom it would bring. At other times, he remembered he was alone on a roadway heading for someplace he had never been to stay with people he didn't know. His pulse quickened at the thought.

He was rapidly learning that things were different now. Posturing with subtle indications of status to establish his place in the world no longer mattered. On the road, the only important goal was to bum a ride. At times, his face flushed with humiliation as he stood on the roadside thumbing rides. At times, it seemed he was not the person standing along the road with his thumb extended outward. After all, he was an executive with credentials, not a vagabond. But now his life had changed, he had to use every ounce of his energy just to survive.

A sense of rejection swept over him every time a car passed without stopping. At first, it seemed like a personal affront. Then, he realized he was now one of those bums he had often seen standing along the highway thumbing a ride. He took a deep breath and swallowed his pride. Finally, a driver pulled to the side of the road and stopped. John rushed to the car and spoke through a rolled down window.

"Where you going?" asked the middle-aged man.

"Taos, New Mexico."

"I'm only going as far as Joliette. The Interstate runs right by there, you can thumb a ride west from there. Get in!"

"Thanks." John said, relieved that someone had stopped, but nervous about riding with a stranger. As the Chevrolet sedan sped down the highway, John glanced at the sideview mirror and watched the Chicago skyline fade into the distance.

## SLOW TANGO IN TAOS

"I'm glad to see Chicago disappear behind us," John said.

"Why? You running from something? You don't look like the type to be hitchhiking."

John smiled but said nothing. A little later, the sedan stopped near an access road leading to the Interstate. John got out of the car, slipped on his backpack and secured the straps around his chest. For a long moment, he stood watching the sedan disappear down the roadway. John took a deep breath, looked up the rampway, and began walking.

Once on the highway, he stuck out his thumb, but none of the approaching cars stopped. He continued walking for a long time. At times, he watched his feet moving him along the roadway. Somehow, they didn't seem to be part of him. Just a pair of hiking boots that moved methodically along the concrete. As he became increasingly tired from the walk, a musical cadence sounded in his head like a mantra that helped him put one foot in front of the other. One…two…one…two…one…two…

As the sun moved higher, the heat of the day increased. He stopped to rest under the shade of a nearby oak tree and wiped sweat from his forehead. He continued sticking out his thumb as cars passed, but each car sped past and disappeared into the distance. He took a sip of water from his canteen and saw a red truck approach. He stuck out his thumb. To his surprise, the old truck pulled onto the shoulder of the road and stopped. John rushed to the pickup.

"Where ya head'n boy?" asked the driver, an old

wizened man.

"Denver."

"Ain't going that fer. Ain't go'n but seventy or so miles down the road. Got a farm to tend to and cattle to feed."

"That's far enough," John said.

The old man didn't say much as they travelled down the highway, but occasionally his brow would wrinkle each time he glanced at John.

Two hours later the truck stopped and John got out. Once more he stood at the edge of the highway. He watched the truck turn onto a side road and disappear into a cloud of dust. The relentless sun bore down on him like a blowtorch. He tried many creative ways to thrust out his thumb, but no matter how he did it, the cars sped past.

John wiped sweat from his brow and looked upward. The sky was a pastel blue that was occasionally interrupted by a fluffy white cloud. As he stood along the highway, a cloud passed overhead casting a welcome bit of shade upon the landscape. It seemed heaven itself had brought welcome relief. Occasionally, when a brief cooling wind blew past, it gave him exquisite pleasure. Marvelous, he thought, how a small gift of shade or wind could mean so much as he stood stranded somewhere on a Kansas highway in the middle of nowhere. After resting a bit, he set out once more in his trek into a new world. Once more he stuck out his thumb to obtain a ride, but, again, the cars continued to speed past.

"Ass hole!" he shouted at a motorist who flashed him

## SLOW TANGO IN TAOS

a finger as he passed by.

After hiking a long distance, he came to an underpass. The shade provided wonderful relief from the stinging heat. Thirsty, tired, and drenched in sweat, he took off his shoes, removed the cap from his canteen and took a long drink of water. Then, he rested against the concrete abutment. His back ached as did every inch of his body.

Fear raced through him at the thought that he might die out here in the middle of nowhere. He could not walk much farther, certainly not all the way to Taos.

*Why did I embark on this hazardous trip? I must be crazy!*

He took a deep breath, closed his aching eyes and fell asleep. When he awoke, he heard to the sound of someone singing the song, Sweet Caroline. He bolted up to see a man wearing a red bandana walking toward him. The man stood about six-foot-tall, and wore a brightly colored red headband and a yellow and purple tie-dyed t-shirt. John focused his attention as the man approached.

"Howdy," said the man when he arrived.

"Hi," John replied, uncertain how to respond. John stood up and studied the stranger.

*Friend or foe?*

"Beautiful day for a walk. Yes indeed. Beautiful day!" The stranger said.

"Yeah, if you're a buzzard!" John replied.

"Buzzards come not hither!" The man laughed.

"Names Jasper. People call me Traveling Jasper

cause I travel a lot."

"Tollifson here. John Tollifson." John extended his hand. The man looked at his hand for a moment, then smiled.

"No, man! That's plastic," he said. Jasper locked thumbs and grasp the back of John's hand. "That's better, man, much better. That's the way we shake hands."

"Glad to meet you." John relaxed and smiled. "Where you headed?"

"West."

"Where, west?" John asked.

"West, man, till I hit the pacific."

"You have friends out there?"

"Yea, lots of friends, but I don't stay long, got to keep moving. You know how it is."

"You're not staying on the west coast?"

"No, man, I'll spend a few days in Berkeley, then I'll leave."

"Where you going then?" John asked.

"East."

"Any specific place?"

"Yea, like until I get to New York. I'll spend a few days in the village, then head on up to Cambridge, then I head back west."

"Back to the west coast?" John asked.

*What a strange man.*

"Yep, but next time, I'll drop down into New Mexico and Arizona on the way back. Gotta keep moving, you know how it is."

## SLOW TANGO IN TAOS

"Yeah. I'm beginning to understand." John shifted his weight.

"Care for a drink?" Jasper pulled a canteen from his olive drab back pack.

"Thanks," John said. He took the canteen and poured some of the liquid into his mouth, sputtered and swallowed hard. "What is this?"

"Thunderbird wine, man, always carry it with me, helps my head." Jasper took the canteen and upended it, then replaced the cap and leaned against the concrete abutment. He reached into his pocket and pulled out a self-rolled cigarette.

"Care to smoke?" Jasper asked.

"Don't smoke."

"You should. This helps calm the spirits."

"What is it?"

"Grass, man. Good weed. Ever smoked?"

"No, never tried it."

"Wow! Far out! Man, I gotta turn you on." He reached into his pocket, pulled out a book of paper matches, and struck one, but the wind blew it out. He stuck another and cupped his hands. A puff of smoke arose as Jasper took a deep drag.

"Hold it in, count to ten, then exhale," Jasper said with a slightly higher pitched voice. "Here give it a try."

John took the cigarette and reluctantly took a drag. Held smoke in his mouth, then blew it out.

"No, man. That's wasteful! Gotta hold it into your

lungs, man!"

John took a deeper drag and inhaled. The acrid smoke burned his lungs and caused him to cough.

"Try again," Jasper laughed.

John took a deep drag. This time he held the smoke in his lungs for several seconds, then exhaled.

"Good! Good!" Jasper said.

He handed the joint back to Jasper. They passed it back and forth until too small to hold in their fingers. Then, Jasper pulled an alligator clip from his top pocket and attached the tip of the clip to the reefer.

"Another drag?"

"No, that's enough." John's head was dizzy from the effects, and his lungs burned like they were on fire.

Jasper held the small remaining end of the reefer to his lips and kept smoking until there was nothing left to smoke.

"Where you coming from?" Jasper asked.

"Chicago," John said with a lilt to his voice.

"Heavy town, man."

"Got fired from my job."

"Groovy, man."

"Yeah," John jerked his head back, surprised by Jasper's response. "It was traumatic for me."

"Wow, a real downer!" Jasper leaned back against the concrete slope, and lit another reefer. "Man, I think a car is going to come by and give us a lift."

"What makes you so certain?"

## SLOW TANGO IN TAOS

"I just know." Jasper sat down on the concrete and waited.

John sat at the foot of the slope, and focused his eyes on a spot of sunlight highlighting a nearby stone. He reached for the particle of light, cupped his hand, and tried to capture it in his palm. He marveled at its transcendental beauty. John found he had acquired a new admiration for ants and flowers and spots of sunlight. The sound of ants shuffling upon the rocks fascinated him. John's concentration was interrupted by the sound of a car pulling up to a stop nearby and a strange voice yelling, "Where you heading?"

John bolted upright to see a bright yellow Volkswagen van at the side of the highway painted with psychedelic flowers, a peace symbol and stars.

"West," Jasper shouted.

"Where?"

"Just west."

"Hop in!"

"Groovy," Jasper said.

"Come on! Get up, man!" Jasper shouted to John.

"Come on, man, we got us a ride."

John gathered up his gear, threw his backpack across his shoulder and clamored into the van.

"Free at last, free at last!" exclaimed Jasper as the brightly-colored Volkswagen sped down the highway.

"Man, I thought we'd never get us a ride," Jasper said. "Glad you good people happened along."

Sitting in the driver's seat was a sandy haired young

man and in the passenger seat was a pretty young blonde woman of about twenty-five years of age. John turned to the blonde.

"What's your name?"

"I'm Bridget," she said, "and this cute hunk of flesh driving is Ryan. We're astrologically engaged. I'm Aquarius and Ryan is a Libra. Our signs are perfectly aligned."

"I'm a Cancer, always on the move," Jasper said.

"Where you two heading?" asked Bridgett.

"West," Jasper replied.

"Taos," John said.

"Taos is beautiful – very spiritual place," Bridget said.

Jasper pulled out two reefers. He lit one and passed it around. Soon, the slightly acrid smell of weed filled the van.

That evening, as the sun disappeared over the horizon, Ryan turned off the interstate and went down a road, with a cloud of dust trailing behind.

"Where we going, man?" Jasper asked.

"To find a place to crash for the night," Ryan said.

Ryan was in his late twenties, about six-foot with a slender frame. When they came to a large cluster of trees on one side of the road, Ryan pulled the van off the road and stopped.

"Everybody out," Ryan said. "Gather fire wood. We'll set up camp here."

John gathered fallen limbs and twigs nearby and dropped them by Ryan.

## SLOW TANGO IN TAOS

Ryan arranged stones he found nearby into a circle. Inside, he placed a small pile of grass kindling, lit it with a match, and then added twigs and larger wood until a fire roared.

Bridget gathered pots, pans and water from containers fastened to the rear of the bus and placed a pot with water into the fire. As soon as the water boiled, she dumped a packet of dried pasta into the pot, and opened a jar of marinara sauce.

Sparks ascended into the heavens as the group sat talking around the campfire while the food cooked. After a while, Bridget dished pasta with a liberal dosage of sauce onto plates and handed them to everyone. John took a plate and smelled the food. He had not realized how hungry he had become. The food tasted as marvelous as it smelled, the best in the world. John finished his pasta and set the plate aside. After dinner, John leaned back against a tree and looked up at the sky.

A full moon highlighted the landscape and silhouetted a coyote on the crest of a nearby hill. Sounds from frogs in a nearby pond, and crickets from an adjoining field filled the warm night air. He turned to Ryan.

"Been on the road long?" John asked.

"Three years." Ryan pushed a partially burned log back into the fire. "While on the road, we've met a lot of interesting people. I learned that every person has a story to tell. If you listen to people, they will reveal fascinating things about themselves. I gained a lot of insight into my own life as well."

John stared at the fire as he thought about what Ryan had said.

"Here, man." Jasper handed John a reefer. John took a deep drag and passed it to Ryan. Ryan took another drag before passing it to Bridget who offered it back to Jasper.

"No, man. I'm cool," Jasper said.

She handed it back to John who took a deep draw and held the smoke in his lungs for a moment before exhaling. His perception changed. The delicate jingle of Bridget's bracelet sounded like an orchestration from heaven. He took another deep drag, then handed the joint to Ryan.

John looked up at the array of stars that seemed to reach into infinity. He couldn't remember a time when he could see so many dots of light spread over the heavens. A streak of light etched its way to the east as a meteor raced across the sky. In the distance, an animal howled at the full moon.

"What was that?" Jasper bolted upright.

"A coyote," Ryan replied.

"Scared the shit out of me!" Jasper lay back down.

"Man, don't let that animal get near me. I've heard things about coyotes, like how they hunt in packs and attack people."

"They won't come near the fire," Ryan said.

"Man, like I keep getting these visions of being mauled by wild animals."

"Maybe we should turn in for the night," Ryan

## SLOW TANGO IN TAOS

suggested.

"Good idea," John said. He spread out his sleeping bag near a tree and climbed inside. He was glad to have had something to eat and looked forward to a good rest.

The next morning John awoke to cool air and a light dew on the ground. He got out of his sleeping bag and added wood to the embers. He blew on them until the wood ignited. As he warmed himself at the fire, he looked out across a field of brown wheat stubble left over from a recent harvest.

Ryan and Bridget slipped out of their sleeping bags and joined John at the fire. Ryan used a piece of wood to push coals to one side, and nestled a coffee pot into the embers.

"Man, I smoked too much last night. I mean like I was stoned." Jasper laughed a silly giggle as he joined them at the fire.

"Tonight, we'll be in Boulder, and you'll be back on the road," Ryan said.

"You're not taking us farther west?" Jasper inquired.

"Denver is as far west as we're going. From Denver, Bridget and I head North."

"You've been gracious," John said. "Can I give you some money to pay for the gas and food--"

"No, no!" Ryan said. "When I offer people a lift, I don't expect them to pay for gas or food. That's on me. If a man is thumbing, it's because he doesn't have a car, and if he doesn't have a car it's because he doesn't have money. As long as I've got money, I'll spread it around."

# Phil Cline

"Be nice if everyone thought like that," John said.

"Man, that's cool!" Jasper lit up another reefer.

"Do you stay stoned all the time?" Ryan asked.

"Oh, no man. I need this one to clear up my head. I always light up first thing in the morning so I can think clearer for the rest of the day. You know how it is, man. It's tough out there on the road."

"Why do you keep traveling if it's so tough?" Ryan asked. "Why don't you stay somewhere and put down roots."

"I got no roots to put down, you know how it is, man. Gotta keep moving."

"Don't you ever have a desire to stay in one place?" John asked.

"Sure, man, but, like, only for a few days. Like, I gotta keep moving. You know how it is, man." he drew smoke from the reefer and expanded his chest to hold it in.

"You never said why you travel so much," John said.

"Tell you, man," Jasper said with a high-pitched voice. "My dad died when he was about my age. Charlie was his name. With his dying breath, he said he wished he'd seen more of the world instead of wasting his life looking at the walls in his office. It was like a prison to him. Man, like a funny thing happened. Two days after he died, a coworker entered my Dad's office and found the metal stem of his chair broken in two. Man, like the metal was two and a half inches thick – steel, man. And somehow it broke! Just like that." He clicked his fingers. "I figured his ghost had come back and destroyed the chair he had sat in all those years.

## SLOW TANGO IN TAOS

Man, like he came back and smashed that damn chair, just to get even."

"So, you're afraid of dying?" Ryan asked.

"No, man!"

"What then?"

"It's personal!"

"Aren't you eating?" John asked.

"No, man, not right now," Jasper said, "I'm going to finish this joint. I'll eat later."

"Suit yourself," John said.

Later that day, the Volkswagen was once more travelling down the highway as intense sun beat down on the metal roof. Vent windows turned outward into the wind provided only partial relief from the sweltering heat. At long last, a sign appeared along the road reading *WELCOME TO COLORFUL COLORADO*. About one hundred miles outside of Denver, the Rocky Mountains appeared on the horizon to the south.

"Look over there!" Bridget pointed to a distant peak

"That's Pikes Peak. It's near Colorado Springs," Ryan said.

John looked in amazement at the snow-covered peak rising in the distance, but just as quickly it disappeared as they went down a gradient in the highway.

"What happened to the peak?" John asked.

"You won't see it again unless you head south. Pikes Peak will appear again just before you get to Colorado Springs," Ryan said.

# Phil Cline

John looked out the window and viewed the rolling hills that drifted by like humps on a herd of buffalo. Only an occasional tree punctuated the vastness of the landscape. Throughout the afternoon, the van inched its way westward. Finally, they arrived outside of Denver at the intersection of Interstates 25 and 70. The van pulled to the side of the road and stopped.

"I'm afraid this is where we part," Ryan said. "We're heading north into Boulder from here."

"Thanks for the ride," John said.

"Good luck," Ryan replied.

"You aren't heading farther west?" Jasper asked.

"No, we're going to see friends in Boulder."

"Well, Goodbye and thanks for the ride. Enjoyed meeting all of you," John said. He grabbed his gear and slid out of the Volkswagen.

"The same." Ryan put the car into gear and drove away.

# CHAPTER 5

A brown fog-like haze hung over Denver obscuring the downtown buildings. Heat curls radiated upward from the pavement in successive waves of torment. Standing along the highway was like standing in front of the open door of a hot oven. They took turns sticking out their thumbs trying to flag a ride.

"Ass Hole!" Jasper shouted as a car sped past. "Man, we've got to get off this highway. Too damn hot out here."

"Any suggestions?"

"Why don't we head into Denver" Jasper said. "We can stay in one of the parks until tonight. When it's cooler we can thumb a---." At that moment a large semi pulled over and stopped.

They momentarily exchanged surprised but delighted glances before racing for the truck.

"Hop in," said the driver, a big burly fellow with red

hair and freckles. The air-conditioned cab of the truck provided welcome relief from the heat.

"Where you fellas heading?"

"West to California," Jasper replied.

"Both you boys heading west?" he asked.

"No, I'm going to Taos," John replied.

"Been a while since I've been in Taos. That's sure some pretty country down there. Them mountains sure are nice. Just curious boys, wouldn't it be quicker to take I-25 to Taos?"

"Yeah," John said, "but Jasper talked me into travelling across the Rockies with him."

The driver tooted his horn at a sedan executing an illegal turn in front of him. "Wish these damn tourists would learn how to drive." He picked up an empty diced tomato can and spit tobacco into it.

"You boys shouldn't get hooked on this stuff. It'll take the hairs right off your chest." He replaced the can on the dash.

"Ever tried--" Jasper said before being stopped by John's sharp elbow.

"Ever tried what, boy?" he asked.

"Ever tried Red Man?" John inserted.

"I don't chew that brand, but I've got a pouch right here that belongs to my wife," he pointed to the pouch of tobacco. "Want a chew?"

"No! No, thanks," Jasper said.

## SLOW TANGO IN TAOS

"Oh, come on. Have a chew. Both of you have some."

"Really, I--" Jasper protested.

John gritted his teeth at the thought as he stared at the package of tobacco.

"Come on, won't hurt you." The tobacco-chewing driver handed the pouch to Jasper, "Stuff some of that in your mouth."

"Actually..." Jasper stammered.

"Now you fellas aren't trying to jostle me, are you? I mean, if a fella is kind enough to give you two a ride…The way I was brought up, if a fellow offers you a friendly chew, it's considered a downright insult to turn 'im down."

"Well…" John took a deep breath. "Since you put it that way, I'll try some."

"Dig right in there," the driver said with a big grin. "That there will put hair on your chest."

John took out a pinch and examined the moist brown tobacco before placing it in his mouth.

"Don't pussyfoot around. Hell, I offered you some good chewing tobacco and you treat it like it might be gold or something. Hell, reach right in there and get a good plug."

John looked over at Jasper who cringed against the passenger door. John reached into the red foil pouch and pinched a larger amount.

"That's better. Now, stick it between your gums and cheeks. My pappy used to like it under his lips. Yes, sir, my pappy was some tobacco-chewing fool," he laughed.

## Phil Cline

John dumped the tobacco into his mouth. A volley of saliva and juice filled his mouth. He reached for the can.

"Don't spit out that tobacco," the driver cautioned.

"Leave it in your mouth. It don't get good for five minutes or so."

He looked at Jasper. "Here, boy, get you some of this."

Jasper hesitantly took the pouch, pulled out a pinch, and placed it in his mouth. He gingerly chewed while turning pale.

"Now, that's being men. I'm proud of you two. Hell, there ain't ten men in a hundred who know how to chew a good plug. Pure heaven, ain't it?"

John strained a smile and nodded as something turned in the pit of his stomach.

"That's some good stuff, ain't it?" The driver turned to Jasper.

Jasper attempted a smile, but pointed to the spit can. The driver handed it to him.

"Spit your juice in here," The driver said,

Jasper opened his mouth and a gusher of black liquid poured into the can.

"So, you guys are headed west? There's some right smart country between here and the coast. You boys been through there before?"

John shook his head.

"Well, it'll be good for you. There's some swell country in these here Rockies. Bought me and the little

## SLOW TANGO IN TAOS

woman a small cabin down south of Cripple Creek alongside a nice stream. Got the purest water you'd ever care to set your eyes on. We go down for a week or two in the summer. It's real cozy in the mountains away from people. Just me and my little woman."

Jasper stared blankly at the road. His face turned paler with each passing mile. John tried to control the growling in his stomach, but to no avail.

"Well, that's Golden coming up ahead of us. I got a load to take to the Coors plant so I'll drop you fellows outside of town. If you want to stay in the area, there's a nice stream and places to camp up this road a spell in Clear Creek Canyon." He pointed down the highway toward the city of Black Hawk.

The truck stopped at an intersection with a filling station to one side and a sign pointing to Golden on the other.

"You fellows take care now, you hear," the driver said.

"Thanks for the ride," John said. He shut the cab door and stepped out. When the truck pulled away, they both spit out the remaining tobacco and rushed to a nearby stream. They stuck their heads into the stream, drew water into their mouths and spit out the remaining tobacco.

"That bastard!" Jasper said. "Man, like he had a big fucking laugh at two guys thumbing a ride."

"Well, at least we got a ride this far." John said.

"So damn fucking mad right now, I could run down

to that Coors plant and punch the bastard!"

"He probably thought he was doing us a favor teaching us how to chew tobacco."

"Bullshit!" shouted Jasper. "Man, I never tasted anything like that crap!"

"Anyway, let's go into Golden and get some provisions for tonight."

"Like what?"

"Like something to eat after my stomach recovers from chewing that damn tobacco." John said. His face flushed crimson and his stomach seemed to continually turn over. He pulled a towel from his backpack, dried his face and took a deep breath. "Let's go."

They passed a city park and crossed a bridge over a clear stream of swift moving water. A large sign on a wooden archway spanning the old downtown street welcomed people to Golden. They walked past an antique store, a bar and a hardware store before arriving at Pop's Grocery Store on the north side of main street. They opened the screen door and entered into an old-fashioned country style store with crude wooden shelves. A large floor fan sent a torrent of cool air across the room that provided limited relief from the heat. The store's shelves were stocked full of canned goods. Nearby, a glass-enclosed counter offered a variety of meats. At the back of the store were a few hardware essentials, such as hammers, screwdrivers, electrical wire and the like. On the walls were nailed old license plates from many different states that hung like

## SLOW TANGO IN TAOS

pictures of former times.

John surveyed the cans on one of the shelves: chili, beans, corn, olives, and many other food items. They walked along each isle while examining the store's offering of canned goods.

"Pork and beans?" John pointed to a can.

"No man! Beans give me gas!"

"How about one of these?" John pointed to the Columbus salami. "We can eat it with bread."

"Cool!" John grabbed two packets of Columbus Sopressata Salami, and a loaf of wheat bread. Then, he placed them on the counter.

After paying for their food, they left. Once on the main roadway, they turned left and headed toward Black Hawk. By the time they found a suitable camp spot alongside the creek, the sun had disappeared behind a mountain peak. With the help of the lights from passing cars, they located a spot to place their sleeping bags among granite boulders that lined the creek.

John placed his backpack on top of a nearby boulder and sat on his sleeping bag.

"You know the name of this stream?"

"Yeah, man. Like it's called Clear Creek," Jasper said.

"This is a great spot!" John looked above the cascading waters of the Creek and marveled at the majesty of the mountains. A full moon highlighted a lone pine tree that clung tenuously to the side of the slope. At the top of the ridge, jagged rocks jutted outward, threatening to tear loose from their moorings and slide down the cliff. Above the mountain top, bright stars punctuated the vastness of the heavens.

John found camping alongside a rushing mountain stream to be somehow magical, almost as though the stream and the mountains were part of him.

"Rushing water makes me relax." Jasper said. He tossed a small rock into the swift moving water, and watched it skip once before going under.

John spread his sleeping bag onto the ground and lay down. He removed a small rock from under the sleeping bag and tossed it aside. A strong wind blew through the canyon.

"Glad we're camping behind these boulders." John said. He pulled a string on his sleeping bag to narrow the opening around his head as a cold wind whipped past.

"Yeah, man, we're safe here. Like…it's beautiful." Jasper said.

"Damn cold here," John said. He looked across the creek. His eyes moved upward to the top of the cliff. He stared at the lone tree at the top of the ridge and thought of his wife and daughter. He wondered about their life in California. Did they miss him? Was he still in their thoughts? Were they disappointed with him? He thought of how his life had changed. How he used to dress in a three-piece worsted wool suit and prepare for work. The pride of walking into his office. The cry of a mountain lion high on the cliff disturbed his thoughts. He pulled his sleeping tighter around him as a

## SLOW TANGO IN TAOS

stiff wind wound its way down the canyon.

As he lay there, his thoughts wandered. He was a nomad without a job, without a future. He was like one of those bums he used to disparage who ask for money and sleep on the sidewalks. He bit his lip and shook his head. His chest tightened. What had he done wrong? He was ambitious, had the right degrees, had good job references, but now he was a vagrant, not knowing from day to day where he would sleep.

Tonight, he camped in a Canyon hunkered down in a warm sleeping bag, but where would he be tomorrow or the day after? Thoughts of failure filled his mind until he sat up, threw a rock as far as he could across the creek and let out a blood curling scream that seemed to come from the very depths of his soul.

"What the fuck!" Jasper exclaimed. "You'll freak out the wildlife."

"Damn!" John buried his head in his hands. "What the hell am I doing here! I had a great career! Shit!"

"It's not so bad here," Jasper said. "It could be a lot worse. I know! I've been in lots of shitty places!"

John took a deep breath and calmed himself by focusing his gaze on the lone Pine tree at the peak of the ridge. He shook his head. A tear slid down his cheek. The unfairness of it all.

"I'll tell you something my friend," Jasper said. "I learned the hard way not to play the 'Poor Me' song. I played that song too much in my life. Got me nowhere! One thing I've learned is there's only one person in this world interested in your career, and that's you. No one else gives a shit."

"You use too much weed," John said. "I don't like this hitchhiking life."

"It's not so bad travelling like this. I'm used to it."

"Of course! Any thoughts about your future?"

"Oh yeah." Jasper took a long drag on a reefer. "One day I might settle down near Taos. Cool place Taos. It's like a spiritual vortex that --" Jasper stopped talking, interrupted by the sound of a jet roaring overhead. "They should ban those noisy beasts."

"Why?"

"They disturb the trees. Trees don't like noise."

"How do you know that?"

"They do. Man, trees hate noise."

Jasper took out another joint and a book of matches. He tore off a match, and struck it. A small ball of fire lit his face. Jasper took a deep drag and handed it to John.

"No, I've had enough escaping. I need to face reality. Get my ass going. I don't need a crutch."

"Man, it's not a crutch. Go ahead! Take it!" Jasper instructed.

John took the reefer, drew smoke into his lungs, and handed it back. To his surprise, his anxiety faded away as he enjoyed the weed.

"No man, you keep it." Jasper pulled out another

## SLOW TANGO IN TAOS

reefer and lit it.

For a long time, John stared at the stars, lost in thought.

"Man, I could fly to the top of that mountain," Jasper laughed.

"Wow!" John let out a silly giggle. "The flowing water sounds like...like a symphony, I can hear the strings, the woodwinds, and all the other instruments. Wonderful!" John moved his arms through the air as though he were conducting a symphony orchestra. Then, he stared at the stars until he fell asleep.

The next morning, John awoke to a cold damp sleeping bag. He looked around to see Jasper washing his face in the stream.

"Jesus Christ!" Jasper screamed. "Damn water is cold as hell!" He looked back at John. "Get up, man! Gotta get back on the road."

John reluctantly slid out of his sleeping bag into the frigid air. "Who picked this spot, anyway?"

"We did. Together! Remember?"

"We should have picked a spot where the sun shines on us in the morning," John said. "It won't shine here until noon, judging from the heights of these peaks." He grabbed his bag and pulled out a toothbrush, shaving gear and a towel.

"You going to shave?"

"Why not?"

"Let your beard grow, man. It's a pain to shave every

day when you're travelling."

"I prefer shaving." John said.

"Suit yourself. Sometimes you won't be able to shave. Then what?"

John ignored his comment. He took a deep breath of cool fresh mountain air before dipping a rag into the icy water. The crisp air smelled of pine trees. He worked up a lather with soap, and washed. Small goosebumps appeared on his skin. He dipped a cup into the water and poured the ice-cold water over his head. Muscles in the back of his neck tightened in protest. He rubbed soap into his hair, worked up a lather, rinsed and shaved.

Later, they ate a quick breakfast of bread and sausage, then headed back toward Golden. After a short walk up the roadway, the sun appeared over a mountain ridge. The rays of heat were a relief from the cold. After a while, Jasper stopped walking.

"Man, I'd swear we didn't walk this far last night."

"We were going downhill," John replied. "It seemed shorter."

"Man, my legs are tired."

"You smoke too much dope! Come on, let's go."

Cool morning air swept past them as they walked, making their hike back up the roadway a little easier. John enjoyed the brisk air that turned his cheeks crimson.

A nearby chipmunk with light and dark brown stripes stood on its hind legs enjoying a nut, but quickly darted behind a tree as they approached. At the edge of the city, a

## SLOW TANGO IN TAOS

barking pit bull from a nearby yard threatened to jump over a chain link fence. John glared back at the dog, hoping to scare him, but that only seemed to further anger the dog. It barked even more fiercely.

"Man, cut it out!" Jasper said. "That dog can jump over the fence if you piss him off."

After a grueling hike, they arrived at the entrance ramp to the interstate highway. They took turns thrusting their thumbs out at cars speeding past. After an hour or so a Ford pickup covered with camouflage paint pulled over and stopped. They picked up their gear and raced to the truck. The driver was a young man in his thirties who wore a pair of faded jeans, sandals and a tie-dyed t-shirt. "Where you headed?"

"California," Jasper said between breaths.

"Not going that far. Just going to Fall Mountain Road. I'll give you a ride to there."

"Where's that?" John asked.

"Up the road a bit. I'll drop you off at the Idaho Springs exit. You can catch a ride from there."

"Thanks, man" Jasper said.

They piled into the pick-up and buckled up. Trees on the hills slid past as they went up one hill and down another. A blue and white truck with its bed filled with lumber slowed near the bottom of a long very steep hill, its brakes smoking from the tortuous descent. John watched as the truck took the exit to Black Hawk, then slowed as it entered a section of roadway restricted to one lane because of construction equipment being used to cut a tunnel through the mountain.

The driver was not a talkative man, but between monosyllables, John learned through several pointed questions that he lived alone at a cabin in York Gulch next to a pond and didn't care much for strangers. He had the perimeter of his cabin ringed with punji sticks laced with poison, and an arsenal of weapons inside.

"This here is where you get off," the driver said as he pulled over and stopped at the Idaho Falls exit. They got out and stood watching as the truck disappeared down the interstate.

"I wouldn't want to be his neighbor," John said.

"He's a crazy dude."

On the opposite side of the roadway, a large wooden wheel painted red, white and blue slowly turned as a cascade of water fell from high above onto the wheel. John took a deep whiff of the heavy Pine scent. He smiled and relished the freedom and excitement. For nearly an hour, they stood at the entrance to the interstate. Finally, the driver of an old dodge van pulled off to the side of the road and stopped.

"Where you headed?" asked the driver, a young Hispanic man of about twenty-five sporting a full beard."

"West coast," Jasper replied.

"We're head'n for the Bay Area. Hop in," said the driver.

"Hot damn," Jasper said. "No more thumbing!"

They scrambled into the vehicle. Inside, several

## SLOW TANGO IN TAOS

Hispanic men were packed in close quarters. John struggled to find a place to sit. Jasper sat on the floorboard and pulled out a joint, lit it and passed it around.

"Both of you going to San Francisco?" The driver asked.

"No, John's going to Taos. Let him off at the Leadville exit," Jasper said.

"No problem," said the driver.

John's muscles tensed and his clamped fists turned white. So many people in the van, so little room. The men spoke amongst themselves in Spanish. John knew basic Spanish, but could not understand all of what they said.

*¿A dónde van ustedes?* Jasper asked. One of the men explained where they were going in Spanish.

John turned to Jasper "What did he say?"

"They're like day laborers. Gonna pick fruit and vegetables in the Central Valley. Man, they're head'n for hard work."

After a short drive, the van went through the Eisenhower Tunnel and descended down a very steep roadway.

"Hang on." The driver said as he applied his brakes to slow the steep descent. At the bottom of the hill, he pulled into a rest stop to examine his smoking rear brakes.

"That smells!" Jasper held his nose.

"Eeez okay," the driver said when he climbed back into the van. He put the van into gear, pulled back onto the road and continued down the highway.

Later, they passed a sign along the road indicating 10 miles to the Leadville exit.

"Your stop coming up," Jasper said.

John grimaced at the thought of being alone again. Soon they came to the exit.

"This is it," Jasper told the driver. "John gets off here."

The driver pulled onto the shoulder of the interstate and stopped.

"Well, man, take care. I might drop down through Taos on the trip back." Jasper said.

"You do that." John opened the door and stepped out.

"Thanks for the ride," John said.

"Eeez okay," replied the driver.

"Thanks guys," John said to the Hispanic men. They waved and said "*adios mi amigo, vi con dios.*"

John smiled and nodded. Jasper waved to John as the van pulled back onto the highway.

# SLOW TANGO IN TAOS

# CHAPTER 6

Dryness developed in John's throat as he watched the van disappear down the ribbon of concrete. He gave a heavy sigh, threw his backpack over his shoulder and headed up the ramp. After several hours of walking, he was exhausted. Leaving the road, he sat down at the edge of a grassy meadow. A single white cloud disturbed the symmetry of the blue skies that lay in silence above him. To the north stood a large mountain peak of granite that glistened in the afternoon sun.

Flecks of light danced across John's face as leaves of a nearby Aspen swayed and turned in the gentle breeze. A small honey bee hovered above his eye. John moved his hand to sweep it away, but that only seemed to excite its interest. The insect paused only inches from his nose.

John leapt up and walked to a nearby stream, but the bee remained with him with an arrogance born of never having been near people. John washed his face with cool refreshing water. Soon, other bees swarmed around him with growing curiosity about the stranger in their midst. John learned not to swat them, but to ignore them. The buzzing of their wings beating the air sounded like natural music. After the bees satisfied their curiosity and flew away, he lay down on the soft meadow grass and inhaled fresh mountain air. The warmth of the sun made him drowsy.

When he opened his eyes, a man stood on the other side of the stream. John watched partly out of fear and partly out of curiosity. The short man had a small tonsorial bald spot on the top of his head. His green camouflage clothing tended to blend in with nearby vegetation. A short time later, he disappeared into the forest.

The thought of being totally alone overcame him like a wild beast stalking the edges of his existence. He became dizzy and his legs were weak. He took a deep breath to calm his nerves. He feared wild animals in the mountains, but remembered the words of his father: *Wild Animals won't bother you if you don't bother them, but always be on the alert because nature is occasionally cruel and deadly.*

John returned to the road and headed up the mountain pass. How long he hiked he didn't know because time has little meaning for an itinerant hiker. He found himself daydreaming frequently and reminiscing of things past. He thought of his daughter, his former wife, business associates and friends. He thought of George, his writer friend. It helped to reflect on old memories because they made him less conscious of his isolation and made time pass quicker.

# SLOW TANGO IN TAOS

As the sun set in the distance, a chill settled in the mountains. He knew he must find shelter. His back ached from the weight of the backpack. His legs were tired from walking. He was hungry but he had neither food nor a place to rest. John wanted to thumb a ride, but no automobiles came along the road. He pondered his lack of preparation from such a long trek through an unfamiliar area.

As he rounded a turn in the road, he saw campfires in the distance, far from the road. John let out a huge breath of relief knowing that other people were near. He came upon a sign that said: *Goose Creek Campground.* An arrow pointed toward the camp in the White River National Forest. As he hiked down the road leading to the campground, he wondered how best to approach strangers in the camp so as not to appear as a beggar, but his hungry, and aching stomach made thoughts of etiquette seem silly.

Camp fires seemed to hang in the distant air as though they were a mirage. The more John walked, the farther away they seemed to be. Soon, the sun disappeared over the mountain and darkness set in. He realized that he no longer looked down at the campfires, but now looked up at them. He scratched his head, but then realized the fires seemed close because he was looking at them across a valley. He had to go down into the valley and up the other side before he could get there.

After a very long hike, John entered the campground located beside a large lake fed by a mountain stream. The excited chatter of children and adult campers filled the air.

## Phil Cline

He remembered the good times he had with his own family. The happy memories made him feel warm inside, but just as quickly, he realized those days were gone forever. His chin began to quiver and he tried to suppress a tear as he stood alone wondering what to do next.

An elderly man with white hair, a full beard and weathered face sat on a canvass chair by the lake. Next to him was a small lantern casting light out onto the water. A red and white bobber on his fishing line floated near the shoreline. John sat on a nearby boulder watching him. Finally, John mustered enough courage to introduce himself.

"Excuse me, sir," John said, as he approached the man.

"What can I do for you, sonny?" The old man looked up at him, his brow wrinkled, questioning.

"My name is John Tollifson. I've been hiking a long distance. I thought I would find a store where I could buy some food, but I didn't pass any."

The old man stared at him. John shifted his stance as his pulse quickened. The very thought of a former executive of a large company dropping so low was painful. After all, he was begging for food.

"I'm hungry," John said. "Can I pay you for a little food?"

The old man studied John but said nothing. John's face flushed and his ears turned red. Finally, John turned to walk away.

"Hold on, sonny," the old man said.

## SLOW TANGO IN TAOS

"I don't like asking for food, but I'm hungry. I've been walking all afternoon."

"Tell you something. I'm not a man who likes giveaways. I've always been against handouts, but then I'm not the kind of man who will turn his back on someone in need. Tell you what I'll do. I'll let you work for your supper."

"Work? What do you want me to do?"

"Stick around, I'll show you," the man replied.

"What's your name?" John asked.

"People call me Tulsa. Like the city."

"Well, Tulsa, what can I do?"

"First of all, we need a fire. I was going to build one myself, but I got to looking out over this nice mountain lake and I just plumb forgot."

"Where do you want it built?"

"Well, now…" Tulsa said as he stroked his chin. "I suppose over there will do." He pointed to a spot near his camper.

"I'll gather some wood," John said. He set his backpack on the ground, and turned to leave.

"Not so quick there, young man, you're going to need a light unless you can see in the dark." He handed John a flashlight. "Can you see in the dark?"

"Not well," John said.

"Go fetch us some fire wood."

John switched on the light and disappeared into the forest. He returned with his arms full of firewood.

# Phil Cline

"That should be enough," Tulsa said. "What we need to do now is a fire pit. Ever done that before?" he asked.

John paused before answering. "No!"

"First off, you dig a trench so the wind won't take the sparks away and start a forest fire." He handed John a shovel. "Dig a trench about two-feet square and about two feet deep."

John took the shovel and tried to push it into the ground.

"You don't dig that way!" The man said. "You dig like this." He put his foot on the shovel, and used his weight to bury it in the soil. "That's how you do it! Where are you from?"

"Chicago."

"I thought so. A city boy."

John thrust the shovel into the ground and applied all his weight to the blade. After several attempts, he began to get the hang of it. Sweat dripped from his brow as he finished digging. He set the shovel aside and examined a large blister on his right hand.

"That's a mighty fine looking firepit," Tulsa said. "What we do now is take some paper, and wade it up like this." He knelt down by the pit. "Hand me some of those smaller pieces of wood. We put small sticks and limbs over the paper, so when the paper catches fire, it'll light the wood. Then we put larger wood over the smaller pieces. That way the larger wood will ignite from the smaller ones. Hand me some larger pieces."

## SLOW TANGO IN TAOS

The old man struck a match and ignited the paper. They watched as the fire ignited twigs, and then larger limbs.

"What we have to do now is catch our supper. Ever fish before?"

"No."

"Well, then you still got a lot to learn. I've got an extra line." Tulsa disappeared inside his camper and returned carrying a rod and reel. The old man picked up his lantern.

"Follow me," he said and led John to the water's edge. He put down the lantern and handed John a rod and reel. "You put your thumb on this little lever right here," he said. "When you cast your line, out far enough, you release it. Here, let me show you how it works. There's already a hook and sinker on this line. I put a float on the line so the hook won't attach onto something in the bottom of the lake. Now, take the rod in your hand."

John held the rod. It had an uncomfortable grip and felt strange.

"Watch me," Tulsa said.

John imitated the way the old man had held the rod and reel.

"Now bring the rod back and flick it with your wrist and when it's about even with you, release the line. Give it a try."

John pointed the rod behind him, and as he prepared to flip the rod, he pushed the lever. The hook and sinker fell to the ground.

"You pushed it too soon. Wind it back up and try

again."

On the next try, the sinker plummeted into the water only inches from the shore.

"I swear, I've never seen anyone like you." Tulsa laughed and slapped his leg. "If you aren't about the biggest city slicker I ever saw."

"Sorry," John replied, his cheeks flushed.

"Well, you keep practicing until you get it right because I've got all night."

After a few practices tries, John successfully cast the line out into the lake.

"That's more like it. Let's bait it up and see what you can catch for supper."

"You mean we're going to eat wild fish?" John asked with dismay.

"They ain't no wilder than those you buy in the stores." Tulsa strung a worm onto John's hook.

"Toss it on out there and see what you can catch."

John pointed the rod behind him, then swung it while flicking his wrist slightly. The cast went well and landed several yards out into the lake.

"A fine job," Tulsa said.

"How did you get the name Tulsa?"

"Well, now…" Tulsa remained in his canvass chair stroking his chin. "I don't rightly know. I've got my given name, but I never cared much for it. I grew up with my folks calling me Tulsa."

"Okay, Tulsa," John grinned.

## SLOW TANGO IN TAOS

"Why don't you bring that wooden folding chair over there," he pointed to a chair leaning against a tree. John got the chair, unfolded it and sat near Tulsa.

"Want a beer?"

"Certainly would!" John said.

"See that ice chest?" Tulsa pointed to a green and white metal ice chest next to his trailer. "Go over there and get us two beers. I'm kinda thirsty myself."

John reached into the icy water chest and pulled out two cans. The temperature of the water stung his hand. He returned and handed one to the old man.

"This will be a meal you'll never forget. I've taken some big fish out of this lake. Darn good eating, too."

"How long does it take to catch fish?" John asked.

"That all depends on the place where you're fishing, the kind of fish, the temperature of the water. Depends on lots of things." Tulsa leaned forward and scanned the lake, lifting his lantern so that it cast light out onto the lake.

"Well, John, I know my bobber is out there because I can see it, but I don't see yours."

"What does that mean?"

"That means, Sonny, that you've probably got a fish."

"What do I do?" John shook with excitement as adrenalin surged through his veins. He scooped up his pole.

"Turn the handle and tighten up the line," Tulsa said.

As he reeled in the surplus line, John felt something tugging at the end. Then the tip of his fishing pole bent downwards.

"You've got one!" shouted Tulsa. "Keep reeling him in."

Soon, a thrashing fish disturbed the tranquil surface of the lake. John kept cranking the handle to reel the fish closer to shore. When it was near the shore, Tulsa dipped his net into the water and retrieved the fish.

"You got yourself a nice bass. It's a dilly!"

The fish flipped around in the net. Tulsa grabbed it, removed the hook, and placed it on a stringer along with two other fish.

"Catching fish is fun," John said. "Mind if I try again?"

"Not at all. We still need to catch two or three more before we'll have enough for our supper."

"This time *you* bait the hook." Tulsa said. John reached into the dark moist glob at the bottom of the can, and pulled out a worm. He grimaced as he pushed the hook into the worm's skin.

"It's not gonna to hurt that worm," Tulsa said with a tinge of disgust. "Go ahead and put him on the hook."

John put the hook through one end of the worm, and then turned to Tulsa for acceptance.

"That's not the way to bait a worm," he said. "The first time a fish comes along it'll take the worm and leave you with an empty hook. Do it this way." He showed John how to make a series of penetrations with the hook into the worm so that it is secure.

"Now, that's the way to bait a hook. Toss it on out

## SLOW TANGO IN TAOS

there and catch our supper."

John tossed his line back into the lake and sat in his chair.

"Yes, sir, Chicago," said Tulsa. "I'll make a fisherman out of you yet."

"First time I've fished."

"I can tell." Tulsa laughed.

"What brings you out this way?"

"Well…one day I got called into my Chairman's office and…"

After telling his long painful story, John took a deep breath and stopped talking.

"Not a pleasant story," Tulsa said. "Think you'll ever go back?"

"Perhaps, one day."

"Don't know if I'd do it," Tulsa said. "My way of thinking is if they did it to you once, they'll do it to you again. By the way, I can't see your cork." He held the lantern high and peered out onto the lake.

John picked up his rod, reeled in the excess line and felt a tug at the end of the line. He brought the fish close to shore and Tulsa plucked it from the water with his net. As soon as he had the fish on the stringer, Tulsa saw his own bobber disappear. He picked up his rod, reeled in a large mouth bass, and placed it on the chain along with the other fish.

"Now there's some mighty fine eating," Tulsa said

with a big smile as he held up the fish.

"What do we do with them now?"

"It would take a city boy like you to ask a question like that."

"I--" John said, before being cut off. His face turning a faint rose color.

"The thing to do now is gut them!" Tulsa said.

"Gut them?"

"Yeah, we cut out their guts out, so they'll be eatable."

"You mean we're going to cut them open?"

"Yep, then we're going to take their guts out."

"You sure we have to do that?"

"Yes, I'm sure. Get me that long knife of mine over there on the table near my camper."

John retrieved it and handed the knife to Tulsa.

"Thanks, Chicago. If you'll bring that lantern over here, we'll clean the fish." Tulsa took a fish off the stringer and placed it on a nearby tree stump.

"Hold the lamp up high, so I'll have plenty of light."

Tulsa held the fish in one hand and the knife in the other. He turned it over with its soft white belly up. Then, he punctured the flesh and made an insertion the length of its belly. John watched with interested amusement.

"Now that's the way you do it." Tulsa held the fish up for John to examine.

"Amazing," John said.

"Your turn now." Tulsa handed him a fish.

## SLOW TANGO IN TAOS

"But I--" John hesitated.

"You want to eat, don't you?"

John nodded. He looked at the fish in his hand, but was uncertain what to do.

"So, clean the fish," Tulsa said.

John grimaced. The fish felt cold, slimy and not of a pleasurable texture.

"Take the knife and slice his belly open," Tulsa said.

John held the blade to the fish's white stomach, but didn't push hard enough to cut into the fish.

"Push harder on the knife. Don't they teach you anything in those big cities!"

John pushed harder and the blade penetrated the skin. He grimaced as the blade buried itself in the soft flesh of the fish.

"Slice toward the head."

John found the process to be interesting but also brutish. Before long, he had cleaned the fish and set it down on a plate. "There," he said.

"Now, we go back to make sure the coals are ready, and we'll cook," Tulsa said.

They returned to the campfire. Tulsa placed a frying pan over the red-hot coals and added oil. He cracked two eggs into a pan, sprinkled corn flower, whipped them up, and rolled the fish in the batter. The oil popped as he dropped the fish into the hot frying pan.

Later, after the fish had cooked, Tulsa dished out the

savory meal onto an aluminum plate. Then, he handed it to John.

"Try this."

John broke off a piece of the fish and blew on it to cool it off. Then put a piece in his mouth and was pleasantly surprised. "Delicious!"

"More tasty when it's fresh," Tulsa said.

"Just curious, Tulsa…where you from?"

"From Sand Springs. It's just outside Tulsa. I come from a long line of tradesmen. My grandfather made the original run into Oklahoma during the Cherokee strip land rush, but by the time he got to the Tulsa area, some claims had already been staked--illegally. Some people--we call them Sooners--slipped over the starting line the previous night. They made their way into what is now Oklahoma and waited until they saw the first people arriving from the Cherokee Strip run. Then they hastened into town to the government office to stake their claims."

"Sounds like cheating."

"Yep, they cheated, and today their offspring own a lot of land. My Grandfather didn't cheat. He worked as a blacksmith. Had a shop in Sand Springs. We were never rich, but we never envied people who owned lots of material things. My parents wanted us to live our lives as we wished, and expected other people to leave us alone."

"Where did the town get its name?" John took a sip of his beer.

"Don't rightly know," Tulsa said. "Lots of places

## SLOW TANGO IN TAOS

around Tulsa have Indian names, but I don't think Sand Springs is one of them. I'm not one to put the Native American down, mind you, like some folks do. I respect their traditions."

"That's good," John said.

"To tell you the truth, Chicago, I never had much schooling. When I was growing up, a man could get a good paying job with a high school diploma. Course things have all changed now-a-days."

"That's right. Many things have changed. People with advanced degrees can't find jobs with the economy the way it is." John sneered.

"You sound a little bitter," Tulsa said. "That bothering you?"

John mulled his words before responding. "I've known a lot of people, but you're one of a very few I've met who isn't phony. You should congratulate yourself."

"Most folks I know are like that," he replied.

"People I know are too concerned with how they can impress people with where they live or what they own. I used to be like that." John paused and thought a moment. "I suppose, I still am. I enjoyed telling people about my yacht and about my Mercedes and about my home on the exclusive North Shore. I used to get a lot of pleasure from watching their envy, but you know what I wasn't doing?"

"What?"

"It wasn't being true to me. It wasn't John Tollifson thinking that way. To tell you the truth, I didn't know who I was."

"I understand," Tulsa said, "but I never had none of them things. Not when I was growing up or even when I had a man's job. Suppose I couldn't afford them things, but I never envied other folks who had lots of stuff."

"I wasn't that way. I had many nice things, but I felt envious if someone else had something better than what I had. I was jealous if another man's boat was just one foot longer than mine. I lived in a very competitive world."

"Tell you," Tulsa said, "where I came from, folks are content if they have a car that starts when they turn the key."

"I envy your world," John said. "It seems warm and simple, removed from the petty malice of upwardly mobile people."

"Upward, what?" he asked.

"The type of people who are anxious to get to the top. People will make a lot of sacrifices to rise in an organization. They think they'll be happy at the peak, but when you're at the top, the only likely route is down. That makes people at the top of the pyramid paranoid. They can't trust anyone."

"You might be right on that one, Chicago. Course I don't know much about such things, but tell me," he continued, "did you enjoy your supper more because you had to work for it?"

"Yes, I did, and besides…I learned how to fish."

"That's a good lesson, Chicago, my boy. There's an

## SLOW TANGO IN TAOS

old saying my pappy used to say: *You can give a man a fish and he will eat one time, but you teach a man to fish and he can feed himself for the rest of his life."*

"I'll remember that," "John replied.

They talked well into the night about different things. John enjoyed Tulsa and listened intently to his life stories. To John, Tulsa opened up a new world to him. A world of simplicity and joy.

As they talked, John became aware of how much he enjoyed being away from the city and living by his wit and being forced to rely on strangers whom he would probably never meet again. He leaned forward and listened with admiration as the old man talked.

"Tell you Chicago, I'm getting tired. Guess I'm getting old. Put your sleeping bag over by the fire to keep warm and I'll see you tomorrow."

Chicago disappeared into his trailer and closed the door. John rolled out his sleeping bag and crawled inside. He gazed into the star-lit heavens and sensed the presence of an infinite universe. The stars seemed to extend forever. The smell of the pines, the wind rustling through the leaves and the sound of water breaking upon the rocks in the creek gave him a sense of excitement and appreciation of this new world. He pulled the cord to tighten the sleeping bag around his neck and smiled with the knowledge that he learned important insights. He felt content and warm inside his sleeping bag. Soon, he fell asleep.

John awoke to the sound of birds singing in the forest

as rays of the morning sun cast their warmth upon the campsite. The brisk air, and the smell of burning wood from other campfires enlivened his senses. He stretched and sat up. The sun's warm rays upon his face made him feel energetic and alive. The smell of coffee and bacon from other campers aroused John's hunger. The aluminum door on Tulsa's camper opened. The old man stepped out, stretched and yawned.

"Why haven't you gotten our breakfast ready?" Tulsa asked.

"Just woke up," John replied. "I'll make the fire."

"Good. You do that."

John rolled up his sleeping bag, and tied it to the bottom of his backpack. He went into the forest and returned with an armful of wood. He put wood on the coals, and blew gently until it ignited.

"Got some eggs, bacon and coffee. That sound good to you?" Tulsa asked.

"Great!"

"Hand me that shovel." Tulsa pointed to an army trenching tool of olive drab paint leaning against his trailer. John grabbed the shovel and gave it to Tulsa who used it to rake coals up against the body of the coffee pot.

"That'll make it boil quicker," he said with a big grin.

"We'll have coffee before you can say jackrabbit."

"Jackrabbit?" John asked, "What's that?"

"Never heard of a jackrabbit?"

"No," John replied.

## SLOW TANGO IN TAOS

"You haven't lived till you've seen a jackrabbit. Why them hop-a-longs get to be the size of a large dog and have ears that stick up nearly a yard. When I was a kid, I saw a jackrabbit that had ears the length of a man's arms. The strangest looking critters you'd ever care to lay eyes on."

"They're in Oklahoma?" John asked.

"Yep, but the really big ones are in Kansas and Texas."

"I'll bet Texas has the largest jackrabbits." John laughed.

"Well, now…" Tulsa stroked his chin." I can't say that you're right, but I'm sure those Texans would make that claim."

Water perked into a glass cap on the top of the pot. The aroma of freshly brewed coffee filled the air.

"Smells great." Tulsa rubbed his hands together.

"Why does everything smell so much better in the mountains?" John asked.

"No air pollution. That's why I like to come here two or three times a year. I like the fresh air. Sometimes I bring the little woman with me, but she don't take much to camping. She prefers staying at home. You know, baking pies or canning home-grown vegetables."

"Sounds like a wonderful life," John replied.

"Nothing better than sitting in your living room and smelling green beans being canned in a pressure cooker. Course the little lady doesn't take too kindly to me enjoying the smells while she's slaving over a hot stove on a summer day. I'll tell you, when we open those jars in the winter and have green vegetables grown in our own garden, boy, I'll tell you, that is something you can't buy with money."

Tulsa stopped talking and pointed to a light blue Volkswagen square-back parked nearby with blue knit curtains covering the windows, and California license plates.

"Looks like a late sleeper over there." Tulsa said.

"Yes sir, them California folks sure know how to make the best of things. Now take that youngster poking his head out between those curtains. I'll bet he's seen more than most folks see at his age."

"Could be." John replied.

A young man with dark brown hair stepped out from the car. He was of moderate height, about twenty-five years old, and wore cut-off jeans.

"That boy doesn't need a camper or anything fancy, just enough room to rest his tired bones." Tulsa shifted the coals to make room for his iron frying pan. He poured bacon grease into the frying pan, and then poured in whipped eggs. John sipped his coffee while waiting for the eggs to cook.

In the meantime, the young man took a towel and a small orange colored tin can down to the water's edge. He dipped the can into the stream and poured water over his head to wash his hair. He shaved, brushed his teeth, and returned to his car.

"Young fellow!" Tulsa shouted. "Would you like to join us for breakfast? We've got a lot more here than either of us will ever eat."

## SLOW TANGO IN TAOS

The young man looked startled, then replied. "Sure."

"Come right over here and get some breakfast."

"Thanks," he said as he walked over to join them.

"Grab yourself a cup over there on the table and have some coffee."

"Thank you," he said. "I'll do that." He picked up a coffee cup and held it up for Tulsa.

"Hold it steady there while I pour." Tulsa held the hot coffee pot with a thick potholder and filled the young man's cup.

"What's your name?" Tulsa asked.

"Name's William, but you can call me Bill."

"You're from California?"

"Yeah. Hayward. It's about fifteen miles south of Oakland in the east bay."

"I know where it is. It's near San Francisco," said Tulsa. "I was stationed at the Alameda Naval Air Station many years ago. It was either go into the Navy or starve, so I went into the military. Grab a plate over there and I'll give you some eggs."

After Tulsa dished out a helping of eggs onto the young man's plate, he opened a tin oven sitting on the coals to retrieve several slices of toast and put them on the plates.

"You two traveling together?" Bill asked.

"No, I'm hitchhiking to Taos," John said. "I stopped here for the night and Tulsa was good enough to offer me food."

"I didn't give you that food," Tulsa corrected. "You

worked for it, and you earned it."

"Anyway, I appreciate what you did," John said.
Tulsa piled scrambled eggs and bacon onto Bill's plate.

"You know," Bill said, as he took a bite of toast,

"I'm heading down to Santa Fe. I could drop you off near Taos, if you need a ride."

"I'd appreciate the lift, that is, if it won't be too much trouble"

"No trouble, it would be nice to have someone to talk to."

"That's good," said Tulsa. "Makes my old heart glow to see people helping each other. That's what the world should be all about, you know, people helping each other. Course you don't get much of a chance to see that any more what with the way the world is now days."

"No, you don't," Bill said.

Yes sir, you two can get to be friends on the way down there to Taos. Several times I made life-long friends when I went on the road. Used to travel a lot like you two. Met a lot of folks down on their luck while I was on the road. Guess that's why I'm so happy to help."

"I'm glad you're that way," John replied.

"I'll say." Bill lifted his cup to salute the old man.

"Here's to your health."

"Have more coffee," Tulsa said. "It'll warm you up on a brisk morning like this."

"My nerves will get jumpy if I drink anymore." Bill patted his stomach. "Thanks, for a great breakfast."

## SLOW TANGO IN TAOS

"You're mighty welcome," Tulsa replied.

After breakfast, Bill returned to his car and rolled up a sleeping bag he had in the back of his car. Then, he walked back to the campfire.

"You about ready to shove off?" Bill asked.

"Yep, ready." John walked to the car and tossed his gear into the Volkswagen.

"Sure, nice meeting the two of you," Tulsa said. A trace of sadness in his voice. "Hope you'll drop by this way again sometime."

"Take care," John shook Tulsa's hand.

"Hold on," Tulsa said. "I want to give you something." He walked back to his camper.

"Take this with you." he handed John a small sack.

"I've made you a fishing kit. It has a line, several hooks, a float and sinker. If you ever get hungry, remember what I taught you. You can get you some bait from the good old earth, and before long you'll be eating as good as you did here."

"Thanks," John said. "I'll do that. Thanks for everything."

"That's good enough for me," Tulsa said with a new lilt in his voice. "When you meet people on your journey, remember one thing even if you forget everything else I taught you…remember that every person has a tale to tell and you can learn his story if you'll just listen," Tulsa said.

"It's something an old friend of mine named Herbert used to say.

# Phil Cline

"I'll remember that." John said.

"One more thing," Tulsa said. "While you're on your journey in life, think of the past as being like a photograph that you can remember, but you can't live in it. Let it go. The future is like a picture you can paint of what you hope it will be like – you can't live there either. The only place you can live is in the present. It's the only thing you have control of, so make the best of the present. Do it for yourself and your loved ones." Tulsa said, his voice cracking.

"I'll remember that," John said. "How I can ever repay you."

"Pass it on to someone you meet who needs help. I'm an old man and all I have to offer is wisdom from mistakes I've made in my own life."

"Take care, my friend," John said. A lump formed in his throat when he noticed a tear rolling down Tulsa's cheek. He shook Tulsa's hand, then got into Bill's Volkswagen.

## CHAPTER 7

The high-pitched exhaust pipes of the Volkswagen came alive as the engine ignited. Bill put the car into gear and eased out of the campground and down an access road. John sighed with the thought that he would probably never see Tulsa again. That bothered him, and he struggled to shake off the thought.

The Volkswagen turned onto the highway and accelerated past a grove of Aspens growing along the side of the road that stood like monuments of nature grasping the morning sunlight in their golden leaves. A morning mist created a light purple haze that hung like translucent silk over the distant peaks. A herd of mountain goats grazed on succulent plants that grew on the rocky slope of a nearby hill.

A sense of wonder overcame John as he watched the scenic countryside slip by. A tinge of hope and excitement filled him. No longer was he a prisoner of the past, but a new and revised John. He felt refreshed with optimism of the future and ready to meet any challenges that might come his way.

"Think your car will make this hill?" John asked as the Volkswagen struggled up a steep incline. Bill downshifted.

"My Volkswagen will make it," he said, "It'll pick up speed when we get over the hill."

After the car crested the ridge, it picked up speed again and regained the speed limit. John sighed with relief.

"What takes you to Santa Fe?" John asked.

"I could ask you the same. What takes you to Taos?"

"To meet with friends of an old college chum," John replied. "And you?"

"Connecting with some people from Big Sur."

"Near Carmel isn't it?" John asked.

"Yeah. It's south of Carmel. Beautiful area, gorgeous sunsets. So, why did you leave Chicago?"

"Long story. I was fired. I walked the streets looking for work, but couldn't find any, so now I'm going to Taos."

"That's cool!" Bill downshifted gears to climb another steep grade. "You'll like Taos. Quaint and interesting. The only problem with Taos is New York City types."

"Big money?"

"They come to Taos and buy local real estate. Drive up prices."

## SLOW TANGO IN TAOS

"People must like it there," John said.

"Great place." Bill shifted back into second gear as the car slowed to a near crawl while going up a steep grade. Bill adjusted the rearview mirror.

"Do you have a job?" John asked.

"I've had a few jobs, but they never worked out. I could never spend a lifetime working 9 to 5. It's like I'm giving up my life. I take a job and it's only a matter of time before I ended up leaving."

For the next few hours, they wound their way along mountain roads heading toward Taos. John gazed out the window, enjoyed the ride.

"So, you were a vice president," Bill said, breaking the silence. John nodded.

"I've met a few corporate executives. Mainly in the Oakland unemployment office. You meet a lot of interesting people in unemployment offices. Oakland doesn't call it an unemployment office, it's called Experience Unlimited."

"Sounds appropriate," John replied as thoughts of his own experience flooded back.

"Yep," he said. "Some people drop out. Others, take up a craft. Any way to make a living. You know the most difficult thing for people to give up?"

"No. What?"

"Pride. That's the hardest thing."

"Yeah, probably so," John said. "I'm told there are many artists in Taos."

"Yep." Bill replied, "There are a lot of art galleries

near the central square. Is your friend an artist?"

"He's a writer."

"Writers are artists. Not much difference between writers and other people in the arts."

John furrowed his brow. "You read a lot of books?"

"Sometimes. Libraries are my main source of relaxation. Whenever I hit a new town, I find out where the main library is. That's usually where I spend my evenings."

"I hadn't thought of using a library like that," John confessed.

"Oh, I use many things for relaxation and recreation, anything that's free. A while back, I was in Colorado Springs. Spent a couple of weeks there. I slept in my car behind a large mound of earth not far from the Cave of the Winds exit on one of the highways. It blocked the bright headlamps of passing autos. I listened to the strong winds at night whipping down through Waldo Canyon. Anyway," he continued, "in the evenings I went to the student union of Colorado College to watch their television."

"No one can condemn you for that," John replied.

"I suppose not," he said as he pulled the Volkswagen off the road and stopped at a filling station. "This is as close to Taos as I'm going. I'm visiting a friend who lives up the road over there. He pointed to a gravel road that snaked its way around a nearby hill. If you keep on this main roadway, you'll soon come to a fork in the road. Stay to the left of the fork in the road and it'll take you to Taos. In a few days, I'm

## SLOW TANGO IN TAOS

going to visit other friends in Ojo Caliente. Good luck."

"Thanks for the lift," John said.

"Sure thing," he replied.

John grabbed his backpack, got out, and watched as the Volkswagen turned off the road and headed up a gravel road. Soon, the high pitch of the exhaust pipes faded as the car disappeared around a bend. John threw on his backpack and opened the door to a convenience store next to the filling station.

"Howdy stranger," replied a heavy-set blond woman in her fifties standing behind the counter. "Don't get many people down here this time of year."

"Used to," said an old man sitting in a rickety rocking chair located near one side of the counter

"In the old days before they got in them confangled new highways, we used to have lots of people pass by. We should'a stayed in Arkansas. Never should'a come out here," he said as he smoked his pipe.

"Well, we're here now, pa. An we're gonna stay." replied the woman.

The convenience store reminded John of an old rural country store similar to those he used to visit with his dad when they were travelling to visit his grandparents in rural Illinois. The store had a slightly musty smell of old tobacco and spilled beer. John surveyed the sparsely stocked shelves. He picked out a few canned goods. Beans, corn, a tin of sardines, crackers, and a small tarp he found in the hardware section. He deposited them on the counter.

The lady rang up the purchases on an old-style brass cash register. When she pulled the handle, a bell sounded and the cash drawer flew open. John paid and put the provisions into his backpack.

"You don't look the type to be hitchhiking mister. You doing it for exercise?"

John fumbled for an answer. "Something like that."

"You one of them professional athletes?" Asked the old man.

"No, I'm not."

"I'll tell you someth'n stranger," said the old man, jabbing the air with his pipe, "only three things can keep a man healthy in this world: whiskey, women and clean air," the old man winked.

"You're right," John chuckled. He opened the door, but his eye caught sight of a white pad of paper.

"How much is this?" John asked, holding up the pad.

"Fifty cents."

John handed her the money, placed the items in his back pack and turned to depart, but remembered his nearly empty canteen.

"Do you have a place where I can refill my canteen? John asked.

"You can fill it over there." The old man pointed to a faucet next to a red coke machine near back of the store. John filled his canteen, slung it over his shoulder and left.

## SLOW TANGO IN TAOS

Several days later, as he trekked down the roadway, he was tired and disheartened. Only a few cars travelled the road, but none of them stopped. He looked out at the distant hills. The sun was quickly disappearing behind a nearby mountain. He knew it would soon be dark and he would need a place to spend the night. The sound of the rushing water came from a mountain stream not far from the road. He walked in the direction of the stream and found a flat area that he felt would be a good place to set up camp. He set his backpack and sleeping bag on the ground.

Then, he found some stones and arranged them in a circle to make a fireplace similar to one he had made as a boy scout on camping trip many years ago. Then, he set out to gather enough firewood to last him through the night. After building a fire, he placed an open tin of pork and beans at the edge of the coals, occasionally stirring them as they heated. The smell made him realize how hungry he had become. After eating, he leaned back against the trunk of a nearby tree and rested. Sounds of animals in the night no longer bothered him. He knew those sounds were just part of the natural beauty of the mountains. He paused to breathe in the mountain air as shadows from the fire danced upon nearby rocks. A sharp sense of excitement and danger shot through him as he realized that he was out here very alone and at the mercy of nature.

He walked to the stream and washed off the grime and sweat of the day, then returned to the campfire to warm himself from the dropping temperature. After eating, he slipped into his sleeping bag. It came as a welcome relief from the cold. He looked at the crystal stars and marveled at their brilliance. There was something magical about the Sangre de Cristo mountains that seemed to stir his creative energy. John reached for his backpack and removed the pad and pencil he had purchased earlier. That night, for some reason, he was overcome by a desire to capture the majesty of the distant horizon highlighted by a full moon. He sketched the scene and tried to capture it on paper. Never before had he felt such a yearning. It was as though something deep within him needed to be released. Perhaps it was from frustration, or perhaps the trauma of his past.

*I'm like a little kid trying to draw*, he muttered after sketching to the best of his ability. He crumpled the paper and throw it into the fire as he realized he possessed only a very basic level of artistic skill.

That night, falling asleep wasn't easy, but when he did, a piercing cry from a wild animal shattered his sense of safety. He retrieved a hunting knife from his backpack and withdrew farther into his sleeping bag. He lay on his back looking at the stars. It was though he was gazing into infinity itself. Wonderful, brilliant, magical.

After a few wakeful hours, he slipped out of his sleeping bag and walked to the stream. The sound of swift water cascading over rocks seemed magical and intriguing. He looked into the moon-cast waters. There, he saw the reflection of a man who bore a distinct likeness to him, but a man tired from a long journey and troubled in spirit.

## SLOW TANGO IN TAOS

As John sat on a boulder at the edge of the stream he descended more and more into depression as he contemplated his life. Then a luminescent rainbow of colors spread out over the water. He blinked in bewilderment. Soon, the colors morphed into small nymphs wearing diaphanous dresses. For a long time, they danced to the music of rushing waters gently caressing rocks. John watched in amazement. Then, the nymphs joined hands and danced in a tight circle. Faster and faster they danced and twirled. Faster and faster they whirled, gyrated and wheeled far into the night. They spun so quickly that their pirouettes produced a whirlpool of color that radiated outward from the stream into the very air of night. Then the dancers disappeared into the depths of the whirlpool they had created.

From the vortex of brilliant colors, arose a vibrant red firebird, its wings extended outward surrounded by a brilliant pulsating band of yellow and crimson. For a long moment, the firebird hovered above the stream as it radiated strength and mystery. John's pulse quickened. His emotions alternated between fear and fascination. Then, a warm loving energy radiated from the apparition that put John at ease. A soft purplish glow surrounded the firebird as it flew from the stream and disappeared into the sky. For a long time, John stood spellbound unable to comprehend what he had just witnessed. With wide eyes and a slack mouth, he shook his head in amazement, and returned to his sleeping bag.

The next morning John awoke to the rays of a new

day. Arriving back at the stream, he wondered if he had been dreaming, or if he had actually seen the mythical phoenix. He washed in the stream, dressed and struck out once more for Taos.

He seemed lighter as he walked, and his feet seemed to move on their own. In the distance, a lone antelope fed on dew filled grass. A mist hung in the air like a mystic vail carrying scent from nearby aspens. What a wonderful new world, he thought. The mountain scenery, distant clouds, wild antelope, deer, and chipmunks all fascinated him. He smiled and drew in a deep breath of fresh air. Something within him had changed, but what?

The cool morning mist soon gave way to a rising sun and increasing heat. After several hours of walking, his enlightened thoughts gave way to growing fatigue and wishes of being somewhere other than on the roadway. He imagined a car would come along, but by late afternoon, he realized no cars were coming.

Sweating and tired, he looked off into the distance, to see grey clouds signaling the approach of a storm. A long sweeping valley separated him from the next mountain, and a misty haze descended along the side of the mountain. Bolts of lightning shot across the heavens, accompanied with peals of rolling thunder. John searched for a place of refuge from the approaching storm. He sprinted to some nearby boulders, pulled the plastic tarp from his backpack, dragged two limbs that had fallen from a nearby tree, and propped them up against one of the rocks. Across the limbs he draped the tarp

## SLOW TANGO IN TAOS

to fashion a lean-to, and placed heavy rocks on the sides of the plastic to keep it from blowing away. Then, he crawled inside.

Soon, the long row of blue-grey clouds rolled across the valley and brought a torrent of rain that lashed against his lean-to, threatening to destroy it, but it held firm. For more than an hour the rain beat down. John retrieved a can of sardines from his backpack and ate them with crackers while the storm raged outside.

When the rain finally stopped, he dismantled his lean-to and laid the tarp out on the ground to dry. The warm afternoon sun felt warm and inviting. He basked in the sun until his clothes dried. Then, he repacked and set out once more for Taos.

As he descended from higher levels in the mountains, the vegetation changed from Douglas Pine and Piñon to Juniper and Sage brush that dotted the landscape.

Two days later, John stood on a ridge overlooking Taos. In the distance, John could see many adobe buildings that formed the town of Taos. He breathed a sigh of relief as he saw the end of his hitchhiking adventure.

# Phil Cline

# CHAPTER 8

John felt a wave of relief as he got closer to Taos. He passed an adobe house with an open field behind the house that extended to the base of a tall mountain. Several goats, a cow and two horses were in the field near a fence blocking them from entering the roadway. The presence of a home with animals gave John a sense of comfort as he descended the final hill leading into Taos. Being that close to his destination after such a long voyage gave him a sense of warmth and security. When he was a short distance outside of Taos, an old Packard automobile rambled past him on the roadway, but the driver ignored John's outstretched thumb as so many others had done. John had stopped being affronted by such drivers, but he remembered when he first left Chicago the personally insult he felt each time a car passed without stopping.

Soon, he crossed an irrigation ditch with a sign that read *Acequia de Juan Manuel*. He pronounced the words out loud, remembering some of the Spanish he had taken in high school. The closer he got to Taos, the more Spanish signs he encountered.

Finally, his outstretched thumb attracted the driver of an old Chevrolet truck from the 1940's. It pulled over to the side of the road and stopped. John quickened his steps.

"Where ya headed?" asked the driver, an older man with tattered overalls.

"Downtown," John said.

"Hop in. I'm going to the Pueblo. I'll drop you at the corner near the filling station."

The man didn't say much as they drove and John was so tired he could not converse without difficulty, so they mostly rode in silence until the truck pulled off the road and stopped.

"Thanks for the ride," John said as he got out of the truck. John glanced up and saw a large sign with an arrow pointing to the Taos Pueblo.

"Keep walking down this street," the man pointed.

"The old square is off to the right. You'll see it."

"Thanks again," John said as he got out. The truck pulled back onto the street and headed down the road toward the pueblo.

Being in a city again felt strange after such a long time on the road. He put his arms through the straps on his backpack, gave a heave to, straighten it, and then started walking.

The smell of exhaust from passing automobiles

## SLOW TANGO IN TAOS

seemed a rude awakening after breathing pure mountain air. The fumes made him cough and look at the cars with scorn. Soon he came to a sidewalk. Good protection from cars, he thought. John marveled at his new surroundings. A young couple held hands as they passed by. Many cars and an occasional bus sped past by on the busy street. Amazing, he thought, how different the high desert buildings of Taos are from those in Chicago. Taos seemed clean and wholesome.

From a nearby city park came laughter of children playing, some frolicking, some on swings. He continued past an assortment of adobe buildings, some with flat roofs, and some with sloped roofs topped by red Spanish tiles. There were shops selling tourist trinkets, some selling hats and textiles, others selling jewelry. Occasionally, he passed a restaurant filled with smartly dressed tourists. He looked down to examine his own slightly tattered clothing and worn boots, as a surge of blood rushed to his face that turned his cheeks a light shade of pink.

Later, he arrived at a downtown square lined with clothing, curio shops and restaurants. Native American men and women wrapped in brightly colored serapes congregated on the square. Children played hide and seek on a concrete gazebo while dogs ran loose in the park. To one side of the square stood an old hotel, the La Fonda de Taos. John walked across the park, past a bronze statue and into the lobby adorned with colorfully painted woodwork carved with intricate designs.

" May I help you?" asked a man at the reception desk.

"I'm looking for Tina Reiner. Do you know her?" John asked.

"Yes," he replied "Are you a friend of hers?"

"Well, not actually. She's a friend of a friend. Perhaps you know George Proctor."

"Certainly, he visits Taos quite often. Is he a friend of yours?"

"Yes, we met at the University. He suggested I come to Taos."

"Oh, Taos is an excellent place. You'll enjoy Taos. Would you like to register for a room?"

"No," John replied. "I need to connect with Tina. Does she have a telephone?"

"Oh, my word, no," replied the manager. "She lives strictly off the grid."

"How do I get to her place from here?"

"Which way did you come in from?"

"From the North."

"Well, you go back out the way you came in. Go out the square to the traffic light. Turn left and go until you get to a fork in the road, there's a filling station--"

"I remember the station," John replied.

"Stay on the road curving to the left and go five or six blocks. You'll see her place on the left. It's a white adobe house with a cottage behind the main house. Do you have a car?"

"No," John replied.

"Perhaps I could find you a ride with someone."

## SLOW TANGO IN TAOS

"Thanks, but I'll walk. You say it's only a few blocks?"

"It's a pleasant walk, and there are several restaurants on the way, if you're hungry."

"Thanks," John replied. He walked from the hotel, crossed the plaza and back onto the main road leading out of Taos. Soon, he came to a restaurant in an adobe building. He paused in front, then decided to go inside. A dog lay near a window on a well-worn oak floor. John sat in a chair at a white Formica table, and placed his backpack on the floor.

"Can I help you?" Asked a young waitress dressed in faded denims jeans. She had a cute set of dimples, blonde hair and wore an elegant turquoise neckless.

"Coffee," John replied.

The waitress left and returned with a cup of hot brew. She set it on the table. John added cream to his drink and listened to conversations drifting across the room. Some spoke of travels, some of visits with friends in New York. Others talked about paintings they had seen or a sculpture they had purchased. He felt at ease in this new environment. Three young people in their early twenties wearing faded denims entered the restaurant and sat at a nearby table.

"Garçon!" shouted a young man in the group, his hair pulled back into a ponytail and secured with a leather band.

"Yes?" asked the waitress.

"Garçon, Garçon s'il vous plaît."

The waitress walked to the table and stood beside them. "Would you like a menu?"

## Phil Cline

"Please," replied a woman wearing a red madras. "Don't mind our friend here, he's a little high."

"You are a pretty woman," said the man, "I'm high, so watch out!" "Actually," explained the woman, "he's a first-rate artist when he's sober, but get him high and he acts crazy."

Amused by the conversations, John smiled and his eyes twinkled. He finished his coffee, paid and left.

After a pleasant walk, he came upon a white adobe house with a single cabin behind. Looks right, he thought. It was a large adobe structure with old weathered wooden beams extending past the roof. The windows and walls of the house were thick with adobe mud.

He walked onto a wooden porch, and looked for a door bell, but found none. John knocked. The door opened and an older Hispanic woman with grey hair stood in the doorway.

"Hola," She said as she looked him over.

"Is this the home of Tina Reiner?" John asked.

The old woman smiled, revealing the absence of a few teeth.

"Si," she replied.

"A friend of mine wanted me to meet Tina," John said.

"Enter," she said with a heavy Spanish accent.

"Thank you," John replied, stepping into the room.

"Sit down. Tina be here soon." She turned and

## SLOW TANGO IN TAOS

disappeared into a back room.

John looked around the room. A colorful rug of southwestern earth colors lay on the floor of old warn oak planks. A couch of aged but good original leather rested against one wall. Above the fireplace, several roughly hewn timbers bearing the mark of an adze stretched across the ceiling. He sat down on a large couch near a window in the living room. Behind the couch was a large oil painting of a young Native American girl with black hair dressed in a rust colored dress. He turned to see the name of Nicolai Fetchin in the lower right-hand corner of the work.

As he waited, a slender man of average height with a scraggly beard knocked once then opened the door and entered. He wore a pair of dirty overalls, stained with numerous colors of paint.

"Who are you?" He asked. John sized him up before answering.

"I'm meeting Tina Reiner," John said.

"This is her pad, why do you want to see her?" He asked.

"My name is John Tollifson, and I--."

"Fantastic! Now what's a John Tollifson?"

John stared at the abrasive young man, grimaced, crossed his arms, then replied. "I wrote Tina a letter telling her--."

"Letter? You from Chicago?"

"That's right."

"You a friend of George Proctor's?"

## Phil Cline

"Yes," John replied.

The man smiled and extended his hand. "Ron is my name. Ron Free. I stay here at Tina's on occasion. That's to say, when I'm not traveling the country trying to sell my work to galleries. George was here not long ago and was worried you might not show up."

"I almost didn't," John said.

"Come, you must be thirsty. Socorro!" he called out. The old woman appeared. "Would you make John one of your fine drinks?" The woman bowed, smiled and disappeared into the back room.

"Socorro makes one of the best drinks. I mean no one, but no one, has ever been able to duplicate her recipe."

"What kind of a drink is it?"

"Taste it when she returns."

"I noticed paint on your clothes. Are you an artist?" John asked.

"I work in a foundry. I make models out of clay and then cast them in bronze."

Socorro returned from the kitchen carrying drinks on a decorative wooden tray.

"You try drink?" She asked.

John took the mug and sipped. It was slightly bitter with a hint of cinnamon, but pleasant to the palate.

"Marvelous drink," John said.

Socorro smiled, pleased.

"She will reveal the recipe for this drink to no one, not even to me," Ron said. "I once offered her one of my

# SLOW TANGO IN TAOS

finest statues. She refused. Me, Ron Free, the greatest sculptor this side of the Mississippi. She turned me down. Said it was a family secret. I told her we could make million dollars if she gave me her recipe. I told her I would talk to my contacts in New York and arrange to sell the stuff, but she wouldn't do it."

"It's a fine drink," John said.

"The after affects are the best," Ron replied.

"Do you know what's in it?"

"No, but I know it has cactus juice, but don't ask me in what proportions or what kind of cactus."

"Interesting," John replied. "Tell me about your factory"

"Factory?" Ron exclaimed. His eyes narrowed and he crossed his arms. "We don't refer to places where art is created as a factory. A factory is a place where automobiles are made, bad automobiles that fall apart. I make art that lasts a lifetime. My bronzes end up in museums."

"I didn't mean to offend you." John replied.

"It's just that I worked in a factory in upstate New York. I know factories. I didn't like working in one. That's why I came out here in search of something new and different. In Taos, I found what I was searching for, creativity. I don't make much money at the foundry, but I wouldn't give up my job for one in New York making two million dollars."

The sound of tires on a gravel road came from outside the house. Ron stood up and peered out the window.

"Looks like Tina's van."

# Phil Cline

John stood and looked out the window. A light-colored Chevrolet van was coming down the gravel driveway. When it stopped, a woman in her 50's with strawberry blonde hair got out. Of average height and slightly plump, she opened the door and entered.

"Ron!" she said. "The foundry must be keeping you busy. Haven't seen you in ages."

"It is," he replied. "Oh," he said, turning to John.

"Tina, I'd like you to meet George Proctor's friend, John Tollifson."

"So, you're the mystery man I've heard so much about," she said. "George was afraid something had happened to you. How was your trip?"

"Very long," John replied.

"George told me you left Chicago. He was in Taos not long ago. He was hoping to be here when you arrived."

"Where is he?"

"George had to go to Beaconsfield, England. He's meeting a producer at Pinewood Studios. They're making a movie of one of his novels

"Great!" John smiled for his friend's success, but thoughts of his own failures turned his smile into a frown.

"If you're tired from your trip," Tina said. "I have a guest cabin out back where you can rest. "

"Socorro!" Tina called out. The old woman appeared from the kitchen.

"Señora," she replied

"Go straighten up the guest house."

## SLOW TANGO IN TAOS

"Si," she replied and disappeared out the front door.

"The guest house is small, but it's adequate."

"Thank you," John said. "I don't want to be a bother."

"You're not," she said with a wave of her hand. "The guest house is empty most of the time anyway. You can stay as long as you like. So, tell me about your trip."

"Not much to say, except the trip was long and grueling. At the same time, I had some unique experiences."

"You'll have to tell me about it sometime," Tina said. Ron set his mug on a redwood burl table with a thud.

"Good, drink, damn good!" He exclaimed. "Well, I must be getting back to my work. Nice meeting you, John."

"Do you have to leave?" Tina asked.

"Yes. The piece I'm working on should be ready by now."

"Are you ready to pour?" Tina asked.

"Not yet. We dipped the wax model in a slip mixed with ground fire bricks. As soon as the piece is baked, we'll pour the bronze."

"I don't know much about bronze making," John confessed.

"Stick around and you will." Ron said. He opened the door and left.

"Ron's a nice man. He gets sort of cocky at times but you'll get used to him," Tina said.

Socorro returned. "Es ready now," she said.

"Your room is ready," Tina said. "Would you like to put your gear in the cabin and relax for a while? You must be exhausted from your trip."

"A rest would be nice," John replied.

"I'll show you to your room."

John picked up his backpack and followed her out the door to a small adobe building behind the main house. Its wooden porch creaked under his weight. Inside, a single twin bed was near a window. It had a colorful orange bedspread and two pillows. On the floor lay a turquoise and white handloomed rug with a red Kokopelli woven into the center. Built into the wall was an adobe fireplace that jutted out a foot or so into the room. The walls of the room were of earth colors of beige with borders of red clay. A simple redwood burl clock hung above the doorway. Tina went to the window and pulled the burgundy curtain to one side.

"You can use this crank to open the window." Tina demonstrated by turning a metal handle with cracked white paint near the bottom of the window.

"I like the paintings you have on the walls," John said.

"Do you know anything about those artists?"

"No. Sorry to say. No, I don't." John shook his head.

"The one over there is by Irving Couse," she said pointing to a painting of young Native American sitting next to an adobe fireplace, the illumination of the fire reflecting on his skin. On the other wall is by Joseph Sharp," she pointed to a painting with a tranquil scene of two horses tied to a railing outside an adobe ranch house. I put them in here

## SLOW TANGO IN TAOS

to liven up the place."

"They remind me of this area," John said.

"They were painted just outside of Taos. Those two artists were founding members of the Taos Society of Artists who were in Taos from about 1914 through the late 1920's. It's a very interesting story. Do you want to hear it?"

"Sure," John nodded.

"Back around 1914, Bert Phillips and Ernest Blumenschein were travelling across Northern New Mexico in a Surry when one of the wheels broke. Blumenschein rode a horse 23 miles into Taos to fix the wheel and liked the area. When he returned with the repaired wheel, he told Phillips about the wonderful effects of light in Taos. Together, they came here, fell in love with the region, and decided to stay. Later, four other artists joined them. Together, they formed the Taos Society of Artists."

"Hope I'm not boring you. I love to talk about art in Taos," she said.

John smiled and shook his head. "I suppose they sold their artwork in the galleries on the square," John mused.

"Not at all. In those days there wasn't a single art gallery in Taos. So, the members took turns taking the group's artwork to Chicago, Kansas City and New York to sell them, something they called the Circuit Shows. Each year, a different member was designated to make the trip."

"That's an interesting story," John said.

"I have other paintings in my house of the Taos

## Phil Cline

Society artists. I received them from a very dear old friend who willed the paintings to me when she died. She knew most of the Taos artists and was a good friend of Ernest Blumenschein whom she visited frequently. He lived in a house on the other side of Taos Square. Bert Phillips, Joseph Sharp and Buck Dunton were also good friends of hers as was Mable Dodge, an heiress to the Dodge fortune. I think they must have given her the paintings because she didn't have much money. She referred to her group of artists as *The Founders*, since they were the six artists who started the Taos Society."

"George told me Taos is an artist colony," John said.

"Taos has always been a mecca for artists. Back in the 1920's the writer D.H. Lawrence lived here. He tried his hand at painting as well. Some of his works are displayed in the La Fonda Hotel down on the square. My opinion is he should have stuck to spending his time writing."

"I don't know how I can thank you enough for giving me a place to stay," John said. "I suppose George told you about my financial situation."

"Most people around here don't have much money," she replied. "George told me you had aspirations of becoming an artist."

"I wasn't aware of that," John said.

"Well, George must have sensed something that you didn't know about yourself. Have you written anything or made any paintings?" she asked.

## SLOW TANGO IN TAOS

"No," John replied, "Too preoccupied with business."

"Pity," she replied. "Do you know how to operate a kerosene lamp?"

"No. I've never used one."

"You'll find a small book of matches over there in the ash tray near the lamp. She removed the glass chimney from the oil lamp. "The lamp is very simple. You roll the wick up like this," she said. She turned a small brass wheel which raised the wick, then touched it with a lighted match. A flame spread out along the wick and lit up the room. She placed the glass back over the wick and locked it into place.

"You have to keep the wick low enough so the glass doesn't get black from carbon. Make yourself at home. There's a small shower stall over there in the corner. It's fed by water from a tank on top of the roof. You can take a shower to freshen up, if you like. I'll be in the main house if you need anything. If you're hungry, come next door and I'll make something for you. Otherwise, come to breakfast in the morning. There is a cord of wood stacked behind the main house, if you want to use the fireplace." She turned to leave, then paused. "By the way, if the flies get too bad in here, there's a fly swatter inside the closet." Tina closed the door and left.

John opened his backpack and laid the contents on his bed. He opened a drawer on an old hand-made walnut dresser at the foot of the bed, and arranged his clothing in the drawers. Then, he undressed and showered. He remained under the showerhead for a long time enjoying the coolness of the water. Afterwards, he lay upon the bed with a towel wrapped around him.

A gentle evening wind coming through the window provided a pleasant relief from the evening heat. The breeze carried with it the smell of piñon that hung in the air like a delicate perfume.

John went to the window to see smoke rising from the chimney of the main house. He ate the last remaining beef jerky he had in his backpack, and then lay down on the bed and fell fast asleep.

The next morning, John showered and dressed, then went next door. Tina was preparing breakfast in the kitchen when he entered. Also, a large man with a well-kept red beard and a Scottish accent was sitting at the table.

"John, glad you're joining us. I want you to meet Reggie Brownell."

"Everyone calls me Red."

"We were talking before you arrived. Red said he's looking for someone for his shop."

"Ya," Red said. "Do ya know how to work a potter's wheel?"

"No. Is it difficult?"

"Depends," Red said. "Some people pick it up fast, others never become good. Would ya like a job turning clay?"

"I'm willing to give it a try," John said, unsure of what the job would be like.

"Well, ya be in luck. One of my workers left last

## SLOW TANGO IN TAOS

week. Ya can fill in for him."

"You offering me a job?"

"Ya," Red said, extending his large hand to John. "Then, it's a deal, shake. When can you start?"

"Tomorrow?"

"Ya, tomorrow would be fine. Do ya know how to get to my shop?"

"I'll show him," Tina said.

"Good. We start work at nine o'clock. Wear old clothes. Clay will get all over ya."

"That's nice of you, Red," Tina said.

"I can tell a good potter when I see 'im," Red winked.

"But, I'm not a potter."

"Ya will be," Red said flashing a big grin as he went out the front door.

"See, all it takes is a little help from friends," said Tina. "That's what we do out here. We help each other."

After they finished eating, Tina picked up Red's plate and utensils and put them in the sink.

"I'll help clean up," John offered.

"No, I wouldn't think of letting a guest help with the dishes," Tina took a plate from John, and set it on the counter.

"But, I would like to help. You're letting me stay here and I should help."

"You're not obligated."

"I would like to help," John repeated.

Tina stood with her hand on her hip and studied John.

"Well, perhaps. Gather up those other things and put them by the sink, and I'll do the washing."

"Deal!" John replied.

Tina drew up a bucket of water, and placed it on a wood fired stove. She used a pot holder to open a door on the stove and threw several more pieces of wood into the fire.

"It'll take about fifteen minutes for the water to get hot. We don't have gas or electricity, but we do have running water."

"How long have you been in Taos?" John asked.

Tina ruffled her brow. "Many years."

"Just curious. If you don't mind my asking…how did you end up in Taos?"

"Long story," Tina said.

"I have time," John set a stack of plates in the sink.

"It began with my divorce in New York. I wanted to get away. I was young and bitter. I had some savings, so I went to Europe for a few months. I was in London where I met a British playwright who told me about Taos. He said he lived in Taos for a while, and was a great admirer of the area. He said Taos had a cleansing effect on the mind, and recommended the area so highly that I decided I had to come here. So, I packed my bags, and headed for New Mexico. When I got here, I was a little disappointed."

"Why?" John asked.

## SLOW TANGO IN TAOS

"I don't know, I suppose I expected to find…" Her voice trailed off. "I don't know what I was looking for. I was about to leave Taos. Then, one night, I went to a little pub down on the square next to the La Fonda. I sat at the bar by myself to drown my troubles when a very handsome man sat next to me. He said he was lonely and needed someone to talk to. I think he felt sorry for me. Anyway, I got to know George quite well. In fact, he helped me get this house. I suppose it's no secret that we were once lovers, but now we're just good friends." For a long moment, she stared at the wall. "I don't know," she said in a low voice. "It's difficult going from lover to a friend. Sometimes it's better to break off the relationship. But, it's different with George and me. Somehow, we managed to remain friends."

# Phil Cline

**SLOW TANGO IN TAOS**

# CHAPTER 9

Lights from nearby homes flickered through leaves in the trees as John left Tina's house after dinner that night and crossed the yard to his cabin. Soft light from a full moon highlighted the great expanse of gentle rolling hills. The smell of piñon wood in nearby fireplaces filled the air. When he opened the door, the room was dark. He retrieved matches from the ashtray sitting on top of the dresser, and removed the glass chimney from the kerosene lamp. He struck the first match, but it failed to light. He struck a second that lit as he fumbled with the small brass wheel that controlled the height of the wick. A yellow flame spread along the edge of the wick as the fluid ignited and created a soft light that filled the room.

Excited by his new life, he looked out the window at bright stars that seemed to extend into infinity. The heavens never seemed so magical. At that moment, something unusual happened. Perhaps it was the piñon smoke, or maybe something mystical that made him aware of something within himself that was strong and alive and beautiful.

He stood spellbound for a glorious moment. He was more and more drawn up into the infinity of the stars. The cool breeze brought him back to his presence in the adobe cabin. As he crossed the room, he noticed a reflection in a mirror hanging on the wall. What he saw was not the stern look of a man heading off to work. This man was different. He had the appearance of someone at peace with himself and with the world. What happened in the past no longer mattered. Only the future seemed important now. John extinguished the lamp, and went to bed.

The next morning, he awoke with a knock at the door. He put on a robe that was in the closet and opened the door.

"Senior Tollifson! Are you awake?"

"Yes, Socorro," he said.

"Breakfast ready in fifteen minutes. You hurry for work at pottery shop."

"I'll be there in a few minutes."

He laid his clothes out on the bed, poured water from a large pitcher into a white ceramic basin, washed, dressed and then walked to the main house.

"Good morning. Did you sleep well?" Tina asked.

"Yes. This mountain air is ideal for sleeping."

Socorro was cooking scrambled eggs in one skillet and making toast in another. After they were sufficiently cooked, she put them onto plates and set them on the table.

## SLOW TANGO IN TAOS

"We eat a lot of eggs. Good source of protein" Tina said. "You'll need lots of energy for work today. Have you ever worked with pottery?" she asked.

"Not since elementary school. I remember I made a small ceramic bowl for my mother. There was a large area of grass next to our house. When I looked out across the field I saw green grass and blue skies. So, when it was time to put on the glaze, I decided to paint the exterior blue like the sky and the interior green like the grass. However, when my teacher saw the bowl she chastised me for not checking with her before selecting colors. She told me blue and green are conflicting colors and don't go together."

"I'll bet your mother liked it."

"She did. She said the bowl was beautiful."

John took a bite of the eggs, and beads of sweat formed or his forehead.

"You'll need to get used to the New Mexican food. Much of it is spicy."

"Ez good, though." Socorro smiled.

"Yes, good." John grimaced and swallowed hard.

Later, as he finished breakfast, his thoughts of walking into a new job and the anxieties it triggered dominated his thinking. He rubbed the back of his neck and shifted in his chair. Then, he left the house with Tina and got into her van. Two cars were getting gas at the corner station as they passed by. They drove past the park and stopped at a light near the downtown square. Then, turned onto the square and parked.

Walking past an assortment of art galleries and curio shops, they stepped upon a long walkway of old wooden planks, John stopped in front of one building and raised an eyebrow. He pointed to its aged wood with small cracks and a slight warping of the planks along the side of the building.

"That's the home of Kit Carson," Tina said. "Carson worked as a scout for the U.S. Army. He's buried out back in the cemetery." Tina said.

Soon, they arrived at the pottery studio. It was in an old adobe building behind an abandoned automotive shop in need of repair.

"This is Red's Pottery shop." She opened the wooden door and peaked inside. John's stomach churned with anxiety. His face flushed. *From an executive to a potter. What a change!*

"Hello!" she called out.

"Come in," came a voice from inside. "Did ya bring the new fellow?"

"I'm here." John stepped inside and looked around. Four potter's wheels stood near the far wall. A sandy haired young man skillfully transformed raw clay into bowls at a potter's wheel. He used his bare feet to push a wooden wheel used to turn a circular platform upon which the clay turned. The wheel clicked with each turn. John took a deep breath. An organic smell of wet clay filled his nostrils.

"Get'n ready to mix mud." Red said. "Did you wear old duds?"

## SLOW TANGO IN TAOS

"The clothes I'm wearing are old," John said.

"Good, lad, put ya hands in here, and help me mix this clay." Red stood beside a large tub containing potter's clay.

"I'll leave you here with Red," Tina said "I'm going downtown to the Chamber of Commerce."

"Is there a meeting today?" Red asked.

"Yes, it's about a permit to build tall apartments near the square."

"Why can't the bloody developers leave our town alone?" Red's face turned red. "Them folks come here to make a quick buck. It destroys our culture. Sometimes I get so damn mad!"

"You're not alone," she replied.

"If you need any help, just yell," Red said. "I'll have my guys down there in fifteen minutes."

"Deal." She opened the door and left.

"It rises my Scottish temper to think those bastards are trying to put an apartment complex right down by the square! Bastards!" Red threw a glob of mud into the water. It splashed brown water onto John's shirt."

"Damn. Sorry. Wipe it with this." He handed John a white rag partly soiled with grey clay. "If ya gonna to work here, ya gotta get used to me. When I'm upset, I'm damn upset!"

"I can tell," John replied.

"We'll mix this mud. Then, I'll show ya around the

shop."

"Where do you get the clay?"

"It's a special mixture from a hill out near the San Ildefonso Pueblo. He reached into the vat and kneaded the clay.

"See the pieces sitting over there?" He pointed with his clay stained finger to unfinished bowls sitting on a long table."

"Yeah," John said.

"Randy made them the other day. He's the guy sitting over at the potter's wheel," Red pointed.

John turned to see Randy who was in his late twenties with blond hair and light blue eyes sitting at the wheel. Then, he returned his attention to the vat of clay. For the next few minutes, John helped Red work the clay into a uniform mixture.

"There," Red said taking his hand out of the mud. "I think that's mixed good enough. Wipe your hands on this, and follow me." Red handed him a cloth and left the vat. John followed him to where Randy sat turning clay on a potter's wheel.

"This is John Tollifson. He's our new apprentice. He's staying at Tina's."

"Hi." Randy looked up momentarily, then returned to his work.

"Show John what you can do, lad," Red said.

"We make all sorts of things with clay. I can flare it

out, like this," Randy spun the clay outward. "Or I can shape it into a long thin column." The clay took on numerous shapes under Randy's expert hands.

"What would you like me to make?"

"Don't know. How about a bowl?" John proffered.

"That's easy." He kicked the lower wheel with his foot and the upper platform turned faster as he shaped the clay. Then, he wrapped a thin nylon string around the bottom of the bowl, pulled the ends of the string and severed the bottom.

"That's all there is to it," he replied. He handed the newly created bowl to Red who carried it to a nearby table and placed it next to others to dry.

"In a few hours, the clay will be ready for the glaze," Red said. "We leave the piece overnight. Then, it goes through the finishing process. That's what Jose over there is doing now. He's very reliable. Always here on time and does great work." At the other side of the shop, Jose sat smoothing the clay's rough edges with a damp cloth and sandpaper. He was in his thirties with dark hair and olive skin.

"After Jose finishes, it goes into the Kiln. Come, I'll show you." They walked out behind the shop to a large brick oven that stood near a tall hackberry tree.

"We keep the kiln out here because it creates a lot of heat." He opened the metal door to reveal two shelves loaded with various sizes of pots, cups and other pottery.

"Follow me back inside the shop." Red said. John

## Phil Cline

followed and they paused in front of a shelf of colorful pottery. "This is where we store the finished product after it comes out of the kiln. From here it goes over to our store. Come on, I'll show you."

John brushed dust from his shirt. They left the shop and walked across the street onto a wooden walkway of old planking. They stopped in front of a shop with an old wooden screen door.

"This is it." Red said and opened the door. "This is where our ceramics become the property of rich tourists."

A bell above the entrance rang out with a series of jingles as they entered. As he looked around the shop, John's first thoughts were of how the display and marketing of the items could be improved.

*Better to put more colorful items out front to attract attention. A hook to get attention of the tourists. That's the Key!*

"How did you get into the pottery business?" John asked.

"At first, I worked with another potter. That's how I learned. Making ceramics doesn't pay much, but it covers rent and expenses. We get along okay. Plus, I employ several people and give 'em an income."

The old wood plank floor of the shop squeaked as John walked around the shop examining the various ceramics. A big boned woman standing behind the counter handed Red a sheet of paper with a tally of the day's sales.

"I'll tally up the total when I get back to the shop,"

# SLOW TANGO IN TAOS

Red said.

He turned to John. "Well, we need to get back to the shop. I'll show ya how to operate the pottery wheel. Maybe ya can turn out something to sell."

Back at the shop, John set about learning how to turn the clay into saucers. At first, he found it unnatural to be turning a wheel with his foot while shaping raw clay with his hands. By the end of the day, he had grown accustomed to the potter's wheel and could even turn out a few bowls

After work, he stopped by Tina's house. She sat in the living room couch reading the newspaper. When John entered the room, she laid her paper aside.

"How was your day?" she asked.

"Making pottery is more difficult than I thought, but I think I'm getting the hang of it."

"I dropped by Red's shop, but he said you had already left. He says you have the makings of a good potter."

*A potter for the rest of my life? This is only temporary.* John paused, as reality sunk in. *This is my life, Get used to it!*

"Red is very colorful. Lots of personality, but he has a temper, that's for sure," John said. "How was your meeting at the Chamber?"

"Oh, don't know how it's going to turn out," Tina said. "Condos near the square would ruin our town. Everyone is up in arms. That is, except the developers. They're pushing hard."

"I need to go back to the cabin," John said as he turned to leave.

## Phil Cline

"Will you join us for dinner?"

"Yes, but first, I need to clean up and change clothes."

# CHAPTER 10

He pushed the window drapes in his cabin to one side to allow more sunlight into the room, then undressed and showered. The water had little pressure owing to the gravity fed water reservoir on the roof. Still, the water felt cool and refreshing, almost cold, but invigorating. John dried off with a towel, lay down on the bed, and rested. He thought of how fortunate he was to be in Taos and away from Chicago. A breeze occasionally moved the diaphanous curtain, providing pleasant relief from the hot afternoon sun as it began its descent behind the peaks of distant mountains. He looked out the window at the rolling hills and shook his head.

*Why did I spend so much time in the corporation? I could have been living outdoors in the mountains. It's beautiful here.*

But, then, other thoughts crept into his mind. *Where is*

*my life going? No money. No future. What has happened to me? Put it aside!* he chided himself. *This is your new life!*

An alarming hoo-hoo-hooooooo drifted in from outside the cabin. John peered out the window. Perched on a limb in a nearby tree was a Great Horned Owl. John detected something peculiar about the owl. Perhaps it was the way the waning light of the sun reflected off its penetrating eyes that seemed to burn deeply into John's soul. He could feel the power of those eyes and their embodiment of something mystical, something universal as though they contained knowledge far beyond the comprehension of mere mortals.

John stared in awe at the bird as goosebumps slid along the base of his neck. His mouth fell slightly open. Then the owl let out a very loud hoo-hoo-hooooooo. Alarmed, John's eyes widened, his heart raced and his skin turned clammy. He withdrew into the room, his heart pounding. After taking several deep breaths, he regained his composure.

*What the hell! Must be from stress.*

He dressed and stepped out onto the porch of his cottage. Baying dogs in the distance alarmed the owl and it flew away. *Fly far away from me*, John muttered. He wondered what the dogs were chasing? Perhaps a mountain lion?

He opened the door to Tina's home.

"Tina?" He called out.

Tina appeared in the doorway of the kitchen. "Have a seat John, we're preparing dinner. Would you like some

## SLOW TANGO IN TAOS

wine?"

"Yes, please," he said, and sat down, still troubled by the owl.

Socorro handed him a glass of wine. John sipped the merlot while thinking about that owl. What was it about the owl that so haunted him? Was it an omen of something? Tina entered the room carrying a cedar splinter with a flame at one end. She ignited the wick of a lamp. "Native Americans believe cedar smoke wards off evil spirits," she said. "I love the smell."

"Wards off evil spirits? Like an owl?" John asked.

"Especially owls," Tina replied.

At that moment, there was a knock on the door and a tall man wearing jeans and a brown canvas coat opened the front door.

"Anyone home?" He asked.

"Oh, hello, Bill. Come on in," Tina said.

"I'm not disturbing anything, am I?" Bill asked

"Oh, John and I were just chitchatting," Tina said.

"I dropped by to show you the latest."

"You finished another one?" Tina asked.

"Yep," Bill said proudly. "Got it outside."

"Well, bring it in, and show us," she said.

Bill returned carrying a large three by four canvas oil painting depicting nothing in particular, but with an assortment of vivid colors arranged in geometric designs with a light blue background. He leaned it against the wall, and turned it so it was illuminated by waning light from the window.

"Marvelous!" Tina said as she studied it. "I think you're finally coming into your own. Abstract Expressionism is definitely your forte," she said with great admiration. "This is a beautiful painting!" She studied each brush stroke, then turned to John. "John, what do you think?"

"I'm afraid I'm at a loss," John replied. "I don't know much about painting."

"It isn't necessary to be well versed in art. Let your emotions do the talking," Tina said. "Your heart, not your mind is the judge of art. If it speaks to you, then it's good."

"Then, I like it," John said.

"Great!" Bill replied, pleased.

"Would you like something to drink?" Tina asked.

"Man, I'm bone dry from working on this painting."

"I bought two bottles of merlot at the package store." She said before disappearing into the kitchen. She returned with a tray of three glasses filled with wine and handed them out.

"Well, here's to your work." She raised her glass in a salute.

"To the resident genius," John offered.

"To a gifted artist," Tina said.

They clinked their glasses together in a toast.

"I worked on this all day trying to finish it," he gushed. "Last night, I lay in bed trying to figure out what was wrong with this painting. You know what? See that

## SLOW TANGO IN TAOS

small blotch of orange paint?" He pointed to the bottom of the painting.

"Yes," Tina replied.

"That was what was wrong!"

"It wasn't supposed to be there?" John asked.

"No, that's not it at all." Bill shook his head and wrinkled his nose.

"It was in the wrong place?" Tina asked.

"No! Like it wasn't there. The orange wasn't in the painting, and it was screwing up the symmetry."

"Oh, yes. Now I see what you mean," Tina said.

"You're right. Without that section of orange, the whole work is out of proportion."

"Bothered me all night. Couldn't get it out of my mind. Just could not figure out what was wrong. Want to know what I did?"

"What?" John asked.

"I was down on the square last night, really distraught. Well, along comes this brightly colored Volkswagen bus with red and orange polka dots. Craziest thing you ever laid eyes on. Well, it didn't sink in all at once. These things take time, you know."

"I understand," Tina replied.

"Well, I went back to my studio and stared at the painting. Suddenly, I remembered that van. Right in front of me was a tube of bright orange paint. I picked up the paint, and smeared it down at the lower right. That made the painting perfect."

# Phil Cline

"That's marvelous, Bill, simply marvelous," Tina said. "The painting looks a little like--"

"Exactly!" Bill said. "Like an abstract whale. Wow, I know the gallery will take this piece, and then, I'm all set for another month. I can use the money. I'm down to eating nothing but catchup and bread."

"Bill," Tina said. "I don't want you to ever do that. There's plenty of food right here and you're welcome any time. I don't want you to go hungry while I have food in my home. Do you hear me!"

"Tina, I ate over here the other night. First real meal I'd had in days. You use your money to buy the food. I don't like being a sponge."

"Don't you ever call yourself that!" she said. "You're creating art and culture. You deserve to be supported while you're working. Don't ever let me hear of you going hungry."

"Yes, mother," Bill joked.

"And don't call me mother! You come into the kitchen while I make you a meal," she said.

Bill turned to John. "She thinks she's my mother," he laughed.

"She's right," John replied. "You shouldn't go hungry."

In the kitchen, Tina took a jar of left-over vegetable stew out of the ice box. Then, stuck her hand back inside the box to test the temperature. "Looks like I need to go down to the ice plant for another block of ice," she said. "I'll do that

## SLOW TANGO IN TAOS

tomorrow."

She placed two pieces of piñon into the wood burning stove, stirred the coals, and poured the contents of the jar into a pot. When it warmed, she emptied it into a bowl and set it on the table.

"Now, sit down and eat," She said.

Later that evening, Tina held an oil lamp close to Bill's painting so that they could examine it better.

"How much will you get for it?" John asked

"Don't know for sure," he replied. "Last time I got one hundred and twenty-five dollars. I hope I'll get one-fifty for this one."

"How much will the gallery get?" John asked.

"Oh, they usually mark it up three hundred percent," Tina said. "They'll start out at about five hundred and come down from there. The art business is slow this year. Not as many tourists, but the gallery is fair. They try to get the best price for the artist."

"When I get money for this painting, I'm going to rush out and buy myself a large juicy steak."

"Bill!" Tina shouted.

"Look, man, like I got these keen incisors that ache to bite into a juicy steak."

"I'll never understand how someone can be an artist and eat meat!" she said. "The very idea of killing a poor innocent animal to eat is disgusting!"

"A man's gotta eat what's good for him. However, that vegetable soup you make is the best in all of New

# Phil Cline

Mexico."

"Thank you," she replied.

"You know," Bill said turning to John. "Tina is the most generous person you'll ever meet."

"Oh, Bill," Tina replied, her cheeks turning crimson.

"The wine is going to your head."

"No, I mean it. You're a swell person. No finer can be found in Taos."

"You don't need to flatter me," Tina said.

"Can I have more wine?" Bill asked.

Tina grabbed the bottle of wine and filled his glass.

"Thank you," Bill said. "Now, that I have more wine, I'll tell you about my style."

"Style?" John asked.

"Yes, don't you recognize my unique style?"

"No, can't say that I do," John grimaced.

"Abstract expressionism," Tina said.

"I've perfected the style of painting used by Jack the dripper!"

"Jack who?" John asked.

"Jackson Pollock," Bill replied. "I could look at his work all day, and never get bored. Jack knew how to paint, and how to live. That is, until he died in a freak car accident."

"Shouldn't you go easy on the wine?" Tina asked.

"No sweet heart!" he replied. "When I get drunk, I'll let you know. Right now, I want to tell you a story. One that

## SLOW TANGO IN TAOS

is important to the world."

"What kind of story? John asked.

"It's a story about whales."

"You mentioned whales the other night," Tina said.

"Come on now, Bill, be serious."

"I am. Whales are much more intelligent than people. They're very organized. They travel in pods. Whales even have sharks working for them. One day I'll publish a novel about them."

"I'd like to see your writing when you finish," Tina replied.

"When I write my best-selling novel, I'm hoping it will pay me a lot because I'm slowly starving by painting."

"Sounds like a good fantasy piece. Perhaps a science fiction publisher will take it," Tina offered.

"I'm tired of not having money. I work all the time painting and developing culture, but what do I get for it? A few measly bucks. Just enough to keep me poor."

"It can't be that bad," John said.

"Really?" Bill raised an eyebrow. "Give it a try. Become a painter. You'll realize what a dog's life an artist leads. If the agents don't rip us off, the galleries will."

"Now, Bill, Betty has been good to you. She's gone out of her way to sell your paintings to wealthy tourists."

"Can I have another glass?" Bill asked.

"Don't you think you've had enough?" she said.

"Yeah, I guess. Can I leave my painting here tonight?"

# Phil Cline

"Of course. I'll take it to the gallery tomorrow."

Bill stood up, a little unsteady on his feet. "Whew, I did have too much to drink. Let me know if my painting sells." He took a few wobbly steps, and disappeared out the door.

# CHAPTER 11

One evening, John felt an overpowering desire to be by himself out under the stars. He left his cabin, walked across a vacant lot into an open field, and climbed to the top of a distant hill. A full moon highlighted the mountain peaks that seemed to rise out of the darkness. An occasional light flickered from a distant home in the foothills. For long moments, he gazed at the Sangre de Cristo mountain range as he stood on the hill. The influence of the mountains that evening made him feel close to nature, and removed from his problems and memories of Chicago.

As a full moon cast its glow over the land, he felt caught up in its beauty. Never before had he felt such a loving warmth as though he had become a part of the rugged mountains, and they a part of him. Never before had the soft rays of the moon stroked his cheeks before gently falling to the ground and carrying with them his fears and painful memories of the past. Looking up at the peak of Taos

# Phil Cline

Mountain, he became surrounded by a soft glow that created in him reflections of times past, of painful memories as well as blissful ones. As he stood on the hill, a soft voice seemed to enter his head: *what happened in the past is as necessary a part of life as breathing. All is well with the world. It is progressing as it should, and you are important part of the universe.* These words repeated in his mind many times as though they were on a recording.

Later, he walked toward his cabin with an awareness that something within him had changed. It was as though the mountains had instilled in him an overpowering desire to accomplish something during his life, something wonderful and mysterious, but without the knowledge of what it was. The fruitlessness of his past came to him with increasing clarity. To have worked so long in the name of profit and greed was wrong. Now that he had gained that insight, he was possessed with an overpowering desire to create. But, it was more than a desire, it was a driving need to create, as though his very sanity depended upon creating something of value.

Light from his distant cabin served as a beacon to guide him as he crossed the field. The nearer he came to the cabin, the warmer and more inviting the light became. He entered his cabin and undressed. Once in bed, sleep came easily.

In the weeks that followed, he worked at the pottery shop during the day. In the evenings, he stayed in his cabin, tirelessly practicing his art, in an attempt to recreate the Taos

## SLOW TANGO IN TAOS

landscape. At times, he was exhilarated. At other times, he was restless. One evening, he crumpled yet one more sketch and tossed it into the trash can. The paper hit the top of the trash can that was filled with wadded paper and rolled onto the floor.

One evening, he left the cabin with drooping shoulders and heavy steps. He walked down to the square, and entered a bar next to the La Fonda. As he drank, he sank deeper and deeper into depression. He sat at the bar with his head buried in his hands when he heard the tavern door open. He turned to see a well-dressed man wearing a wool overcoat, a light gray cashmere scarf and a fedora enter the room. The balding slightly rotund man took off his coat and hung it on a rack. When he turned around, John was surprised to see it was his friend, George Proctor. He waved and joined John at the bar.

"Glad so see you," George said with a warm handshake.

"Likewise. Heard you were in Beaconsfield, England."

"Finished my work there. Thought I'd return to Taos."

"How are things in England?"

"The weather there was simply marvelous, especially after an unusually hot and oppressive summer. Oppressive, that is, for England." He signaled to the bartender for a drink. "Tina told me I could probably find you here. I was relieved to hear you arrived in Taos. I was worried you might stay in Chicago."

"I'm glad I left. I've got a job working at Red's pottery shop."

"Good. Tina tells me you're doing well there."

"I suppose I am." John said. A wave of darkness swept over him at that moment as he considered George's comment.

George tilted his head. "Is something wrong?"

"No." John grimaced and toyed with his beer a moment before replying. "It's nothing…It's just…I don't want to burden you."

"We've been friends for a long time," George said.

"Tell me what's bothering you."

"I need another drink," John downed the remainder of his beer, and signaled to the waiter. "Two more beers." Then, he turned to George. "I was wondering if I'd see you here in Taos."

"Sorry I wasn't here when you arrived, but I was tied up on a film shoot. "

"Must be nice." John sipped his beer. "I was hitchhiking and camping in the mountains. Quite a change from Chicago."

The bartender placed two bottles of beer on the table with two clean glasses. George filled a mug with beer and handed it to John, then filled his own mug.

"I've done some hitchhiking myself in my youth. The experience can be rewarding."

# SLOW TANGO IN TAOS

"I suppose," John grimaced.

"So, what do you think of Taos?"

"I like it here," he paused. "So many things have happened since I left Chicago."

"Oh?" George raised eyebrow. "How so?"

"Difficult to explain. Something seems to be happening in my head."

"I don't follow," George said.

"Lately, I've been frustrated. Like something is lacking in my life."

"Do you miss your job in Chicago?"

"No, that isn't it."

"Your family?"

"Sure, I miss them, but this is different. It's like I need to create something beautiful."

"Tell me more." George's brow furrowed.

"I don't know. Often, I've lain awake at night thinking…I've never been like this before. Like there's a deep chasm."

"This sounds serious." George frowned.

"I used to have confidence in myself. I used to be a gung-ho corporate executive. Now, I'm an artisan making pottery."

"Everyone goes through changes. It's natural," George said.

"That may be, but I've never gone through anything like."

"Did your job mean that much to you?"

## Phil Cline

"It used to mean everything to me, but not anymore. The way I lived in Chicago now seems artificial."

"I'm still not following you."

"It's as though a flame has developed within me. An all-consuming passion for life. I can't seem to control it…it's making me irritable and antisocial."

"Have you told Tina what you're going through?"

"No," John said.

"You should. Other people need to understand. Otherwise, they might think you're rejecting them."

"I hadn't thought of that," John admitted.

"Tina told me you're going through some kind of crisis. She's very perceptive. She's the same way with me. She can detect my every mood."

"You're fortunate to have her," John replied. "The two of you make a good couple."

"I wouldn't go so far as to say that," he laughed. "We have differences which I don't think could be resolved with marriage."

John poured the remaining beer into his mug. "Want to hear something odd?"

"Odd?" George arched his eye-brow. "Like what?"

"In the evenings," John confessed, "Sometimes, I lay awake at night, thinking. Then, I'll take my sketch-book and begin drawing…scribbling away like a school boy far into the night."

"There's nothing wrong with developing a new skill."

"I'm embarrassed to let word get around that I'm

## SLOW TANGO IN TAOS

learning to draw."

"Embarrassed? Why?"

"Because grown men don't do things like that."

"Learning new skills isn't limited to kids! Honestly, you surprise me!"

John's face flushed red. "You're right," he admitted. "Hiding in my room, and scribbling is silly."

"There are plenty of artists in Taos who would be glad to give you instructions on the mechanics of drawing, or for painting or sculpting for that matter. You shouldn't be ashamed. A whole new world is opening for you. Don't fight it."

"Perhaps. I shouldn't have said anything." John took another drink and stared at the ornate shelf filled with bottles of liquor behind the bar.

"No, no!" George raised his hands in protest. "You did right in telling me. You shouldn't keep such things tucked away. Don't isolate yourself. People are a vital link to a struggling artist."

"An artist must earn the title. How can I call myself an artist?"

"You're a struggling artist."

"Struggling. Yes, that's what I'm doing." John managed a wry chuckle. He reached for his beer. "That, my friend, is what I'm doing--struggling."

"Then concentrate your energies, and develop new skills. You must get some pleasure out of drawing or you wouldn't be spending your nights sketching."

John thought a moment. "You might be right," he replied. "What would you suggest?"

"Many artists live in this area. Just ask them for help."

"I don't know…"

"Tina has an unusual skill. She's a little like Gertrude Stein in Paris during the 1920's. Gertrude had a talent for accumulating around her a wide circle of talented people, such as Hemmingway, Fitzgerald, and, painters like Picasso, Matisse as well as other artists. She would draw artists around her and help them develop their talents. That's a rarer talent than artistic ability alone. Tina is the foundation of the Taos art community. When you get back to your place, ask Tina for help."

John considered his words for a long moment. "I'll do that, but do me a favor."

George raised one eyebrow and tilted his head.

"Which is?"

"Don't tell Tina about our conversation. I'll work this out myself."

"All right," George replied. "Only on one condition…that you not cut yourself off like you've been doing."

"I'll try," John replied.

"No. Promise me you won't cut yourself off."

"All right," John agreed. "I promise."

"Good! Let's go back to Tina's. I told her I'd collect you, and come right back."

## SLOW TANGO IN TAOS

John finished his beer and set the mug on the bar. "I'm ready to leave." John waved to the waiter, and reached for his wallet, but George stopped him.

"Oh, no!" George said. "When you get back on your feet, you can pay for my drinks, but as long as you're my guest, I'll pay the bill."

"But you joined me. You're my guest."

"Doesn't change anything." George handed money to the bartender, and asked him, "Are you an artist?" He asked.

"I'm a poet" the bartender replied. "This job pays my bills"

"Here's a little extra. Keep the change." George handed him a five-dollar tip.

"Thank you , sir."

They left the bar, and stepped out into a cold night. George tightened a grey cashmere scarf around his neck.

"Damn cold out here," George said. He put on his gloves. "I hope you're getting used to this weather."

"Look!" John pointed to snow-flakes highlighted by the street lights as they fell to the ground. "The flakes are large."

"We'd better get a move on." George said. "I've seen weather like this before. This is how a large snowfall begins, and I'm in no mood for walking in a lot of snow."

They hastened their steps, but before they reached Tina's house, several inches of snow had fallen. Upon reaching Tina's porch, they stamped their feet upon the planks to dislodge snow.

# Phil Cline

Tina opened the door. "I wondered who was making all that noise."

"It's just us," George said. "This snow makes me think of the good old days back when…"

"I was thinking the same thing," she smiled. "The weather report says we're going to get several more inches tonight. Use that over there." She pointed to a broom resting against the wall. "Brush the snow from your shoes and come on in. I have a warm meal waiting."

They brushed away the snow, and went inside. The fireplace was warm and inviting.

"You two want a hot drink?" Tina asked. George nodded. He took off his coat and shoes, and held his feet close to the fireplace to dry his socks.

"The temperature is dropping to the low twenties. You know what that means?" Tina asked.

"Piñons?" George replied.

"Soon we can go out and harvest piñon nuts." Tina said.

"Gads!" George said.

"It'll be fun gathering the nuts," Tina said.

George nudged John. "What she calls fun I call sheer terror. You ever gathered piñon nuts?"

"No, is it difficult?"

"Tina," George smiled, "we need to initiate John into the art of piñon picking."

*I don't like the sound of this.* John shifted in his chair. *Am I being set up for some kind of trick?*

## SLOW TANGO IN TAOS

"What do I do?" John asked.

"Did you hear that?" George winked at Tina. "We have a recruit. John, you're in for a real treat!"

"Somehow," John said. "I feel like I'm going to get the worst of this."

"Nonsense," Tina replied, "We'll all work together. You'll enjoy yourself even if you do get a little sticky."

"Sticky?"

"We'll get sticky sap all over us." George said. "Someone has to climb up into the trees to gather the cones. The nuts are located inside the cones. Sap from the tree will get on whoever does the climbing."

"Oh!" John replied.

"Don't worry, we have plenty of old rags to tie around your head. It'll keep sap out of your hair."

*Doesn't sound pleasant!*

"Ah, the aroma of Piñon," George replied. "What a luxury! It hangs in the air so pleasantly on a crisp fall day."

Tina handed George a ceramic mug of hot grog.

"You smell piñon smoke everywhere in Taos. After a while, you get so used to the smell that you're not aware of it."

Logs in the fireplace crackled as sap exploded sending small cinders against a metal screen. Flames leaped up both sides of the logs as warmth spread into the room.

John got up from his chair and walked to the window with his mug of grog. He put the tasty liquid to his lips and gazed at large flakes of snow falling upon the moonlit landscape. Smoke from distant chimneys arose in the air briefly before bending down and caressing the ground.

George set his mug on a table. "John told me he's interested in taking art lessons."

"I'm glad you mentioned that," Tina said. "Socorro emptied John's trash can this morning and showed me some of his sketches. I was impressed! The landscape sketch I saw was wonderful. Very original!"

*Oh no! Not those!* John winced and turned from the window.

"I intended to dump the trash last night, but forgot." His cheeks flushed.

"I can give you some pointers," Tina said. "You should never work in secret."

"I learn the hard way," John said.

"Show us more of your work," Tina pleaded.

"I really can't. It's juvenile," John said, his face fully crimson.

"Please," Tina pleaded.

"Come on, show us your work," George said. "You've got to come out of the closet sooner or later. You're safe with us. We're friends."

"Okay, I'll be right back."

Once in his cabin, John glanced at a window left partially open. A thin covering of white powder lay on the floor near the window where snow had drifted in. He closed the window, grabbed his sketch book, and returned.

"Here it is," he said handing the black sketch book to

## SLOW TANGO IN TAOS

Tina. She thumbed through it, stopping occasionally to study a sketch before continuing.

"You're right," she said. "They are puerile and undisciplined to be sure, but something about them intrigues me."

"None of them are very good," John proffered, a nervous twitch crossing his cheek.

"Let me be the judge of that. When did you draw this one?" Tina pointed to a drawing of a red firebird perched on a rock in a stream.

"A while back," John replied.

"It has a strange energy." She said, examining it more closely.

"I had a vision of that while in the mountains," John said. "I tried to replicate it."

"Really? " she replied. "What happened?"

"Well…" John went on to explain about the firebird he saw that night in the mountains while camping along a stream. Tina listened intently as he told the story.

"You may have a secret muse," Tina said.

"A muse?" John asked.

"A little genie who whispers sweet things in your ear, and prompts you to get on with your craft," George laughed.

Tina examined other drawings. One of a mountain range, one of a deer crossing a field, one of a moonlit meadow and others, each containing a hint of mysticism.

"John, I'm impressed," Tina said. "You have talent. Why didn't you study painting in school?"

"My focus was on business, not art," John said.

"A waste of talent!" Tina said.

John shrugged and downed the last bit of grog, and set the mug on a table.

"I'll get more," Tina said. "The pot is warming on the stove."

Tina disappeared into the kitchen, and returned carrying a brightly colored yellow ceramic bowl and a ladle. She set the pot on a table and filled their mugs with additional warm brew.

"I'm impressed with your drawings," she said.

"I think my sketches are pathetic," John said.

"It takes years to develop skill in any of the arts," George replied.

"I know." John shifted in his chair. "George, how long will you be in Taos?"

"I haven't decided, but I need to meet an artist out at the pueblo."

"George sometimes acts as an art broker for one of the New York galleries," Tina said with pride.

"A friend of mine owns an art gallery in New York," George explained. "When I told him I was on my way to Taos, he asked me to drop in on the daughter of an Elder at the Taos pueblo. She studied art in New York and gained the attention of the owners of the gallery I'm representing. She's works in a medium called Native American mysticism."

"Is that Maya?" Tina asked.

"They told me her name is Running Bear," George

## SLOW TANGO IN TAOS

said. "That's the way she signs her paintings."

"That's her Native American name," Tina explained.

"People around town call her Maya. That's the name she was given when she enrolled in the public school. She's attractive and talented."

"I'm looking forward to meeting her," George said, then turned to John. "Why don't you go with me tomorrow out to the Pueblo. That is, if you can get off from your work for a few hours."

John thought a moment. "I think so. Business has been slow lately."

"I'm sure Red won't mind if you took a couple of hours off," Tina said. "He's probably down at the pub having his bitters. People say he's turning into a lush."

"Red is a sensitive fellow," George replied. "I hope he finds himself before it's too late. Wasn't he in Washington before he came out here?"

"Yes," Tina said. "He told me he could no longer perpetuate an unjust system, so one day he quit his research job, left Washington, came to Taos, and stayed."

"Red is an interesting man," John said.

"He's full of odd ideas," Tina replied.

"But they're original," George added. "He could be a first-rate writer, if only he would write."

"We've tried to get him to write a novel or short story many times." She sipped her drink. "He's too bitter to listen."

"A bitter fellow lives a lonely life," George said.

"It's tragic," Tina said.

## Phil Cline

"Yes, well…" George looked at his wristwatch. "We should get some rest. A busy day tomorrow."

SLOW TANGO IN TAOS

# CHAPTER 12

The next morning, John awakened with a knock on the door of his cabin. Tina opened the door. "Are you awake?"

"Barely," John responded, rubbing his eyes.

"You should hurry. George is putting things into the car, getting ready to go out to the Pueblo. He wants to go after breakfast. Get up and come to breakfast." She closed the door and left.

John got out of bed and looked out the window to a landscape blanketed with newly fallen snow. Tracks of birds were visible in the snow beside the cabin. Two cardinals and several blue jays fought over grain that Tina had placed in a birdbath near her house. A deer had been in the yard earlier leaving hoof prints in the fresh snow.

George and Tina were in the Kitchen drinking coffee when John arrived.

"Hope I'm not late." John said as he sat at the table.

# Phil Cline

"Tina and I were just talking about old times." George said. "Tina says you've never been out to the Pueblo."

"I haven't," John admitted.

"Maya's dad believes in doing things the old traditional way," George said.

"He and his daughter have had fierce arguments," Tina added.

"That's what I've heard," George said. "Going to New York to study art must have really set off the old man."

"Oh, he was furious," she said. "It took a diplomatic mission from the town folks to convince him not to disown her. He wanted her to stay at the pueblo and learn the old ways. The Chief said she could learn how to paint at the pueblo, but she was determined to go to New York to study art. She's a very strong-minded young woman."

"When you've finish eating, we'll go," George said.

"I'm finished." John swallowed the remainder of his coffee and stood to leave.

When they arrived at the van, it was blanketed with a thick layer of snow. They brushed it off and got in. George pushed the clutch, put it into gear, and started up the driveway. Before they reached the main road, the wheels lost traction and began spinning. He gunned the engine, but the rear of the van slid to one side. He lifted his foot from the gas pedal and waited. Then, he dropped the gearshift back into low and pushed down on the accelerator. Again, the rear tires spun and the van threatened to slide sideways into a

## SLOW TANGO IN TAOS

ditch alongside the driveway.

"I'll try getting a run at the hill," George said.

He dropped it into reverse and backed down the driveway. He stopped near the house, then dropped it back into first gear and accelerated up the incline. This time, the van went onto the highway.

"That was close," George replied. "I've been telling Tina for years that she needs something with four-wheel drive."

They drove past three-foot banks of snow piled up alongside the roadway from snow plows that came earlier. The van moved easily along the roadway before passing a filling station and turning onto a roadway leading to the pueblo. A wall of sundried mud bricks formed a perimeter around the pueblo area. They entered the pueblo grounds, and parked alongside one of the ancient buildings.

Getting out of the car, they walked past numerous adobe dwellings constructed side by side and one on top of the other. Wooden ladders stood against the lower walls, allowing access to the upper homes. Large weathered timbers protruded from the adobe roofs, remnants of a long-gone era.

"What are those?" John pointed to several small adobe domes that stood under a structure of poles and loosely assembled limbs.

"They're hornos," George said. "That's where they bake bread."

Many residents of the Pueblo were out in a common

area enjoying the fresh mountain air, some baking bread, some bundling herbs, and others gathering water from the stream and carrying ceramic pots into their homes.

"How old is this pueblo?" John asked in amazement.

"The Anasazi established it around the tenth century."

"What's it like inside the homes?" John queried.

"They're all a little different. Most have two rooms. One room for general living and sleeping, and the other for cooking and eating. There are no passageways between the homes. No running water, no electricity. Living is much like it was several hundred years ago."

George pointed to a building with beads and other jewelry hanging outside the doorway. "We'll go into that curio shop over there and ask about Running Bear's dad."

They entered the jewelry shop. Its ceiling was supported by a series of rough-hewn timbered vigas crisscrossed by smaller wooden lattillas. The hard dirt floor had been compacted by centuries of moccasin-clad residents. Displayed for tourists on rough wood tables were bracelets, rings and necklaces of silver and turquoise.

"Where can I find the chief?" George asked the proprietor, an older pueblo woman wearing a buck-skin dress and colorful beaded moccasins.

"Out there." She walked to the entrance and pointed to an old Native American man standing not far from the store.

The Chief had a weather-worn face and a stern

composure. He wore a scuffed pair of army boots with the tops left open. On his forehead was a red and white band, and draped over his shoulder was a bright colored serape of turquoise, red, and yellow.

"Good morning, chief," George said. "You probably don't remember me, but we met several years ago."

"I remember." The chief said, his face lined with wrinkles. "How are your books?"

"Good," George replied. "That was quite a snowfall last night."

"Yes. Much snow. Today, we gather piñon nuts from sacred mountain." He pointed to Taos Mountain behind the pueblo. "Last night, hard freeze."

"Yes, very hard freeze. The reason we came out here is to talk with Running Bear," George said.

He stepped backward, shook his head and muttered,

"Why you want her?"

"A friend asked me to look at her paintings."

The old man's stern composure telegraphed his displeasure. "My daughter deserted our people. She became impure with the ways of the white man. She no longer lives in the pueblo. She lives with a friend on ranch, at the base of Má-ha-lu."

"Where?"

"Out the highway five miles away," he pointed. "At the Bustamante ranch. Many artists live there."

"Thank you, I know where it is." George replied.

"Hope you find lots of Piñon nuts."

## Phil Cline

As they turned to leave, a large brown and white Great Horned Owl lit on the top rung of a nearby ladder leaning against one of the dwellings.

The chief's eyes widened, he stepped backward, his mouth agape and pointing to the bird. "Köwéna!" He shouted backing further away. His face flushed, and his hands trembled. "Bad omen!"

"What's going on?" John asked, puzzled by the chief's behavior.

"Köwéna!" The chief shouted again, and ran into a nearby adobe building. He reappeared holding a small bundle of sage. He ignited the bundle and waved streamers of smoke between him and the owl.

Others members of the Pueblo also ran into nearby buildings and emerged waving burning bundles of sage. In unison they chanted *Köwéna* until the bird flew away.

"You must leave!" the chief said. "You bring bad omen!"

George and John looked at each other. John shrugged. George tilted his head toward the van. "Let's go."

They drove back down the Taos Pueblo road, and turned at the filling station onto the state highway. The snow on the side of the roadway had partially melted from warm rays of the sun and had turned into a soft mixture of dirt and snow that sloshed under the tires as they drove by.

"What happened back there?" John asked.

"Owls are harbingers of death," George said. "When an owl perches on someone's house, it's believed someone in that family will die."

"The Chief seemed to think we brought the owl," John said.

Suddenly, John's thoughts flashed back to the owl in the tree outside his cabin. He remembered how frightened he was that night. He remembered the eyes and the strange power they seemed to possess.

"The Chief might be right," George said. "We may have brought the owl."

"Does that mean we'll die?" John asked.

"Not necessarily. It could mean something else."

"Like what?"

"It could mean the death of a previous life, and the beginning of a new one."

As they travelled down the highway, John's thoughts were of the owl and what it might portend. Finally, George broke the silence.

"The Bustamante ranch was a hotbed of writers back in the twenties. He wanted artists of all kinds to stay at his ranch. It's about a twenty-minute drive from here."

They traveled along blacktop for many miles, then turned off onto a road of compacted gravel that had recently been plowed.

"Most folks living up this way use four-wheel drive vehicles with snow tires, not a two-wheel drive van."

"Does that mean we're going to get stuck?"

"We'll know soon enough," George said.

"How far to the house?"

# Phil Cline

"That's it up on the right." George pointed to a silver building with triangular sides.

"A geodesic dome?"

"They're popular nowadays," George said.

# SLOW TANGO IN TAOS

# CHAPTER 13

They turned onto a narrow gravel driveway, stopped in front of the domed building, and got out of the van. George knocked on the door. A tall young slender brunette opened the yellow door. "I'm looking for Running Bear. Does she live here?" George asked.

"Running Bear?" she said in a huff. "Do you mean Maya?"

"Yes, is she here?" George asked.

"Why do you want her?" She asked, her arms folded.

"My name is George Proctor. I represent an art gallery in New York," George said. "I was asked by the gallery owner to speak with Maya to see if she would be interested in selling some of her paintings through their gallery."

The young woman unfolded her arms, smiled, and stepped back. "Oh," she seemed relieved. "Please, come in."

"Maya!" she called out. "Someone to see you."

# Phil Cline

"Who is it?" came a voice from another room.

"Two men." The tall brunette tossed her long hair to one side as she turned.

"To see me?" Came a whimsical reply from another room. Appearing in the doorway was a slender dark-haired young woman in her early thirties with a symmetrical face and high cheek bones that gave her the look of a high-fashion model.

"Who are you, and what do you want?" Maya asked.

"Tom Ahern of Ahern and Cohen Galleries asked me to look at your work," George replied.

"Oh!" She stepped forward with a broad smiled. "I spoke to Mister Ahern while I was in the city. They want to see my paintings?"

"Yes. Do you have some you could show me?"

"Of course," she said, somewhat out of breath.

"Come."

They followed her into a room that smelled of turpentine. Paintings hung from triangular sections of the wall. An easel at one side of the room held a canvass of Native Americans dancing next to a turquoise lake. Scattered around the room were tubes of paint, watercolors and an assortment of brushes. The floor was a kaleidoscope of multicolored paint splatters.

"Are you working in oils?" George asked.

"Yeah, mainly, but I also do charcoal, watercolor, lithographs, etchings, engravings, you name it. I'll get some of my work." She walked to a shelf, selected several sheets

## SLOW TANGO IN TAOS

of heavy gage paper, as well as two oils on canvass, and spread them out on a large table.

George studied the artworks. An acrid smell hung in the air from a mixture of oils and paint thinners. A whisk of cold air swept through the room and lifted the edge of one lithograph.

"I need to close that window," Maya said. "I opened it to let out the fumes."

"Your theme of mysticism is intriguing," George said. "It runs throughout your work."

"Comes from my upbringing at the Pueblo," Maya replied.

John found it difficult to keep his attention on the artworks. To John, the most beautiful art he saw was Maya, the beautiful dark-haired perfectly shaped maiden, with full lips and dark eyes. John glanced at one of her landscape paintings lying on the floor, but as he looked up, he caught Maya's eye. She returned his gaze with an intensity that John found flattering. Maya diverted her eyes. Her cheeks flushed.

"I like that painting over there on your wall." John indicated to a large painting showing the spirit of an old man in the side of a mountain.

"I worked on the Taos Mountain spirit a long time before I achieved what I wanted. "

"Maya," George said. "Do you have samples of your graphics?"

"Oh, gee, I'm sorry. I took most of them down to the plaza. But, let me look."

## Phil Cline

She rummaged through an assortment of boxes and drawers. "Oh." she pulled out a print. "I have a mezzotint, also I have a plate for a dry point engraving. I could run off a print if you'd care to wait."

"Will it take long?" George asked.

"No, it's just a matter of inking the plate and printing. It's of a flower. I'll set up the press."

John helped her move cardboard boxes away from a hand press near the wall. As he reached out to move a box, their hands touched. A momentary surge of electrical pleasure surged through his whole being. He looked into Maya's eyes and saw a universe of beauty and wonder.

"Sorry, I didn't mean to…" John said.

"It's all right," she smiled.

She mounted a copper plate onto the press, poured red ink onto a glass palette, then worked it with a wide putty knife to get the desired thinness, before pushing a rubber roller across the plate. She then used the roller to transfer ink onto the copper plate.

"Ink that's too thick will really mess up a print. It has to be just right."

"Looks complicated." John said.

"This is a copper dry point plate. It's an engraving that gives the print soft contours. I'll show you in a moment."

She slid paper onto the press, then turned a crank that pressed the paper against a copper plate. "This is basic rag

# SLOW TANGO IN TAOS

paper. I sometimes use Arches or Japon paper, but it's expensive. Costly paper won't bring any higher prices in the gallery. Anyone who thinks money is not important to an artist is wrong. Truth is, we need money to live and continue our work."

"You like money?" John asked.

"I like nice things, and I like being able to buy them. For years, I sold paintings at the pueblo and lived off tourists. I admired their fine clothes, their cars, and the expensive cameras they used to take pictures of us. I told myself that one day I would be like them."

She lifted a long wooden handle on one side of the press, and removed the paper. Imprinted was a soft image of a red rose with delicate leaves. She gingerly lifted the paper and waited for the ink to dry. Then, she handed it to George.

George examined the print. "Very nice. I'll take it back to New York and show it to the Gallery."

"Wait a minute," she said. She rummaged through her art supplies, then returned with a pencil. She signed the graphic and wrote "A.P." in the bottom left hand portion of the paper. "That stands for Artist Proof," she said.

"Would you like something to drink? We have tea on the stove if you'd like some," Maya said with an inviting smile.

"How can we resist?" George replied.

"Carol and I will prepare the tea. You two can go into the living room and sit down."

"I want to take photographs of your artwork to show

the gallery," George said. "I'll join you in a moment."

After photographing Maya's paintings, George joined John who was sitting in the living room on an old couch draped with a bright multicolored cotton throw. As they sat, laughter drifted from the kitchen.

"I think one of us is being discussed," George said.

John leaned forward to better hear the conversations, and caught a few flattering words about himself. Soon, Maya and Carol returned from the kitchen. Carol carried a tray with cups and cookies. Maya carried a large brown pot of earthenware that she set on a table made from a wooden cable reel that was formerly used by the local utility company. Carol poured a brew of light-yellow tea into the cups.

A little later, Maya left the room, then reappeared wearing a brightly colored print blouse with flowing sleeves. She had let down her hair.

"I wanted to freshen up, and clean the oil from my hands," she explained.

Maya smiled. John gazed briefly into her eyes before breaking off contact.

"Are you also a writer as well?" Maya asked.

"No," John replied. "I've never written novels like George."

"What do you do?" she asked. "Are you in the arts?"

John thought a moment. "I suppose I am," he replied. "I'm a potter."

"Really?" Maya replied with great enthusiasm. Her

## SLOW TANGO IN TAOS

jet-black hair accentuated her perfectly straight white teeth.

"Yes, I work with Red Brownell down at the Pottery Works."

"I didn't know Red had taken on help," Carol replied.

"Is he getting any better?"

"You mean with his drinking?" John asked.

"That and his bitterness," Carol said. "I stopped seeing him because I couldn't take his cynicism anymore. I would come home depressed after an evening out with him."

"Maya, I would like to stop by and take photos of your works in the Taos Gallery, if that's alright with you," George said.

"Please do," Maya said.

Later, as they stood to leave, John turned to Maya.

"I really like your paintings. Perhaps I could come down to the gallery sometime and you could show me more of your work." John's pulse quickened, his heart raced and his mouth turned to cotton.

Maya studied John for a long moment before speaking. "I'll be at the Chimayo Gallery tomorrow afternoon. Meet me there at 4:30?"

"I'll be there."

As they drove back down the gravel road, John felt a warm glow cascade over him. He smiled and his pulse quickened. His eyes sparkled with the thought of meeting Maya again.

"She's quite a beautiful woman," George said.

"Yes. Quite beautiful."

"Very talented too," George said.

"Yes, very," John said as he envisioned being out on a date with her.

SLOW TANGO IN TAOS

# CHAPTER 14

Embankments of snow created by plows along the sides of the highway slipped past as they travelled down the roadway. Douglas fir and piñon trees extended as far as the eye could see in either direction, their limbs bowed by a thick layer of snow. John's thoughts were not about the drive, nor the scenery. The possibility of meeting Maya dominated his thoughts as he stared out the window, smiling.

"I'm leaving for New York in a few days," George said, breaking the silence. "Tina will drive me to the Albuquerque airport."

"You're leaving so soon?"

"I need to meet my agent in New York. He says my publisher wants me to write another book."

"Busy schedule," John replied. His thoughts shifted back to the days not so long ago when he too kept a busy schedule.

# Phil Cline

"A man has to make a living." George maneuvered the van around a tight turn in the road.

"I'm glad you've done so well," John said. "Back in college, I thought only a madman would want to make a career out of writing."

"There are a lot of interesting people in my profession," George replied.

"Back in college, I thought a person had to work for a large corporation to succeed," John said.

"When I decided to become a writer," George said, "I had no illusions. I knew the odds, but I was willing to take a chance."

"You must have been certain of your abilities."

"You're wrong. I liked writing, so I followed my interests. Success didn't come easy. As a beginning writer, I had my room decorated with rejection slips. Every time I'd get a new rejection slip, I'd use a bottle of white paper glue to paste it to the wall. Two years later, I didn't have a vacant spot on the wall."

"Didn't you get depressed?" John asked.

"At times. At one point, I was so depressed I couldn't take it anymore. Fortunately, I had understanding friends. I might not be here speaking with you today without them."

"You mean..."

"I might have ended it, as some writers do."

The van pulled into the Tina's driveway, and stopped. A ribbon of soft white smoke wafted from the chimney.

# SLOW TANGO IN TAOS

"Well, let's see what Tina is doing," George said.

When they entered, Tina was using a mop to scrub the floor. George looked around for Socorro.

"Socorro had other work to do," Tina explained. "How was your day?"

"Good," George replied. "I think John came out the better for our trip."

"Oh, what happened?" she asked.

"Running Bear," George said.

"Ah, ha." she said as she put the mop aside. You two go into the kitchen. I have some food set out for you."

Later, John stood on the porch of Tina's house. Newly fallen snow cast a magical glow upon the quiet Taos community as it fell in hushed silence. John stood gazing at his magical surroundings. Headlights from passing automobiles revealed thick flakes falling to the ground. He closed his coat tighter around his neck.

"Quite an evening," George said as he joined John on the porch.

"It's pleasant out here," John replied. "Pleasant, but cold."

"I treasure nights like this," George said. "Memories of Taos come to me often when I'm away."

"Why don't you live in Taos if you like it so much here?"

"Oh, I've thought many times of permanently living in Taos, "George replied. "I don't believe I would appreciate Taos as much if I lived here."

# Phil Cline

George folded his arms to stay warm and looked at smoke arising from a neighbor's chimney. "Funny, I had forgotten how smoke from a chimney rises a short distance and then drops sleepily to the ground. It only does that when it's very cold."

"Your literary talents are showing through," John laughed.

"My age is showing through as well. I can't stay out here much longer--I'm freezing. I'll see you tomorrow." He wrapped his scarf tighter around his neck and returned to the warmth of Tina's home.

John walked across the snow to his cabin. He placed a few logs into the fireplace, struck a match and lit the kindling. A flame crept up the logs as the room became warm and cozy.

He pulled a sheet of drawing paper from a drawer, then stood by the window, and studied the moon-swept landscape of newly fallen snow. He sketched the scene of a lone tree, barren of leaves, standing on a steep hill in a blanket of snow with a pack of wolves silhouetted on the distant hills.

He drew the oil lamp closer and examined his sketch. It seemed to him that his artistic skills had improved. A creative fever prompted him to sketch another, and yet another well into the night.

The next day, after work, John showed up promptly at the Chimayo Gallery. When he entered, Maya was talking to an elderly woman at the back of the gallery. She saw him

## SLOW TANGO IN TAOS

and waved.

"Glad you could make it," Maya said. "My works are over there." She pointed to a series of paintings hanging on the wall. They were of a surrealist influence that bordered on the metaphysical. She showed him several paintings and explained each one. Most had the figure of a Native American shaman and a background of Taos Mountain. John listened intently as she described her work, but his gaze was more on her eyes and finely chiseled face. Her eyes caught his gaze. She stopped talking.

"Are you listening?" She smiled, showing her dimples.

John looked into her eyes for a long moment before speaking. "Would you like to have dinner with me sometime?"

Maya studied him and touched her mouth, before answering. Then smiled. "There's a milonga this Saturday at the Old Martinez Hall. Why don't you meet me there?"

John raised an eyebrow, his heart raced, cheeks flushed.

"It's a dance. It starts at eight," Maya explained. "I'll give you my number. You can call me if you have any questions." She wrote her telephone number on a piece of paper, folded it, and handed it to John.

"I'll be there." He put it into his shirt pocket.

Later that evening, over dinner with Tina, John told her of his gallery meeting with Maya.

"She wants to meet at a dance next Saturday in a

place called the Old Martinez Hall. Do you know where it is?" John asked.

"It's across the street from the old adobe church, the San Francisco de Assis," Tina said, delighted. "Call her and go to the dance."

"I believe I will," he said as he took a bite of food.

A few days later, John entered Tina's house to find George's suitcase sitting near the door with his heavy overcoat draped over it.

"Good morning," John said. "I see you're packed."

"We're leaving after breakfast."

"I hate to see him go," Tina said.

"I hate to leave, but I have no choice," George replied.

"You two can sit and talk while I prepare breakfast." Tina returned to the Kitchen. John sat next to George in the living room. The soft smell of piñon filled the room as they warmed themselves before the fireplace.

"Sorry to see you go," John said.

"I stayed as long as I could," George replied. He sipped coffee from a ceramic mug. John stared into the fire, lost in thought.

"Something on your mind?" George asked.

"I've been thinking," John said. "I need to get a place of my own. I hate relying on Tina. I don't like relying on someone for meals and a place to stay."

"You pay her rent, and give her money for food, don't you?"

## SLOW TANGO IN TAOS

"Yes, but she gives me a big break on the rent and food." He ran his fingers through his hair. "It's like I'm a dependent child. Damn, I'm beginning to worry if I'll ever come out of this."

"Are you thinking about going back to Chicago?"

"No."

"What then?" George asked.

"I don't know. I don't like imposing on Tina. I've become like a permanent house guest."

"Do you have enough money for a place of your own?" George asked.

"No, but I can't continue relying on Tina."

"So, what do you have in mind?"

"Red's health is not good, and his business is failing. I've decided to talk to him about letting me take over the pottery shop. I could pay him a percentage of the sales, say, ten to fifteen percent."

"That sounds reasonable. How do you think he will react to your offer?"

John's muscles tightened as sap from a burning log popped like a loud firecracker, sending an enfilade of glowing embers against the fireplace screen.

"He's well on his way to bankruptcy," John said. "After he's paid us and the supplies, he's lucky to breakeven. If I can improve the quality and get the guys to produce more, I can use my marketing skills to sell more product."

"So, talk with Red. He might welcome a chance to get out and still have an income."

# Phil Cline

"Breakfast is ready." Tina announced. She stood in the kitchen doorway, wiping her hands on a dish towel.

The smell of bacon and freshly brewed coffee greeted them as they entered the kitchen. Both George and John ladled scrambled eggs onto their plates, and grabbed slices of toast.

Later, George loaded his suitcase into the van. Then, all three climbed aboard. John got into the back seat.

Traffic was unusually light that morning as they drove into town. They stopped at a red-light near the plaza, and John stepped out onto wet pavement. Cold air bit his cheeks. The scent of exotic perfume from a woman walking in the nearby crosswalk greeted him as he stood outside the open passenger window.

"Take care of yourself," George said.

"You do the same," John replied. "Hurry back! We'll have lots of things to catch up on."

Tina put the van into gear and pulled away. John's cheeks burned from the cold wind that swept down the street. He paused on the way to work and observed a poorly placed pottery display in the outlet store window.

When he arrived at work, he was met with the normal earthy smell of fresh clay. He searched for Red, but he wasn't in the shop. The others were busy at work shaping clay into bowls, dishes and cups. John examined the backlog of work. When he opened the door of the kiln, he found two days of ceramics waiting to be fired.

Just before noon that day, Red staggered in. His face

## SLOW TANGO IN TAOS

sallow, his clothing tattered and hair unkempt. He went immediately into his office. John waited a few minutes, then knocked and entered.

"We're waiting for the kiln to--" John began.

Red held up his hand. John stopped mid-sentence. The room smelled of Jack Daniels and decay. Red drained the remainder of the fifth, then tossed it into a trash can overflowing with empty bottles.

"Red, I--" John began.

"Don't ya say it!" Red said, slurring his speech. "Ya think I'm a lush, don't ya?"

"We need to talk, but it can wait." John said, knowing how contentious Red had become.

"Ya mean ya want me sober when we talk? Well, I'm not drunk!" Red steadied himself against the desk. His face lined and grey as though life itself were slowly being wrung out of him.

"Yes, I do," John replied. "But, it can wait."

"Come on. Come on!" Red demanded. "Tell me!" He plodded forward with unsteady steps. He reached for the edge of the desk to steady himself, then bent over, dry-heaving.

John sighed with sympathy as he watched Red retching, then wrinkled his nose in disgust. "Not now." John said He stepped backward to the door, ready to leave.

"I ain't gonna be here all day," Red mumbled. "Ya want to talk, do it now!" His blood-shot eyes were a chronicle of his many days of drink with little food.

# Phil Cline

"We need to fire the pottery," John said. "We have a lot of backlog."

"So, fire up the kiln!" Red said, holding onto the desk.

"That's your job," John said.

Red straightened upright and looked John in the eye. "Ya think you can run this shop better than me?" Red said, then paused. "Ya think you're better than me, don't ya? Big executive!"

"I'll talk to you after you sober up."

"Fuck ya! I'm not drunk!"

John shook his head, left the office, and closed the door. The other workers stared through the office windows.

"Okay, guys, let's get back to work," John said.

He went outside to the large kiln and opened the door to reveal several rows of pottery waiting to be fired. He ignited the kiln, and watched the gage as the temperature increased.

*1600 degrees should do it.*

John had watched Red fire the kiln many times, but this was the first time he had actually done it. After successfully starting the kiln, John returned to the office, but Red had already gone.

"He's having a hard time, man," Randy said. "He left when you went outside. Said he's not coming back."

"Where did he go?"

"Out," Jose replied with a shrug.

# CHAPTER 15

Days later, John left the shop and walked across the street and into the local curio shop to use their telephone. He picked up the receiver from its cradle and dialed Maya's number. His heart pounded as he waited for her to answer her phone.

"Maya? John Tollifson here."

"Oh hi," she said.

John's mouth turned to cotton, and his heart pounded. "I called to find out more about the dance."

"I'm glad you did. It's Argentine Tango. A lot of people will be there. It'll be fun."

"I don't know—" John hesitated.

*How can I impress Maya when I can't dance?*

"Tell me you'll come to the dance," she pleaded.

A wave of anxiety poured over him as he imagined himself a fool on the dance floor. He took a deep breath, and gathered his courage. John's throat tightened at the thought of being on the dance floor with the most beautiful woman he had ever seen, but not being able to dance.

He swallowed hard and said, "I'll be there."

The following days seemed to drag. He was seized alternatively between anxiety about dancing and a great desire to be with Maya. His heart pounded with each thought of her.

The day of the dance, he closed up shop and walked home. When he arrived, he washed the grime of clay off his skin from the day's work, changed into black dress slacks, a new red shirt and black leather soled shoes he had purchased at a local thrift store. Then, he went to Tina's house.

"You look nice," Tina said. "You'll fit in well. Everyone dresses up for the milongas."

"I'm nervous. I know nothing about Tango."

"There's a one-hour lesson before the Milonga begins. You'll learn enough to get out on the dance floor. Go ahead and eat your dinner. I'll drive you to the dance."

"I'm like a teenager going out on a first date," John said.

"It's normal to be nervous. Finish your dinner."

Later that evening, Tina stopped in front of a large earth tone adobe building that might have once been a hotel. A long portico with wooden posts adorned the front of the building. Butterflies lined John's stomach as he stepped out of the van. He glanced across the street at the old adobe church then back at Tina.

"Have fun," she said.

## SLOW TANGO IN TAOS

John strained a smile as Tina started the van and drove away. He walked to a set of large oak doors, and paused before entering. He took a deep breath, opened the door and walked inside. Several dancers were setting in chairs along the side of a large rectangular hardwood floor. Others were practicing on the dance floor.

Above the dance floor was an old Spanish style balcony with an ornate oak balustrade that allowed spectators to view the dancers below. John looked around for Maya, but she had not arrived.

At the far end of the room was a dark-haired Latino man with an Argentine accent speaking to a group of people. As John approached the group, the man looked at him, sizing him up. "You here for the lesson?"

John nodded and grimaced a nervous smile.

"Have you danced tango before?"

"No. This is my first time," John replied, trying his best to hide his mounting anxiety.

"Good." The man clasped his hands together and announced: "Everyone who is here for the Tango lesson, gather in front of me."

Six smartly dressed couples arose from their chairs and walked onto the dance floor. The men wore dark suits, some wearing spats. The women wore long sleek tight-fitting red or black dresses with slits up the side all the way to their hips. The smell of perfume filled the air giving the room a sense of exotic excitement.

"My name is Roberto. My partner is Alexandria,"

# Phil Cline

Roberto said. "We're here to teach you the basics of Argentine Tango. As you probably know, the Tango dance originated in Argentina with lonely cowboys who danced with each other. The music is sad and melancholic for good reason. They had no women to dance with." A soft rumble of laughter arose from the group.

"I want everyone to form a straight line across the dance floor," Roberto instructed. "The movement of your feet is extremely important to the dance, so for the first few minutes we're going to practice the walk. When dancing the Tango, you don't lift your feet as you walk. You slide your feet like this."

Roberto demonstrated by sliding his feet forward while his dance shoes remained on the floor in a type of shuffle. He also demonstrated how to walk backwards with a similar sliding of the shoes. Then he turned to the group. "I want everyone to practice the Tango walk down to the other end of the dance floor."

For several minutes, the group of neophyte dancers practiced the tango walk. The women seemed to pick up the technique with ease, but the men not so easily.

Alexandria watched John. He awkwardly tried to execute the walk, but he tended to a normal walk. "Don't lift your feet. Slide your feet forward," Alexandria instructed.

John tried to walk as instructed, but the movement was strange and awkward. Sliding his feet along the floor seemed unnatural, then his thoughts turned to Maya and how he wanted to please her. He turned his concentration to the

# SLOW TANGO IN TAOS

Tango walk and tried his best to master the odd movement.

After the group reached the far end of the room, Roberto said. "Now, I want you to walk backwards using the same technique. Walking backwards is especially important for the women, as we'll demonstrate later."

Walking forward had seemed odd, but walking backwards was not only strange but more difficult as well. John focused his attention and diligently practiced. He often looked behind only to find he had veered to the left or right, rather than moving backward in a straight line.

After half an hour, Roberto clapped his hands. "Now, for the next part of the lesson, I want you to pair up with a partner. We have an odd number, so Alexandra will partner with this gentleman." Roberto pointed to John.

"Alexandra and I will demonstrate the next movement. Alexandra, if you will join me."

The dance instructors moved into what they called the open position with arms bent only slightly, creating distance between them.

"The man moves forward and the woman walks backward like we're doing," Roberto explained. "We're going to practice moving forward for the men and walking backward for the women. During the last few minutes of the lesson, we'll show you how to execute a backward ocho. Now, get with your partner and practice."

All the dancers rejoined with their partners. John returned to the dark-haired Argentinian instructor and put his left hand in her right hand and his right hand on her left hip.

# Phil Cline

"You need to maintain firm contact with your arms," Alexandra explained. "Lean forward slightly and push forward with your chest as you move."

This movement was strange and unsettling to John, and his head was swimming with confusion, but once more he thought of Maya and focused his attention.

"Good," Alexandria said. "I think you're getting the technique. Have you danced the Tango before?"

"No, but I did a little ballroom dancing when I was in high school," John said.

"That's good. It shows."

"Why is it called an ocho?" John asked.

"Because the movement looks like a figure eight. Ocho is the number eight in Spanish."

"How do we do the backward ocho?" John asked.

"I'll show you. As we move, slide your feet to either side of mine. I'll guide you through the movement. At the same time, you control me by moving your shoulders back and forth. Since our embrace is firm, when you move your right shoulder, it will force me to move to your left, and when you move your left shoulder, you'll force me to move to the right. Keep your arms firm and turn your shoulders with the upper part of your body." Alexandria demonstrated the movement. "Now, let's try doing the backward ocho."

Alexandria stepped backward with her left foot to her right side while pivoting on the ball of her left foot before swinging her right foot to her left side and then pivoting to her right side and landing on the ball of her right foot and

## SLOW TANGO IN TAOS

again pivoting. Then, once more back to her left side, pivoting on the ball of her left foot. This movement was repeated as they progressed down the dance floor. John was surprised that he was actually dancing the Tango.

*Helps to have an instructor to dance with.*

Later, when the dance lesson ended, John saw Maya entering the dance hall. She was dressed in a tight red dress with black fringe and an opening cut up the side of the dress all the way to her hip. His heart skipped a beat.

She sat down, opened a small black bag, and put on a pair of red tango shoes with high heels.

When the lesson ended, John walked across the dance floor.

"Hello," John said. He sat next to Maya. "You look stunning."

"Thank you. Enjoy the lesson?"

"Yes, but it was difficult."

"It gets easier with practice. I'll show you a few more moves when we get on the dance floor."

Promptly at eight o'clock the Milonga began with music by Astor Piazzolla. Butterflies returned to John's stomach – it was time for him to perform.

"What's the name of this music?"

"It's called Todo Buenos Aires. It's a beautiful piece." She looked into John's eyes and said, "Let's dance."

"Okay," John said, but he was reluctant to get out on the dance floor.

"The Tango is a dance of the heart," Maya said as she

led John onto the dance floor, and stopped. Maya held up her right hand. John joined hers with his left hand. She placed his right hand around her waist. Her perfume was intoxicating and put John into a world he had never known.

"One of the rules in Tango," she said, "is always move in the line of dance which is counter clockwise. That way we won't run into other dancers."

"We practiced the open embrace during the lesson," John said.

"That's a good start, but when you approach a woman to dance, you let her determine whether she prefers open or close-embrace. Many women dancing for the first time with a man will want to keep distance between them, so they prefer the open-embrace. At least for the first dance or two. With you, we'll dance the close embrace."

"How do we do that?"

"I'll show you."

"Now, lean forward slightly so that the distance between us forms a slight "A" shape. Keep your right arm around my back the palm of hand on the right side of my back. Bend your left elbow into a right angle while holding my hand. Keep a little tension in your left arm so you can control my movements. When you move me forward, lead out with your chest."

John's heart skipped a few beats as they danced. His movements were awkward, and a wave of relief swept over him when the Piazzola piece finally ended. They left the dance floor, and remained seated while awaiting the next selection. When the music began, John's pulse rate increased again.

"This music is very fast," John said. "What's the name of this piece?"

"It's called a Milonga," Maya explained. "It's danced with quick steps."

"I'm confused," John confessed. "I thought the dance event is called a Milonga."

"It is. The word Milonga refers to two different things. It's the name of the Tango dance event, but it is also the name of a type of Tango danced with quick steps. It's more difficult to dance. We can sit this one out."

John watched as a wave of lithe bodies swept across the floor, twisting, turning and spinning in sleek undulating movements. A kaleidoscope of bright colors filled the room as he sat transfixed. The beauty and sensuality of the dance fascinated him as the dancers swept across the floor, the women in bright dresses and the alpha males in double-breasted dark suits, black shoes and white spats. The couples remained locked together in a sensual embrace as they danced.

"Excellent dancers," John remarked.

"Most of them have been dancing a long time," Maya said.

When the next dance began, it was much slower, an intense piece of music, yet surprising in its beauty.

"What's the name of this one?" John asked.

"It's nuevo tango. The song is called Tango Santa

Maria. This piece is perfect for dancing."

They returned to the dance floor and embraced. John lead out with his chest as instructed, and they moved along the line of dance.

"I'm afraid I might step on your feet," John said.

"That won't happen if you push forward with your chest," she said.

He found the close embrace to be more difficult than with the open embrace to judge the location of Maya's feet.

"Now, put me into a backward ocho," she instructed.

He moved his shoulders rhythmically from side to side while sliding his feet to either side of Maya's. The movement felt awkward, but he succeeded in putting her into a backward ocho.

"Very good. You're a fast learner," she said.

On the balcony, spectators leaned over the railing, watching. The men watching from above wore dark three-piece suits, some with fedoras. The women wore brightly colored and alluring dresses. All leaned forward to watch the beauty unfolding below them on the dance floor.

"Very good!" Maya said. "I'll show you another movement. While I'm in the backward ocho, move me to your right side and prevent me from moving forward by stopping my foot with your right foot. It's called a parada. Then, bump me lightly with your hip and I'll do a gancho."

As instructed John moved her to his right side, slid his right foot to her right shoe and bumped her hip. In response, her left leg hooked outward in a beautiful quick

## SLOW TANGO IN TAOS

movement.

"You're doing very well, John. You dance very well for this to be your first Milonga," she said.

John smiled, but his eyes followed other dancers moving like graceful swans across the dance floor.

"Don't look at them. You're dancing with me."

"All those fancy moves," John mused.

"Takes practice. You feel the music and your body reacts."

"Is that the way it's danced in South America?" John asked.

In Argentina, the Tango is danced slowly. No one executes fancy movements. The dancers in Buenos Aires fall into the mood of the music. That's important. Personally, I prefer dancing the slow Tango."

"Slow Tango in Taos," John mused.

John's anxiety slowly disappeared as he gradually fell into the flow of the music. To his amazement, he enjoyed the dance.

As the night progressed, he found he was falling more and more for Maya. Her perfume filled his mind with fanciful thoughts. Her perfect body pressing against him during the close embrace released romantic emotions. She seemed to sense his reaction and pressed closer.

When the final song finished, John wished the dance could have continue into the night, and reluctantly left the dance floor. Once they reached their seats, Maya retrieved a black bag from under her chair and changed into her street shoes.

"Tina told me you may need a ride home." Maya said as she slipped on her shoes.

"I could use a ride," John replied. "I don't have a car."

"I'll give you a ride," she said.

Later that night, Maya stopped her Jeep in front of Tina's house.

"Thanks for a wonderful evening," Maya said.

"It was wonderful. Hope my dancing didn't embarrass you."

"You dance very well...for a beginner." Maya paused a moment. "I'm going to a demonstration this Thursday. Would you like to join me?"

"Demonstration?"

"Yes, against the new apartment buildings planned for the square."

"Yes, I would like to go with you." John replied as he thought it a wonderful way to spend more time with Maya.

"I'll meet you at the La Fonda. Say five o'clock?"

"Great. I'll be there," John said.

"I had a lot of fun tonight." Maya smiled.

"So, did I," John replied. He gave her a quick goodnight kiss and got out of the car. She waved, backed the jeep up the drive and turned onto the road. John walked back into his cabin, undressed and crawled into bed.

# CHAPTER 16

The following days seemed to drag for John. He kept thinking of Maya and remembering the smell of her perfume and the feel of her firm body against him. He couldn't concentrate very well on his art work or on daily activities at the ceramics shop because his thoughts were of Maya.

Finally, the day arrived. He left the shop and headed to the downtown square. Snow crunched under his feet as it gave way to the weight of his footsteps. The air was bitterly cold, but that didn't bother him.

When he got to the plaza, an angry crowd had gathered. Several people held signs of protest. Some read *Down with the Mayor*! Others read *You sold us out!* He looked around for Maya, but she had not arrived, so he went into a bar near the La Fonda to wait. He sat on a stool at a well-crafted cherry wood bar.

"What can ah do for you, honey?" Asked a middle-aged blonde waitress.

"A draft."

"A draft for this young man," she said to the barkeep.

The bartender pulled one of the long draft handles behind bar and filled a pint mug with beer. He put it on the bar. John sat at the bar nursing his drink and waiting for Maya.

He had nearly finished his beer, and was lifting the mug to his lips to drain the final drops when something disturbed him. His brow wrinkled. He looked behind the bar at the rows of alcohol bottles of various shapes, sizes and colors. In a large mirror behind the bottles, he could see an image of himself sitting at the bar with a beer mug in his hand. Then, his eyes moved up the rows of shelving to the very top. There they focused on a Great Horned Owl sculpted of Carrara marble that perched on a small ledge at the very peak of a decorative fleur-de-lis carved into the wood.

It had a round face with forward-looking eyes and stone-cold feathers forming a disc around its eyes. As he looked at the bird, it appeared to change color and texture into that of a live owl that stretched its wings. John blinked and his face turned ashen. Multiple colors swirled around the owl. It had blazing red eyes that seemed to bore into him. He could feel the power of those eyes. They seemed to peer through his mind and touch his thoughts. John's heartbeat hastened and his eyes widened. Beads of sweat formed on his forehead. He diverted his eyes, and set his mug on the

## SLOW TANGO IN TAOS

bar. As much as he could, he avoided looking at the sculpture, but he could still feel its presence.

At long last, John saw a reflection in the mirror of Maya entering the bar. He turned to her. "Maya!" he called out, relieved that she had finally arrived. She waved and walked over to him.

"It's so cold outside," she said. "Didn't you freeze walking here?"

"No. I'm getting used to the cold." John checked his watch and nervously glanced back at the owl, relieved that it had returned to its original cold-stone state, but avoided saying anything to Maya about what he had seen. "The demonstration starts at six," he said. "We have some time. Would you like a drink?"

"Yes, something to drink would be nice."

"There's a table over there." John pointed. "Let's get it.."

He picked up his beer and moved to a nearby table. Maya unwrapped a vermillion scarf from around her head, and stuffed her bright fuchsia wool gloves into her coat pocket. John helped Maya remove her coat. He placed it on a coat rack, and motioned for the waitress who came to the table.

"Would y'all like to order?"

"I'd like a glass of water." Maya said.

"One water coming up. And for you?"

"I'll have another draft."

"Be right back, honey." She winked and left.

"Honey?" Maya kidded. "You know her?"

"Met her when I ordered a beer." John said. "You don't drink alcohol?"

"I don't like the taste of alcohol."

"But you're--."

"Native American?" she interrupted. John nodded.

"I've heard that before. It doesn't bother me."

"I've been thinking about you ever since the dance," John said.

She smiled and wiggled slightly in her chair. "Been thinking of you too," she replied. "In fact, I created a serigraph of you."

"I'm flattered."

"I have a favor to ask," she said.

"What?" John asked as he leaned forward, intrigued by the nuances of her voice.

"I need your help with a project I'm working on."

"Oh?"

"I need you as a model." She smiled, her cheeks flushed.

*Did I hear that correctly?*

"Of course, it will be strictly a professional relationship between artist and model," she asserted.

"Oh, of course." The corner of his mouth turned into a mischievous smile.

The waitress put a glass of water and a beer on the table. "Y'all have a nice time now, ya hear? Let me know if ya need anything else." Then, she left.

## SLOW TANGO IN TAOS

"I hope I haven't embarrassed you," Maya said as she took a sip of water.

"There are other men."

"None with your facial qualities," she said. "I want to capture your spiritual aura on canvass. You have a magnificent aura. That's what attracted me to you."

"I don't understand."

"I can see things that other people can't see."

"What's an aura?"

"It's a circle of colorful energy that surrounds your body. The more spiritually advanced someone is, the farther out the aura extends, and the more brilliant the colors. The aura leaves the body at death and returns to the universe."

John took another sip of beer and thought a moment.

"You sound a little like my friend George," he remarked.

"Is my voice that deep?" She kidded.

"No," he said. "You're a beautiful woman." John looked into her eyes and longed to touch her. He reached for her hand. She responded with a smile, a squeeze of his hand and a wink in her twinkling eyes.

"Tina told me you want to be an artist," she said.

"Tell me about your work," she said.

"There isn't much to tell, only I'm improving, at least, I think so." He glanced nervously back at the owl. Something about the eyes – they seemed to stare deeply into his soul. John shifted uneasily.

"It's good that you're improving. Would you like

some instruction?" she asked.

"Well, I--" he began.

"I'd like to help you," she said.

He paused a moment to consider. "I would like--"

A growing quarrel between a woman of hard features and a slender Hispanic man in worn denim jeans, cut into their conversation.

"What's going on?" Maya whispered. John shrugged.

The man was with a woman of late thirties sitting at the bar. She seemed angry and shouted for the man to leave her alone. The bartender, a large man wearing a white apron ducked around the bar and confronted the man.

"Leave the woman alone!" The bartender demanded.

"But--" protested the little man.

"What's your name?"

"Jose," he replied. "She's my girlfriend!"

"I never saw that shrimp before!" The woman said with a raucous voice that echoed years of drunken nights.

"Listen, Jose, leave her alone or I'll throw you out of here!" he warned.

As the bartender returned to the bar, Jose again approached her. This time she flailed at him. He stepped back, but the barkeeper returned and grabbed him by the arm.

"Get out of here and stay out of here!" the bartender ordered. The man went through the lobby and disappeared out the door.

"I feel sorry for that little man," Maya said.

## SLOW TANGO IN TAOS

"Don't know what their quarrel was about," John said.

"Where were we," Maya said.

"Talking about art."

"Oh yes, I was just--." she began before stopping mid-sentence. John turned to see Jose reentering the bar. The barman grabbed him by the arm.

"My beer! I left my beer!"

"I told you to get out and stay out!" He said as two other men came to assist the bartender. Together they escorted the protesting man out of the bar.

"I think the bartender overreacted," Maya said "He didn't have a chance against those three men. And he couldn't have caused much of a problem for that large woman either."

"You're right," John replied.

"I'm going over to that woman and tell her off," Maya said.

"Don't," John said. "You'll only create another scene. Let's go outside and join the protest."

They finished their drinks and left the bar. Outside, the frigid air bit at John's cheeks as he stood with Maya in the town plaza. He shifted his weight back and forth to stay warm. Other people meandered into the plaza to join the group of protestors. Soon, the plaza was filled with people, some holding signs that read: *Get out of Taos! We don't need no stinking condos!*

Soon a stretch Lincoln pulled up alongside the square

and stopped. Out stepped a tall distinguished looking man, the mayor of Taos. He was a man of athletic build with patches of grey interspersed throughout his dark hair. He wore a wool topcoat with a light grey scarf. He waved to the crowd as he walked up the concrete steps of a gazebo in the middle of the plaza. As he did so, a wave of anger erupted from the crowd. The Mayor held out his hand to calm them, but as he spoke the crowd broke into a chant of: *Sell out! Sell out! You're selling us out!*

The Mayor once more held up his hand to try to silence the crowd, and then as loudly as he could, he said: "Development is the future of Taos. We can't remain a backward city, forever looking to the past with—" The crowd cut him off with chants of *Sell out! Sell Out! You're selling us out!*

"Please! The development plans for the new apartments are not yet final. They must be approved by the city council."

"How much money did the developer give you!" yelled one burly man wearing a dark wide-brimmed leather hat.

"I'm not making any money on this project," the mayor retorted.

"Like hell!" Yelled another man, "How are you buying that new house of yours?"

Soon, counter protestors carrying signs of support for the development entered the square. As the crowd's anger increased, John motioned to Maya.

## SLOW TANGO IN TAOS

"Let's leave," he said.

They left the square and walked around to a side street where Maya had parked her car.

"Hop in, I'll give you a ride," she said.

When they arrived at John's cabin, he turned to her.

"I'd like to see you again," John said. "Perhaps we could go out to dinner, or…"

"I'd like that," she replied. "There's a Milonga every Friday. Call me."

He got out and stood beside the driver's door. She winked at him before placing the car into gear. John watched as she went up the driveway. Then, he turned and walked to his cabin.

The next Friday they met again at the Old Martina's Place for the weekly Milonga. This time, John was much more confident of his dancing skills, but still he watched as dancers in brightly colored clothing moved effortlessly in graceful undulating motions across the dance floor. He wished he could dance like them.

"Don't fret," Maya said as she observed John's pensive gaze. "I'll teach you to dance just like them."

"They seem to move so gracefully. The dance is so beautiful," he said.

"Yes, but you'll learn. I'm going to teach you," she said.

That night and other dance nights that followed, Maya did teach John many of the movements, and in time, he learned to move almost as gracefully along the dance floor as the other dancers. Each time as he danced with Maya in close embrace, and felt her body pressed against his, thoughts of romance danced in his head.

# CHAPTER 17

One evening, as white flakes of winter fell on Taos, John and Maya were once more walking hand-in-hand. As they strolled past shops on the Plaza. John turned to Maya. "What would you like to do?"

"Oh, I don't know. Any suggestions?" She smiled mischievously, and placed her hand inside John's coat pocket.

"We could go across the plaza to that little restaurant. We've eaten there several times," he replied.

"A restaurant! Oh, John!" she stated in disgust.

"Can't you think of a place that would be nice and cozy and pleasant. Someplace where we could be…alone?"

"My place?"

"Great! My car's over there." she said. Maya fumbled inside her purse. "I can never find my keys." She walked under a light so that she could see inside her purse. Finally, she found the keys and handed them to John. When they arrived at her car, he unlocked the Jeep and held her door open. She slid inside.

The motor turned three or four times before igniting with a soft roar. He placed the car into gear and stopped at a traffic light at the entrance to the square. When the light changed, he pushed the accelerator and the Jeep sped forward.

When they arrived at John's cabin, they got out and went inside. Maya pulled her coat tighter around her. "I'm cold."

"I'll get the fire going," John said. "The room should be warm in a few minutes."

"Oh, hurry!" she pleaded.

John placed several logs into the fireplace. He knelt down and blew on the coals until a flame licked the sides of the wood. Soon, the logs were ablaze and the chill subsided.

"I love your cabin," she said.

They looked at each other with passion-filled eyes. Then, as though some great magnet drew them together, they became locked in a passionate lovers' embrace. He kissed her neck, ears and face.

"Do you think this is too soon?" Maya whispered.

"I've dreamed of this ever since I first laid eyes on you," John replied.

"I've longed for you too," Maya panted. "I've been going crazy thinking about you, and what it would be like being together like this."

## SLOW TANGO IN TAOS

"You're beautiful," John said between passionate breaths as he loosened the top button of her blouse.

"I can't believe we're doing this," Maya laughed with pleasure.

Her heaving breaths pressed tightly against her blouse threatening to jettison the buttons. John's eager fingers skillfully removed each button, then removed her blouse and let it fall to the floor. Her heaving chest begged to be relieved from the restraint of her bra. He removed the snaps. The bra flew apart as though exploding from passion. John tossed the bra to the floor. Before him were two beautiful heaving breasts with protruding nipples begging to be kissed. He reached down and kissed each gently and longingly. Overcome with passion, they slipped out of their remaining clothes.

He examined her naked beauty, more perfect than any piece of art in the best of museums. She smiled and raised her arms toward him. They engaged in a long embrace. The moment was perfect. His lips wandered wistfully and delicately along the golden contours of her body. She moaned as his meandering kisses grew more desirous.

His mouth encircled the contours of her breasts and he sucked gently upon her nipples. They became rigid and erect. His kisses moved along her neck while his caressing hands moved along her thighs.

She moaned as his hands caressed the contours of her groin. A great passion welled up within both of them screaming for relief. He moved on top of her as she arched her body, begging and caressing. Her eyes rolled backward and her mouth opened with a series of whimpers as he inched inward. Maya turned her head from side to side moaning and whispering delicate secrets of passion into his ear as he moved rhythmically. Beads of sweat poured from his face. Her breasts formed suction cups which popped when their bodies pressed and released. Their passion increased as her moment grew nearer.

" John!" she cried, pulling him closer and closer while sucking on his neck. Her body stiffened. She grew more and more impassioned, and more and more rigid and panting and wanting him,

"Harder, harder," she pleaded with bated breaths.

Suddenly, a warm glowing sensation overcame him as their moment approached and their passions exploded in unison.

"Don't move," she pleaded as the crucial moment passed. She clutched him as if her whole existence depended upon it. He ran his finger over the contours of her face and across her body. She smiled and kissed his hand.

"That was wonderful," she cooed.

They lay in exhausted silence for long minutes as burning embers crackled in the fireplace. How wonderful, he thought, to be loved by a woman as young and beautiful as Maya. John's world was warm and aglow. He wished they could lie in each other's arms forever.

A little later, Maya lifted up on one elbow and looked

at him. "Tina told me you wanted to get a place of your own. I was thinking…" Maya mused.

"About what?"

"Well…we could get a place together…you know…and share expenses. We could have two studies, one for you and one for me. That way, we wouldn't bother each other, but we'd still be close." She said. "I have a friend who has an old farm not far from Taos. It isn't in good shape, but if we moved in and fixed it up, we could make it really nice."

"Where is this place?"

"Oh, John...it's beautiful with large trees, a sweeping landscape, a small brook. It would be perfect for us. It has wild animals, its own private well, and…you'll think about it, won't you?"

"Our own little farm," he mumbled.

"With cows and chickens and horses." she added.

"And you know what's really nice about it?"

"What?"

"We would be alone…really alone."

"Oh," he replied, "and what would we do when we we're really alone?"

"Well," she replied lifting herself slightly above John and looking down at him, "if we were alone--"

"Yes," he added.

"If we were alone. then no one would bother us, and if no one bothered us," she said, her voice purring.

"Yes, what would we do that no one would bother us?"

# Phil Cline

"Anytime we have the urge, we could…"

## SLOW TANGO IN TAOS

# CHAPTER 18

One evening, as flakes of snow fell outside, John and Maya warmed themselves in John's cottage. Aroma from piñon logs filled the room and an occasional explosion of sap sent embers flying against the fire screen. As they held each other, there was a loud knock on the door. John got out of bed, threw on a robe, and opened the door. Tina stood in the doorway pale and gasping for air.

"John, something terrible has happened." Her voice cracked. "It's Red"

"What happened?" John asked.

"Oh, it's horrible," she sobbed uncontrollably. "One of the men from the shop came by and told me. Red's in the hospital…in Santa Fe…intensive care." she said between sobs. "He's not expected…to live!"

"Was he in an accident?" John asked.

Tina shook her head. "Red has been binge

drinking…at bars in Santa Fe…his liver is shot." Tears streamed down her cheeks. "The doctor warned Red…about his drinking, but he…wouldn't listen," She burst into tears again.

"Let's go to Santa Fe. We can take my Jeep." Maya said as she joined them, wrapped in a blanket.

John dressed, threw on his coat and sprinted across the snow-laden yard to warm the Jeep's engine. A little later, Maya and Tina joined him and climbed in. John drove from the driveway onto the street and headed south toward Santa Fe. He sped through a red light near the Plaza, and headed down U.S. Highway 64 toward Santa Fe.

Maya held Tina to comfort her as they drove.

"John, be careful," Maya warned. "There are dangerous turns in the road."

"Keep your eyes open and let me know when we're coming to a sharp curve," John said.

"I'll try," Maya replied, "but I usually travel during the day. Everything looks so different at night."

"Try," he pleaded.

"Okay," Maya said. She leaned forward and studied the road as the silent white countryside slipped past them in the darkness. They continued down the narrow two-lane road as occasional patches of black ice slipped past them on the roadway. As they entered the Rio Grande gorge, the roadway became a series of sharp serpentine turns. Around one bend they ran over a large area of black ice that stretched across the roadway.

## SLOW TANGO IN TAOS

"Damn!" John said, realizing too late that he was travelling too fast. He hit the brakes in quick succession trying to regain control of the Jeep as it skidded sideways. John steered into the direction of the skid in an effort to control the Jeep, but it left the highway, plowed into a snowbank and came to an abrupt halt.

"Didn't notice the ice until it was too late," he said, his heart pounding.

"You were driving too fast! It doesn't matter if it takes us a little longer," Maya chided.

"Everyone okay?" John asked.

"We're okay," Tina said. "Only a little shaken. I thought we were going off that!" She pointed to a cliff in front of the jeep that dropped sharply down into the Rio Grande River.

"My Jeep has snow tires that should pull us out." Maya said as she looked outside.

"Let's see what happens," John said. He placed the jeep into four-wheel drive and put it into reverse. The vehicle moved slightly, but stopped. He pushed harder on the accelerator, but the tires spun freely in the snow.

He alternated between inching the jeep forward until the wheels slipped and then reversing in an effort to rock the vehicle out of its bondage of snow. A cloud of black smoke arose from the wheels as they spun freely. John got out, and examined the Jeep. Realizing they were stuck in a deep snow bank, he got back into the vehicle.

"Looks like the snow lifted the Jeep so the tires can't

get traction," he said.

"What are we going to do?" Tina asked.

"I don't know," John said, "I'm stupid for driving so fast!" He got out again and used a broken piece of a limb he found beside the road to dig around the tires in an effort to free the Jeep. To no avail. They remained stuck in snow for more than an hour. Finally, a pair of head lights appeared over the ridge behind them.

"Maybe we can get the car to stop." John said. He stepped outside and waved. The approaching pickup slowed and stopped. The driver rolled down his window.

"What's the trouble fellow?" asked the driver.

"We hit some ice and I lost control," John said.

"Car damaged?"

"Don't think so."

"Ain't no problem, then," replied the driver. "Grab the hook on the wench in front of my truck and attach it to the back of your car. I'll release it." John grabbed the hook and walked backward as the cable unwound. When several feet of cable had unwound, the wench stopped.

"A little more," John shouted.

The driver activated the motor on the wrench once more and unwound more cable. John got on his knees, scooped snow from under the bumper and hooked it to the frame.

"All right," he said. "It's attached."

"Get in your Jeep, put it into reverse and see if you

can back it out," the man said. "I don't want to put too much strain on my cable. I busted it once already."

"Okay," John signaled to the pickup. He slid behind the steering wheel.

"That's Brian Stuart," Tina said. "He lives up the road a spell."

A moan arose from under the car as the steel cable tightened. John put the car into reverse and accelerated the engine. The wheels spun, and black smoke arose around the car. Then the Jeep slowly began moving. Finally, they were back on the pavement.

"Whew!" John exclaimed. "That was close."

John got out, and removed the hook. "Rewind the cable," he shouted to the pickup driver. The driver activated the wench and the cable slowly rewound onto the front of the truck.

"I can't thank you enough, friend," John said.

"Not a problem. Glad to help. This four-wheel drive pickup comes in handy at times. It's old, but gets the job done," replied the man.

"Brian!" Tina shouted as she stuck her head through the car window.

"That you, Tina?" asked the man. He got out of his truck and walked to the window.

"Listen, thank you for pulling us out," Tina said.

"That's all right," he said.

"Why don't you come by for dinner one night," Tina said.

"Sure thing. I like your cooking. Get tired of mine," he laughed.

"Have you heard about Red Brownell?" she asked.

"No. What happened?"

"He's in the hospital in Santa Fe. That's where we're going. Red was drinking too much."

"Damn." he said, as he spit brown splatters of tobacco onto the white snow. "Just goes to show you, a man can't abuse his body and get away with it for long."

"He's got problems," Tina replied.

"Yeah, I guess he does. Sorry about Red. Been meaning to stop by his shop, but haven't gotten around to it. Hell, I've got to get my old buggy back to my place and feed the cows. Get 'em bedded down before it gets too late. I'll try getting down to the hospital in a day or two. In the meantime, tell old Red we're thinking about him. "

"I'll do that," she replied. "Thanks for your help."

"No problem," he replied. He returned to his truck and sped away.

John slid into the driver's seat and shut the door.

"Nice guy. Not many people would stop to help."

Later that night, they pulled into the parking lot of the Santa Fe Hospital, an adobe style building located on the outskirts of Santa Fe. They parked and walked into the lobby. A nurse seated behind a receptionist desk looked up when they entered. "May I help you?" she asked.

"We're here to visit Red Brownell," John said.

"Do you know what room he's in?" she asked. Tina

shook her head.

The nurse thumbed through some papers on her desk before holding one in her hand.

"Oh, yes," she said finally. "He's on the second floor, in room 244, but you'll have to make it short. Visiting hours are almost over."

"We've come all the way from Taos, "John said.

"We're friends. Could you tell us anything about his condition?"

"I'm sorry, but I can't reveal that information," she said.

"Would you call his doctor and ask? We're close friends."

"I'm sorry. We're not allowed to do that. You can check with his nurse on the ward."

John turned to Tina and Maya. "Let's go to Red's room," John said.

They followed a series of wall signs with room numbers. Finally, they paused outside of room 244. They took deep breaths, and gathered courage to go inside.

"Can I help you?" asked a nurse as she walked by.

"We just spoke with the receptionist," John said.

"She said it would be all right to visit Mister Brownell. Could you tell us if he is awake?"

"Hold on. I'll check," She stuck her head in the room, then returned.

"He's resting, but you can go in to see him if you remain quiet.

"I'm frightened," Tina said.

Red was asleep when they entered the room. A bottle of saline solution hung from a stand near his bed. A long plastic tube connected Red to the bag. He appeared much smaller and frail than John remembered. Tina began to cry. The sound of her sobbing awoke Red. His eye lids flew open.

"Spiders!" He shouted, "they're crawling all over me!" Tina grabbed one of his hands while Maya held the other.

"Don't be afraid, Red. We're here with you." Tina said. Her words seemed to comfort him.

"Maggie, I've missed you so much!" he cried out.

"It's all right, Red. We're here," Tina said in a soothing voice. As she rubbed his forehead, he relaxed and fell asleep.

A little later, Red regained consciousness and opened his eyes. "Why ya here. What happened?" He looked around the room in a daze. "What happened, man?" He lifted his arm and looked at the attached tubes.

"The doctors want to keep you under observation for a while," Tina said.

"Why? Something's wrong, or I wouldn't be here!"

"You've been drinking too much," Tina replied.

Red laid back and stared at the ceiling. "Now I remember," he said. "Doc said this would happen."

"Oh, Red," Tina wept, "why did you keep drinking? Why?"

## SLOW TANGO IN TAOS

He shook his head. "I don't feel so good," he said as a gurgling noise came from his throat.

"Get a nurse!" Tina screamed.

John ran to the door and yelled for a nurse. A nurse at the circular ward counter rushed into the room. She did a quick examination of Red.

"He'll be going through a series of these episodes," the nurse said. She left the room and returned with a hypodermic that she filled with fluid from a small bottle. She pulled up the sleeve of Red's hospital gown and gave him an injection.

"You'd better leave now and let him rest. It's important that he gets a lot of rest."

"When will he be well enough for us to visit?" John asked.

"I don't know," she said as she ushered them out of the room.

"Is the cafeteria open?" John asked.

"No, but there's a self-serving canteen across from the cafeteria. You can buy coffee and snacks there."

Later, as they sat a table in the cafeteria, Tina wiped tears from her eyes. "I'm sad about Red," She said.

"Why?" Maya asked, "You had nothing to do with his drinking."

"If only I had done more. If only I had--"

"You did all anyone could do," Maya said. "Red is the only person who could help Red. We all tried to help him, but he ended up in the hospital anyway."

"He became so bitter, so cynical." Tina slumped in her chair, toying with her paper cup of coffee.

"I've known a few people who ended up the same way," Maya said, "not only from the Pueblo, but from other reservations who drank themselves to death."

"But Red isn't Native American," John said.

"Alcoholics are all alike," Maya said. "Some drink until they run out of money. When they could no longer afford alcohol, they turn to drinking Vitalis hair tonic, or anything else that would give them a high. I've tried talking to them, but it's no use. They escape into alcohol and drugs."

The next morning, as the sun arose, they walked back upstairs and past a medicine cart in the hallway. The smell of rubbing alcohol filled the air. Sounds of monitors beeping in the rooms resonated down a hallway active with nurses caring for patients. As they approached Red's room, a tall red-haired nurse wearing a neatly pressed white uniform stood outside his door in the hallway.

"Can I help you?" She asked.

"We're friends of Red Brownell. We would like to see him. Is he any better?"

"The doctor saw him about fifteen minutes ago. He's resting now."

"Is he awake?" Tina asked. "Can we see him?"

The nurse shook her head. "Perhaps, later this afternoon."

"What do we do?" Tina asked.

## SLOW TANGO IN TAOS

"Why don't you go home. I'll call if his condition changes," the nurse said.

Maya wrote her number on a card and handed it to the nurse, "Please call me if his condition changes."

The nurse took the paper and looked at it. "I'll call if there is any change."

"Thank you," Maya said.

On the return trip to Taos, John forced himself to remain awake as he drove. It was welcome relief to see the buildings of Taos appear in the distance as he topped a hill. Later, as John stopped in front of Tina's house he turned around to look in the back seat. Tina was fast asleep. "Tina," John called.

Maya shook Tina who opened her eyes. "Where are we?"

"We're home," John said.

"Let me know if you hear from the hospital," Tina said as she got out.

"We'll let you know if we hear anything," Maya said.

"Thank you," Tina said as she got out and went into her house.

# Phil Cline

# CHAPTER 19

While Red was in the hospital, John busied himself with organizing work at the shop to make certain customer deliveries were made on time. Keeping the new orders filled was more difficult than John had realized. Maya had done a great job of redesigning their ceramic wares. As a result, business was brisk and new customer orders were flooding in. Most days, John went to the shop to make sure customer orders were being filled on time. Other times, he left Jose in charge of overseeing the filling of new orders

One evening, there was a knock on his cabin door. He opened it to find Maya standing in the doorway.

"The nurse called from the hospital," Maya said. "Red's condition has improved. The nurse said his doctor gave him some new type of medicine. Red was still a little groggy, but much better. The nurse let me talk with him. He was kidding around with me. Red gets playful when he's scared."

"He should be scared," John replied. "He came very close to meeting the grim reaper."

"The nurse said the doctor should release him soon. She said Red is anxious to return to Taos."

"He didn't leave a good impression with the men at the shop," John said. "Don't know how that will work out. If he returns, I don't know how I'll fit in at the shop. Anyway, come on out of the cold."

Maya entered and sat on the bed. She motioned for John to sit next to her.

"I've been thinking," Maya said.

"About what?"

"About us."

John raised an eyebrow. "Yes, and..."

"Well, I was thinking. If you quit your work and we moved in together, we could live on with what I earn. Then, you would have time to develop your art. It would be a win for both of us."

"Move in together? I can't move in with you and your roommate."

"You wouldn't have to. I've been looking for a new place for the two of us."

"I'm listening."

"There's an abandoned ranch house. It's about eight miles outside Taos. It's run down, but I think we can make the repairs ourselves. It's not much to look at, but it has potential. I want to show it to you."

## SLOW TANGO IN TAOS

"Maybe after work tomorrow I could—"
"No! Not tomorrow. Tonight. Let's go look at it."
"Now?" he asked. "It's dark. We can't see at night."
"It's a full moon. It'll be perfect for us."
He thought a moment, then replied, "Okay, let's go."
They drove north and west out of Taos up U.S. highway 64, veered onto Highway 522, and turned onto San Cristobal Road. After travelling past Juniper and Sage brush growing along a rough gravel road, they turned onto a dirt driveway that had occasional clumps of grass growing in it. They stopped in front of a gate made of barbed wire. John got out, lifted a circular wire connecting the gate to a permanent fence post, and dragged the barbed wire gate to one side of the roadway. He motioned for Maya to drive forward. As she drove over the cattle guard, the tires made a series of clacking sounds as they rolled over six-inch diameter metal pipes crossing the entrance that had prevented livestock from getting out. She drove through the entrance and stopped. John pulled the gate back to its original place, secured he post, and then got back into the Jeep.

Maya drove a short distance down the driveway and stopped at the top of a hill. A full moon illuminated the landscape. In the distance was a deserted house, and behind it an old barn of weathering wood. Alongside the barn lay an old plow, a hay bailer and other discarded farm equipment that stood rusting in the weather.

"This is it!" She said with a sweep of her hand

# Phil Cline

John said nothing for a while, but took in the view. Then, a subtle thrill of electricity surged up his back.

"It has potential," he said. "I can see why you like this place." John said as he looked over the snow-laden landscape. Beyond the barn, reflecting light danced upon a stream of water glistening in the moonlight.

"I used to bathe in a stream at the pueblo when I was younger." She said.

She nudged closer to him. "Care for a swim?"

"A swim? Now?"

"Yes, now!"

He looked into her eager eyes that seemed to beg for excitement. "You're crazy. It's freezing out there."

"Everyone's a little crazy. Besides," she said with a mischievous smile. "Artists are supposed to be crazy."

"But I'm not an--"

"Hush." She placed her hand upon his mouth. "You will be. Do you feel daring?"

"I suppose, but I--"

"That's better," she said. She put the Jeep into gear and she stopped near the stream. She took off her coat, slipped out of her dress and smiled at John. "You're not getting cold feet, are you?"

"You're crazy," he said, a chill running through his body.

"Then, let's do it," she said. "Show me how brave you are."

A flurry of thoughts raced through his head as he

## SLOW TANGO IN TAOS

considered his next move. It was a crazy idea. He looked at Maya sitting nude next to him. She smiled and beckoned him with a twinkle in her eyes.

What the hell, he thought. Then, a thrill ran through his body as he undressed and sat nude in the Jeep with Maya. "On the count of three," she said, "one."

"Are you sure you want to do this?" he asked.

"I'll leave the Jeep running so we can warm up. Two!"

"This is insane!"

"Yes, quite!" she said reaching for the door handle.

"Three! Let's go!"

They threw open the doors and raced to the stream. The shock of freezing temperature upon his naked body was like a bolt of electricity running through his muscles.

"Wait, Maya," he shouted as he fought his way through the snow."

"Come on! You can do it!" she encouraged.

She paused at the edge of the stream, waiting for John to catch up, then walked into the icy water.

"This is insane!" He fought his instincts not to go into the currents, but passion gave way and he forced himself. He gingerly walked upon the pebbles until he reached Maya. His leg muscles tightened from the icy waters. All feeling in his feet left him.

"Don't think about the coldness. Learn to control your mind," she said as swift water flowed past them. It was as though he had entered a dream, and before him was a beautiful maiden beckoning him to come farther into the stream.

"Come," she said with a smile, but the voice was not that of Maya. It seemed to be the voice of eternity calling to him. He waded with her farther into the stream until they were waist deep.

"Hold me," she said. Her lips quivered as he put his arms around her. Their bodies blended together. Her body was warm and inviting. He wrapped his arms around her and kissed her deeply, passionately, as a full moon highlighted the nearby hills.

Nothing else seemed to matter at that moment. Only Maya and her beautiful body. For long silent moments they embraced. John felt himself slipping into an alternate reality. He forgot about the icy waters raging about him. He felt warm, relaxed, and free. His mind suddenly darted back to the corporation in Chicago, and he wondered how he would have reacted then if he had seen himself standing waist deep in a mountain stream with a Native American maiden on a cold October night.

Maya smiled. "You passed the test," she said. "Let's go." She grabbed his hand and led him back out of the stream. John followed quite automatically, and from an impulse he didn't understand. She beckoned him to follow. Somehow, the ambient air seemed warm and comfortable.

When they got back into the car, a blast of hot air from the heater hit them. It seemed as though he was in a hot furnace. After they dressed, they held each other and

## SLOW TANGO IN TAOS

watched water in the stream glistening in the moonlight. After long moments of silence, Maya said, "it shouldn't be too difficult to fix up this ranch house."

"In the winter?" John asked.

"We'll have to make whatever repairs we can and wait until spring for major ones," Maya said.

"If you say we can live in it, I'm okay with it."

"You mean you trust my judgement?"

"I trust you to the end of the world," he replied.

"Well, don't trust me that far. Keep an occasional eye on me because I tend to wander."

*Wander? He thought as he pandered her words.*

"Would you drift away from me?"

"Oh," she said. "I might."

"You would?"

"Of course not," she replied. I'll never leave you, but you might leave me."

"Never!" he responded. "We'll stick it out together!"

## Phil Cline

# CHAPTER 20

As John placed new clay into the vat and was kneading it, Maya entered the pottery shop. She waited near the entrance. John saw her, pulled his hand out of the clay and washed off in the basin. As he was drying his hands, he motioned for Maya. She sprinted toward him.

"I spoke…to the property owners," Maya said between breaths, "the place is ours."

"When can we move in?"

"Today. I'm going back to my place to start packing," Maya said. "I'll take some things out to the ranch this afternoon. I'll come by and pick you up at about five."

"Okay, I'll be waiting," John said. She left and he returned to kneading the clay, then placed it next to Jose to use on his potter's wheel. Later, he placed several dried but unfired bowls into the kiln. As he worked, his thoughts were more on Maya and less on what he was doing.

# Phil Cline

The hours seemed to drag by. He kept looking at the yellow wooden clock hanging above the entrance to the shop. Finally, five o'clock arrived. As soon as workers had gone, he closed the shop. Then, he waited anxious minutes. Soon, Maya pulled up in her Jeep. John secured the padlock on the door, and got into the car.

"I'm so excited we got the ranch," Maya said.

"But what are we going to tell Tina? I hate to say anything that would upset her."

"She's a strong woman. You don't need to worry."

When they stopped in front of Tina's house, John mulled what he would say. He took a deep breath before opening the door.

"Tina?" He called out.

"I'm in the kitchen. Make yourself at home. I'll be right out."

"Thanks, we'll wait," he said. John and Maya entered the house and sat on the sofa. Maya bit her lower lip. Wood was burning in the fireplace, and the smell of piñon filled the room. John looked with some sadness at the rug, the table, chairs and other items in the room that had become so familiar to him.

Tina tilted her head slightly when she entered the room. "You two look like Cheshire cats. What's up?"

Maya turned to John. "Well…" John shifted uneasily in his chair. "Maya and I…well…" he stammered. "Maya located a house north of here on a ranch."

## SLOW TANGO IN TAOS

"The old Wells place," Maya said.

"That ranch hasn't been occupied for years," Tina said. "Is it livable?"

"It'll require some work," Maya said.

"And you and Maya want to move out to the Wells property? In the middle of winter? Have you lost your senses?" Tina asked.

"I went into the ranch house yesterday. It's not that bad," Maya said.

Maya and John exchanged glances. John took a deep breath before speaking. "We didn't want to hurt you," John said.

"Don't worry about me," she said. "I've been taking care of myself for a long time. When are you thinking about moving to the ranch?"

"Don't know, but soon," Maya said.

"I'll be hurt if you move away and not come back to visit me," she said. "You know we have a dinner here once a month, and everyone is invited. You must come back once and a while to visit me." She wiped her hands on her apron.

"Listen, I knew you two would hit it off. You make a nice couple."

"We'll be making several trips out to the ranch over the next few days to move our things," John said.

"Next few days," she sighed.

"Will that cause you any problems?" John asked.

Tina paused a moment, "No," she replied, "it's just that...Well, I sometimes wish things wouldn't change.

## Phil Cline

Wished things would remain the same, but they never do."

"I know you miss your husband," Maya said. "It must be hard for you."

"Andy and I had a wonderful life. I do miss him. I miss him so much," Tina said, a tear rolling down her cheek. She took a deep breath and composed herself. "He suffered so much with the cancer. I felt so helpless..." Tina wiped a tear from her eye with the bottom of her apron.

"Tina. I didn't mean to bring up...." Maya said.

"Change is something we all have to get used to. If you want to move out, that's fine with me. Will you stay and have dinner with me?"

"Okay," Maya nodded. "I'll help with dinner."

John remained in the living room. He pulled a chair up next to the warm fire and watched red cinders crackle as the logs burned. A stream of memories flooded through his head. The slightly acrid smell of piñon caused his thoughts to wander back to the night he spent in the mountains with the old man. He wondered how Tulsa was doing, and if he would meet him again.

\* \* \*

Several days later, John packed up his belongings and tossed them into the back of Maya's jeep.

"Well, this is it," he said. "Let's go."

When they arrived at the ranch Maya stopped the car on a knoll overlooking the ranch. They sat in silence as they admired the beauty of the rolling hills under a blanket of snow highlighted by moonlight.

## SLOW TANGO IN TAOS

"It's beautiful," John said.

"The crisp clearness of the night, with the snow and the moonlight falling on the ranch. I want to capture this scene on canvas," Maya said.

"That's because you're an artist, but, one thing bothers me. How are we going to survive tonight?"

"Carol and I came out this afternoon and stocked the house with firewood. We cleaned the house and moved in a few pieces of furniture."

"You could have waited. I would have helped," John said.

"We're not helpless, you know," Maya said.

"I know. You've very capable."

They parked and went inside. Maya held a flashlight and illuminated her way to an old oil lamp. She struck a match and lit the lamp. As she raised the wick, the room filled with light.

"The owners said there's a generator out back, but it doesn't work. You know anything about repairing a broken generator?"

"Don't know. Maybe I could fix it."

"There's no running water. We'll have to carry it from the well."

"Primitive," he replied.

"Would you mind starting a fire? I'm cold," Maya said.

He folded some newspaper and shoved it under a log in the adobe fireplace, then lit a match and ignited the paper.

Soon, a fire was roaring as the room warmed to the glow.

Later, they examined a large crack in the adobe wall of one room that allowed outside air to enter. The gap was about four feet long and varied between three to five inches wide.

"The adobe must have fallen away on the outside of the wall," Maya said. That's the problem with adobe. You need to put on new adobe mud every year because the outside layer dissolves in the rain. You can see old adobe buildings that haven't been maintained -- they're falling apart."

"We could seal the crack with blankets for tonight. It will keep us warmer," John said.

"I only brought enough blankets for us," Maya replied. "Look out in the barn. You might find something out there to use."

He threw on his heavy coat and walked out into the frigid air. The moon was full and cast a soft light. He trudged through deep snow that clung to his pant legs. At the entrance to the barn were two well-weathered wooden doors. The center section of one door had splintered and fallen off, but the main body remained fully attached to the barn. The other door clung to the barn by a single hinge. Drifts against both doors were deep and blocked him from opening the doors. John found a rusty shovel leaning against the barn, and used it to remove enough of the snow to enable him to open one of the doors. After he entered the barn, he brushed snow off his pant legs and looked around.

## SLOW TANGO IN TAOS

Coiled sections of aging rope hung from nails that had been driven into the timbers. The smell of manure and musty hay filled the room. A metal beam extended through an opening in the upper loft that had once been used to bring in hay. Now it stood rusted and abandoned. An old plow with a rusty patina laid discarded in a manger once used by horses.

As he opened a storage room door, it fell from its hinge, nearly striking him. It made a soft thud when it landed on the dirt floor. The sudden noise of small feet upon wood caused him to spin around and shine his light at the loft above. He saw nothing more than weathered boards and small streamers of hay hanging between the timbers.

He climbed a ladder leading to the loft and cast his light to see mice scurrying for safety. Lying in the loft was a spool of bailing wire. To one side of the ladder was a stack of empty jute feed sacks. He held one up. On the side was printed *Tidewater Feed and supplies*. He grabbed several bags and trudged his way back to the house. He kicked snow from his shoes before entering. He rejoined Maya, and tossed the feed sacks onto the floor.

"These might work," he replied. "Do we have A hammer and some nails?"

"I doubt it. I'll look." Maya disappeared into a back room, and soon returned holding a few nails in her hand.

"Will these do?" She asked.

"They'll help," he replied, "you didn't find a hammer?"

"No."

"I need something to pound with," John said.

"I'll look in the front room. She left and returned carrying a rusty iron from the days before electrical cords.

John rolled the feed sacks tightly together and shoved them into the void. With the heavy metal iron, he drove several nails through the jute sacks and into the adobe to hold them in place.

"That should keep us a little warmer," he said. John held his hand up to the crevice. "Cold air is still coming in, but that's the best we can do for now."

The next day, John searched the ranch land for clay, but the snow made finding it difficult. At first, he searched a nearby hill, then the flatland and finally located a source of clay near the stream. He dug into the soft wet gooey soil and put it into a bucket. Then, he brought it into the house. After placing it near the fireplace to warm, he added a little more water and kneaded it as though it were bread dough. When the consistency was right, he carried the bucket into the back room and set it near the crack.

A cold breeze slid around the feed sacks numbing his fingers as he stuffed clay into the opening. He grabbed several handfuls and stuffed more and more clay into the crevice until the gap was filled.

"At last!" he said with satisfaction. "No more cold air coming through."

The following days, they arranged the furnishings, unpacked their clothing and deciding on which of the back

## SLOW TANGO IN TAOS

rooms to use for studios. Maya picked the larger room with more natural light.

Together, they unpacked art supplies Maya and Carol had brought to the house a few days earlier that included scores of paint brushes, sketch pads, arches paper for watercolors, and canvas for oils. She laid out tubes of paint in a variety of colors upon a make-shift table and arranged her brushes in neat rows.

After arranging Maya's studio, John heaved a sigh of relief. "It's exciting being out here on the ranch and braving the perils of the weather," he said as he looked out a window. "I can't get over how much energy I feel." He scratched ice from the inside surface of the window. "I had nearly forgotten what it was like to be free and in love."

"In love with me?"

"With you and with everything about my new life," John said.

"Remember the other night when we skinny dipped in the creek?" Maya asked. "Like to do that again?"

"I was crazy then, but I'm not crazy now," John said.

"Too damn cold! Anyway, the fireplace needs more wood, and I need to fetch water from the well. I'll bring in a few logs from the pile outside."

He grabbed a clean five-gallon bucket in the kitchen and left the house. He brushed snow from stones forming a circle around the well and set his bucket on the rocks. Then he untied a rope securing a long six-inch diameter tin cylinder. He released the rope and the cylinder fell into the

# Phil Cline

depth of darkness. There was momentary silence, then he heard a splash. He waited a few seconds for water to enter the cylinder, then pulled the rope on a large pulley and dragged the heavy water-filled container back to the surface. He secured the rope again around a dowel jutting out of a wooden beam and swung the cylinder into his bucket. At the upper end of the cylinder was a ring that he pulled to release water into the bucket. He returned to the house carrying a bucket full of water and placed it in the kitchen.

    Later, he placed more logs on the fire and blew on the embers. A tinge of excitement ran through him as the logs ignited. "At last!" he said. They watched as the flames grew larger, and rejoiced when the room became warm.

# CHAPTER 21

The next morning, as he dressed, he watched Maya lying asleep on the bed. He bent down to kiss her. She smiled faintly but did not open her eyes. He put more logs on the fire, then left the house. When he turned the key in the ignition, the car's engine turned over several times before starting. He let the engine warm up before putting the car into gear and heading into town. When he arrived at the shop, two of the workmen stood outside waiting to be let in."

"Been freezing our fannies off out here," Jose scolded.

"Sorry I'm a little late. Been fixing up a ranch house with Maya."

"We know that story. No need to explain," said the other.

John unlocked the shop, turned on the lights and

made sure the men knew what was needed to be accomplished for work that day before walking to the ceramics shop where he studied the pottery display and arranged it differently so tourists would be more apt to make purchases. Then, he continued on to the plaza. He entered a small restaurant, and sat at an oak table for two. A yellow rose with a pleasant scent was in a vase on the table.

"Help you, sir?" asked the waitress.

"Two eggs and coffee," he replied.

"How would you like the eggs?"

"Scrambled."

He took papers from his folio and began going over financial figures he had created for expanding Red's business. The waitress brought a cup of coffee and set it on the table. John added cream and sugar. The coffee had a rich full-bodied flavor. He sipped it as he studied the figures. He was engrossed in the figures, oblivious to his surroundings, when he heard a voice from behind him.

"John Tollifson?"

John turned to see a tall bearded man wearing a sheepskin coat standing in near him.

"Remember me? Ron Free. We met at Tina's when you first arrived in Taos."

"Oh yes." John shook the man's hand. "You're the *bronze man*, the one who casts statues."

"That's right." he replied with a broad smile.

"Please," John said indicating toward the chair next to him. "Why don't you join me."

# SLOW TANGO IN TAOS

"Don't mind if I do. Thanks."

"You still living out at Tina's?" he asked.

"No," John replied. "I'm living with Maya out on a ranch.

"Say, that sounds like an interesting arrangement. She's a wonderful person. By the way, I went by the hospital down in Santa Fe and saw Red. A friend called me and told me ol' Red had once more gone on the booze trail, so I dropped by for a visit. Doc says he's improving. Red said to tell everyone hello. He can't wait to return to Taos."

"He came really close this time," John said.

"That's for sure. Who took over his shop?"

"I did. At least, until he returns."

"If I know Red very well, which I think I do," Ron said as he leaned forward. "He'll stay sober until the next bad thing happens. Then, he'll go on another drinking binge. I'm afraid at that point, it'll be all over for him. I hate to say it, but Red doesn't have long to live unless he mends his way."

"Why don't you join me for breakfast. Have you eaten?"

"Actually…no," he mumbled as he stared at John's plate of eggs. John noticed a familiar look in Ron's eyes. John had seen that look in the past when he looked into a mirror. A look of poverty and hunger.

"Waitress," John signaled. She came to the table.

"Bring my friend here whatever he wants."

A warm smile swept across Ron's face as he took off his coat and sat down.

## Phil Cline

"You're paying for my breakfast?"

"That I am," John said. The waitress stood ready to take the order.

"Two eggs, over easy," he ordered. "Two slices of bacon, toast and coffee."

"Got it." The waitress said, then left.

"Tell me more about Red. Was he in good spirits?"

"You know Red. I haven't seen him in good spirits in years. Today he was complaining of the air pollution in Santa Fe. Los Angeles has an air pollution problem, Santa Fe does not."

"Sure, Chicago also has a problem."

"All large cities have pollution, but Red was complaining of the approaching doom of air pollution in Santa Fe."

"It sounds as though his health is improving."

The waitress returned with a cup in one hand and a coffee pot in the other. She put the cup in front of Ron and filled it with coffee. "Eggs are about ready," she said. "I'll get them." She left, then returned with a plate of food, and set it on the table.

"Don't get your hopes up." Ron said tearing into his food and talking between bites, "Red is Red, and he'll always be Red. He's a nice guy, and he has a lot of good points, but flexibility isn't one of them."

"I need to go back down and visit him," John said, "but Maya and I are busy. We're moving into our new place."

## SLOW TANGO IN TAOS

"I envy you. Running Bear is an attractive young lady."

"Yes, she is," John replied, "and speaking of Maya, I've got to run. You going to be in town long?"

"A couple of days,"

"If you get a chance, come out to the ranch. Maya will be glad to see you."

"No, she won't!" Ron replied flatly.

"Why is that?"

"Because I used to date her, and we parted on a sour note," he replied.

"Oh well, I hope to see you before you leave," John said.

"I'll be spending a few days at Tina's," he said.

"We might drop by to visit." John signaled for the waitress to bring the check.

"Nice seeing you, Ron." John handed money to the waitress and left.

Later that day, after finishing work at the pottery shop, John got into the Jeep and drove home. When he arrived, Maya was arranging supplies in her studio.

"Hi, honey," Maya said, as he entered. "How were things at work?"

"Good. Today we put out a lot of ceramics. I was surprised by the high quality we're producing. I was thinking, we need to keep changing the ceramic designs to sell more product. Perhaps you could help us create new designs for our ceramics like you did before."

# Phil Cline

"I'd be glad to," she said. "How do you like my studio arrangement?"

He looked around at the neatly arranged art supplies. All the tubes of paint were neatly arranged on a large wooden tray, the arches paper was neatly stacked, but the floor had a few additional splashes of color. "Very nice," he replied. "From the looks of the floor, you've also been busy painting."

"I'm trying to decide if I should put the drawing table over near that window," she said pointing to the far end of the room. "There's better light over there. Also, I put some of my supplies in your studio for you to use, like tubes of paint, brushes, and paper. I'll make an artist out of you in no time."

"Maybe," he replied. "The patch I made the other day is cracking. The clay is poor quality, so I brought potter's clay from the shop. I'll use it to patch the crack while you work in here."

"Ok, honey. I have water heating on the stove. We'll have tea in a few minutes."

He went outside, opened the back door of the Jeep, lifted a two-gallon bucket of potter's clay, and took it Inside. He removed part of the old clay from the crevice and stacked it on the floor. Then, he reached into the bucket, pulled out a handful of clay and stuck it into the crack.

Later, as his fingers scraped the bottom of the bucket, he applied the last remaining clay. He ran his fingers lightly over the cold wet clay and smoothed it so that it matched the wall. Job completed, he returned to the living room and closed the door.

He warmed himself in front of the fire in the living room. Maya joined him on the couch with warm tea.

"You know," she said as she set her cup upon the rough cedar table, "I sometimes worry that I might not become a good enough artist to make a living. Do you ever have fears like that?" she asked.

John thought a moment before answering. "I have one fear," he replied finally.

"Oh?"

"Age. I'm not getting any younger. Lately, I've been thinking back upon my life. I'm aware of all the years I lost."

"That's all in the past, you have a new future now. Think positive thoughts," she said.

"I wish I had been more like George. He found his calling early, and he's been with it ever since."

"Dwelling on something in the past that you can't change isn't healthy. All that's behind you now."

"George and I are very much alike, but at the same time, different. We became roommates because the school assigned us to the same room. I guess it was from George that I discovered that I had a natural interest in art, but I never had an interest in becoming an artist, until recently. I first realized that I had an urge to create while I was hiking in the mountains. It dawned on me as I hiked that I wasted much of my life following a false dream."

"The dream of becoming a successful executive?"

she asked.

"Yes. I did become successful in business, but I was never satisfied. It wasn't until I was fired that my thinking changed. Before that, I thought happiness was the next promotion."

"That shows insight," she said.

He sipped his tea before continuing. "Some men my age pass away from heart attacks and cancer. I realize that I have only a limited amount of time left. Thanks to you, I discovered something within myself that is beautiful. Something that is alive and free."

"You'll live up to your potential, and you'll be a good artist. You have many good years left. You'll probably outlive me!"

"I doubt that." He thought a moment as he drank the remainder of his tea. Maya observed his pensive mood and went into the Kitchen to retrieve the kettle. She poured more steaming liquid into his cup, and then filled her own.

"Look at it this way, John," Maya said. "It doesn't matter what direction you take in life, you will still be John Tollifson. Not someone else. Taking a different path will not change you into another person. It's healthy for a person to try something different every few years."

John leaned back on the sofa and thought about what Maya had said. "You're right."

# CHAPTER 22

Days later, John stood by a window looking out at the snow-packed peaks of the Sangre de Cristo mountain range. The crackling of a fire in the living room, and the smell of burning piñon sent a thrill of adventure throughout his body.

He laid his pad on the table and studied his sketch. It contained sketches of a fairyland scene of butterflies and small people among multicolor mushrooms in the fanciful land of his imagination. Then, he turned to a clean page and began sketching.

For hours he sketched with a charcoal pencil until the light from the departing sun was too dim to work. He put down his sketch pad and went into Maya's studio. Maya was engrossed with a dreamlike painting of a Native American spirit in the side of a mountain cliff. He watched her, but she was unaware of his presence.

John left and brought back two oil lamps, lit them and

set one on a bench near Maya to illuminate her workbench, but she did not notice him, nor did he break her concentration.

John took the remaining lamp and returned to his studio, and set the lamp on the table where he continued sketching. Soon, he became so engrossed in his work that he lost tract of time. When he once more became conscious of the hour, it was nearly midnight. He put down his pencil and returned to Maya's studio. She was still engrossed in her work.

"Maya," John said as he stood beside her. She turned to him, smiled faintly, then returned to her work.

"It's majestic," he said.

"You like it?" she asked in a dreamlike state.

"Yes. It's lovely. What is it?"

"It appeared in a vision. Beautiful images, beautiful colors…transcendental music…as though my muse is speaking to me," she said as though she were only partially conscious.

"Maya." John shook her gently. She smiled and her eyes cleared as though she had been in a trance. "Where am I?" She asked.

"In your studio," John said.

"I'm cold," she said.

John pulled a blanket from a shelf and draped it around her shoulders.

"Let's go into the living room where it's warmer.

## SLOW TANGO IN TAOS

You shouldn't work so much," he said.

"But," she replied, "I love my work. It's a part of me."

He escorted her to the living room. He set her on the bed, then placed new logs on the fire. He stirred the coals until flames curled upward along the logs.

"It's wonderful. It's like being in love. It's like…" She stopped talking and stared vacantly into the distance as she sat on the edge of the bed. Then she lay down and closed her eyes. John covered her with a blanket, before he laid beside her and closed his eyes.

When he opened his eyes, a kaleidoscope of colors swirled around the room. Maya stood near the fireplace wrapped in a Native American turquoise blanket with red triangles. As though a mirage, she beckoned him with a wave of her hand, unwrapped the blanket and let it drop to the floor. She stood naked before him with hands outstretched, beckoning, surrounded with a purple glow that radiated from her perfect body.

He watched as she grew more and more radiant with a delicate purplish glow. He arose from the bed and stood beside her. As they touched hands, a warm sensation surged up his arm and throughout his body. Maya turned and walked to the door. She paused at the entrance, turned, and beckoned for him to follow.

Outside, John found the frigid winter wind to be strangely warm and soft. The newly fallen snow was as warm as sand on a summer beach. They walked to the stream holding hands. At the water's edge Maya kissed him, then walked into the stream. When she was midway into the waters, she turned and beckoned. As if in a trance, he obeyed, and entered the water.

Suddenly, he found himself sitting on the bed with Maya. He shook her. "Maya," he called out.

"What?" She muttered as she awoke and sat up.

"I had a strange dream," he said.

"So did I," she said.

Above the fireplace on the wall hung one of her mystical paintings. Both of them sat nude staring at the painting's mystical beauty.

"It's magnificent!" she replied in a soft radiant voice.

"Yes, a masterpiece," he replied, "one day perhaps."

"Yes, you too may produce a masterpiece."

"One day, perhaps," he said.

"You will," she replied as she kissed him. "I know you will."

Outside, large flakes of snow blew horizontally past the window as the wind caused the weathered barn door to bang as it swung from the howling wind. John suddenly awoke from the banging. He looked at Maya who lay asleep curled up under a wool blanket as shadows cast by the fire danced upon the walls. *Wow, what a crazy dream.*

# CHAPTER 23

The next morning when he awoke, the logs had partially burned away and the smell of piñon filled the room. John sat up and rubbed his eyes, then leaned over and kissed Maya. She opened her eyes and smiled. He looked at a painting hanging on the wall of Native Americans dancing in a circle near a lake.

"Your painting is very powerful," John said. "The brilliant colors of their clothing…"

"They're conducting a sacred ritual at Blue lake," she replied. "It's not original, I copied the style of Dorothy Brett."

"Could I visit Blue lake?" he asked.

"No white man has ever seen the ritual, and no white man will ever see it, unless…" she said before pausing.

"Unless what?"

"An ancient spirit resides in Taos mountain. Only if

the spirit gives you a vision will you be able to visit the lake and know the mysteries of its waters."

"And how does someone go about contacting this spirit?" he winked.

"Don't mock the spirit!" she scolded.

"I'm not," he replied. "Can I contact the spirit of Blue Lake?"

"Why do you want to?" she asked.

"I'm curious."

"It's off-limits to non-tribal people. White men have attempted to see the sacred rites. Some slipped in with cameras, but none lived to tell about it."

"Murdered?"

"No one knows. They just disappeared."

"The Pueblo Indians are very protective of their culture."

"Orgies?"

"That's the town gossip. That's the way white men think. Always, they think of sensual pleasures, and material rewards."

John thought a moment. "You're right, I apologize."

"There is something that can help you with the vision..." Her voice trailed off.

"Like what?" he asked after a moment's hesitation.

"It's a tribal secret. I've pledged to keep it and other things secret. The knowledge is sacred. It's been in our tribe for centuries. I would receive the curse of my ancestors if I revealed it."

## SLOW TANGO IN TAOS

"But, could I learn the secret by taking your magical medicine."

"No!" she said sternly. "Peyote is to be used only for religious ceremonies."

"But I thought--"

"It's up to the great spirit to reveal his secrets. You must first prove yourself. If the spirit thinks you're worthy, he might reveal sacred knowledge.
"How do I do that?"

"By showing that you truly want to make the world more beautiful and leave the world better that you found it. You must make yourself a medium for universal truths, the wisdom of the universe."

"Is that why your paintings seem mystical?"

"Symbolism is the highest form of language. That's why paintings are a perfect medium for universal truths."

John furrowed his brow, questioning.

"When your spirit is sufficiently developed, you might receive such truths."

"You know, Maya." he replied, "you're the strangest woman I've ever known, but I love you."

Later that night, Maya was in the kitchen looking for something to fix for supper when John entered.

"What do we have to eat?" John asked.

"We don't have much to choose from. Just some canned goods."

"Oh," he laughed, "maybe some wild rabbit sauté in olive oil with piñon nuts."

# Phil Cline

"Where did you learn about that?" she asked with a curious tilt of her head.

"I made it up."

"That's a favorite of my tribe, but we don't use olive oil," she said. "Tell you what, you go out and catch a wild rabbit, and I'll prepare the piñon nuts."

"And how am I to catch a rabbit?"

"You'll think of something."

"Come on now, let's be serious!"

"For centuries, rabbits were part of my ancestors' diet. Tell you what, I'll give you a knife and you go out and trap a rabbit. Show yourself to be a man. If you look out in the barn I'm sure you'll find some rabbits seeking shelter."

"Suppose I find a rabbit, where will we get the piñon nuts?"

"That's easy. I brought some with me," she said.

"I can't catch a rabbit with a knife!"

"I'll go with you."

"This is crazy, Maya! Grown people don't go out mugging rabbits in the middle of night!"

"It isn't the middle of the night. It's only after sundown, and we're not mugging them. We're catching them for food!"

"OK! OK!" He threw up his hands, "let's go. Get your coat."

"Get a large knife from the kitchen," she instructed.

John returned with a slightly rusted butcher knife. He stuck it under his belt and put on his coat. Maya zipped up her coat, and pulled the hood over her head.

"Are you ready?" She stood in front of the fire with an impish smile.

"You're crazy!" he said.

"Isn't that the reason you like me?"

He thought a moment before replying. "That must be part of it."

"Then let's get crazy together," she said. "You lead the way."

John opened the door and stepped into the biting cold air that stung his cheeks. He turned to Maya standing in the doorway. "John," she called out. "We forgot something."

"What?"

"A light." She went back into the house and returned carrying a silver flashlight. He shook his head and walked to the barn where he paused and looked around. "So where are the rabbits?"

Maya focused light from her flashlight alongside the barn. "See those little tracks. At the end of those tracks you'll find a rabbit."

"Great, and how do we get the rabbit to stand still long enough for us to capture it."

"Easy. Look there." She cast the light onto a pile of six-inch diameter pipes. "See the rabbit tracks leading to the end of that pipe?" She shone her flashlight on one of the pipes. "Those tracks are fresh."

"How do you know they're fresh?"

# Phil Cline

"Because it's still snowing! Honestly!"

"I don t know anything about hunting rabbits," John admitted.

"You'll learn. Get a feed sack from the barn. Find one that doesn't have a hole in it."

They went into the barn that smelled of moldy hay. John climbed up the wooden ladder into the loft, shone his light on the floor of the loft, and onto a pile of sacks he had seen earlier. He picked out a feed sack. "This should work," he said as he held it up for Maya to see.

"Now," she continued, "We need a long pole. Do you see any up there?"

"There are several cane poles near the wall."

"Bring one down."

"Okay," he said.

He picked out a pole that seemed the sturdiest of the group and handed it to Maya. Then, he climbed back down the ladder.

"Let's go outside to those pipes," she said.

Outside, John knelt down and focused the flashlight into the darkness of the pipe. Looking back at him were a pair of red eyes.

"He's in there all right," John said.

"Let me look," Maya knelt down and focused the light into the pipe.

"Yep, he's in there."

"So, now what do we do?" John asked.

## SLOW TANGO IN TAOS

"I'll wrap the sack around the other end of the pipe, so that when he runs out, he'll run into our sack. You stay here and push the large end of that cane pole into the pipe, and force the rabbit to run out the other end into our sack."

John took the pole and shoved one end into the pipe.

"Not yet!" she yelled. "Wait until I tell you. I have to tie the sack to the end of the pipe."

John waited. The coldness of the night heightened his excitement of the hunt. Perhaps, he thought, his excitement was some primitive instinct still latent in his genes.

"What if he comes out this end?" John asked.

"He won't." Maya said. She wrapped the sack around one end of the pipe.

"Okay, push."

John shoved the pole into the pipe until it stopped. He pulled it back toward him a few inches and then pushed it back in, but again it stopped.

"It won't go in any farther," he said.

"Push harder! He'll move."

John pushed harder. The pole gave way, and the rabbit exited the pipe into the sack, but one side of the bag was not secure. The rabbit found the opening, and scampered off into the snow-filled night.

"I've lost my appetite for rabbit," John said. "Let's go over to Tina's for dinner. She gave us an open invitation."

He slipped his hands into the pockets of his jacket to protect them from the frigid air. Then, they returned to the house. Inside, he warmed his hands by the fire and thought of his rabbit capturing failure. Maya joined him by the fire.

"Well," she shook her head and muttered. "We won't have sauté rabbit tonight, but we have things to eat."

"Like what?" he asked.

"Lentils" she replied, "I'll put some on the stove."

When they had heated, Maya poured lentils into the bowl, and buttered some home-made bread. She put the plate in front of John. "I can't believe we went through the whole charade of catching a rabbit for dinner, and it got away," John said. His eyes lit up with a twinkle as he thought of the rabbit. "That was quite an adventure," he chuckled.

"I wanted to teach you how to catch a rabbit," Maya said. "It's an important skill to have. One day you might find yourself in the forest without anything to eat."

"Okay, now I know how to catch a rabbit, or rather how not to catch a rabbit."

"Any Native American should have good hunting skills."

"I'm not Native American." He took another bite of lentils.

"One day, I might be able to get you honorary membership in my tribe," she kidded.

"George said it's impossible for a white man to belong to the Taos pueblo," John said.

"It is," she replied. "So, eat your lentils before they get cold."

"You're a strange woman, Maya," he said.

## SLOW TANGO IN TAOS

"It's the--"

"Native American in you," he interrupted.

Later, they retired to the living room as embers exploding in the fireplace provided the only sound in an otherwise quiet room. John placed more piñon logs on the fire. They sat next to each other and sipped herbal tea. As the fire burned, sap in the logs exploded, sending embers flying up the chimney.

John sat in silence for a long-time watching flames in the fireplace. He set his cup aside and turned to Maya. "I'm glad the rabbit got away."

She smiled and kissed him. "So am I. It isn't right to kill an animal unless you're starving and need nutrition. Otherwise, we should leave nature to its own course."

"I agree." He picked up his cup and took another sip as he watched snow-flakes falling past the window onto a landscape highlighted by a full moon.

# Phil Cline

# CHAPTER 24

In the weeks that followed, John followed a schedule that varied little from day to day. Much of his time was taken with art lessons that Maya gave him. At first, he found the painting techniques puzzling and pinched his lips together with each lesson. Day after day, he practiced his art until he became more proficient as his skills sharpened. In the late spring of the following year John was working in his studio one afternoon when Maya ran into his studio.

"John! John!" Maya cried as she raced into the room. Startled by her excitement, he dropped a tube of paint. As it hit the floor, bright orange paint squirted onto John's pant leg.

"What is it!" He picked the tube off the floor and used a rag to wipe his clothing.

"Oh John!" She ran toward him. "The most wonderful thing has happened."

"What?" he asked.

# Phil Cline

" I stopped by the gallery to talk with Cindy this afternoon and a New York art dealer was there. He saw our work and wants to give us a private showing in his studio in SoHo."

"Our paintings are going to New York?"

"Yes, they're going to be exhibited. Isn't that great!"

"Great! That's fantastic!" He said. His pulse quickened.

He tossed the tube of paint onto the table and rushed to Maya. They laughed and danced around the paint spattered room.

"Finally!" She exclaimed. "After all, Finally--" John stopped dancing. His smile disappeared. "Is that a major gallery in New York?" he asked.

"Yes, the owner came out here to look at the local talent. He's an art buyer. He selects paintings here in Taos for display in New York, London and Paris. It's all consigned."

*Wait a minute!*

"How much did you have to do with his decision to exhibit my work."

"Honey, the agent was very impressed with your artwork."

"Maya!" John asked. "Is he taking my work because you asked him to?"

"No, John " she said, stamping her foot. "He was talking to Cindy about your work when I went into her gallery. He was examining your work. Not mine!"

"Was he really interested in my work?" John asked,

wide eyed. His brow wrinkled and he stared blankly out the window. "They're interested in my work! Do you think there's a chance?"

"Yes, John," she said cheerfully, "You're going to make it. I told you you'd make it as an artist."

"They want my work. They want my work!" He repeated. "I can't believe they really want my work…our work!"

"Yes, and we'll be exhibited together, side by side in New York!" she exclaimed.

"Honey, this calls for a celebration. Let's break out a bottle of wine."

Maya went into the kitchen and returned holding a bottle of cheap wine and two glasses. John opened the bottle and filled the glasses.

"A salute to us. To our success," John said as he proposed a toast.

"I can see it now,", he said, gesturing with his hands. "Our art will hang on the walls of museums. We'll be known throughout the world. We'll be known in New York, and Washington, and Los Angeles, San Francisco, London, Paris,"

"Moscow and Madrid!" she interjected.

"Yes, and many more places. We'll be famous," he said.

"World Famous!" she replied

"Let's go to Tina's tonight and tell her the good news, then to the plaza where we can…"

# Phil Cline

He noticed Maya wasn't smiling, but was staring at the floor.

"What's wrong?" he asked.

"I can't go to Tina's tonight," Maya said.

"Can't go? Why not?" he asked.

"I promised the dealer I'd go with him back to New York. He's leaving tomorrow morning. I'm to meet him at nine o'clock in the lobby of the La Fonda."

"What?" John asked dismayed, "New York? But what about your work here?"

"It'll only be for a month," she said.

"A month!" His mouth was agape. "Why do you have to go to New York for a month?"

John's eyes narrowed and his lips pursed.

"Oh John! Can't you see that it's necessary…for our careers!"

"Our careers! Why does he want you in New York?"

"To help open the show. He wants me there to meet clients."

John's face flushed and his jaw clinched. Anger and disappointment welled within him as he fought to maintain his composure. "Is that all he wants?"

"John!" she shouted, "how can you even think such a thing!"

"Because I know what bastards those art dealers are!"

"This one is different. Oh, John, I have to go. Can't you understand, it means the difference between my getting

# SLOW TANGO IN TAOS

known and being stuck out here forever as an unknown. This is my big chance."

"Your big chance? Only a second ago you were saying it was our big chance."

"John, you have to look at this realistically! I've been an artist for years, I studied in New York, and my work is known." she paused. "I've taught you nearly everything I know about art, you're good, believe me you're making great progress. This is my big chance, but it's also yours. Can't you understand that?"

He filled his glass with more wine and took a large gulp. He stared blankly at the floor. A deep set of creases disrupted his otherwise smooth forehead. For long minutes John remained motionless in his studio staring at the floor. He listened to the sounds of Maya in the other room readying herself for the trip to New York. He was distressed by the thought of her leaving him. How it was that within the short period of a few months his life could have been so radically altered. He stared at the landscape painting of the high desert he had worked on earlier in the afternoon. The idea that he too would be exhibited in the New York galleries now seemed unimportant. The most important art in his life was in the other room packing for a trip to New York.

"John," Maya called. He did not answer. "John," she called again. A dark weight seemed to engulf him. He placed his hands on the top of his head as he walked to the window.

"John," she called again. She stood at the entrance to his studio. He stared blankly out the window. She said not a word, but watched.

"Honey," she said softly. She walked over and kissed him.

"Don't leave me," he pleaded.

"Come on, John. It's only for a short time. I'll return and everything will be the same as now."

"No," he replied, "nothing is ever the same. Everything changes."

"But it will be the same," she replied, "I'll return and we'll be together."

"Nothing is ever the same," he repeated. "Don't leave me. I love you."

"John!" She stomped her foot. "It's necessary for me to go to New York. It's important."

"I've learned so much from you," he said as he hugged her. "You've taught me things I was never aware of. It's like all my life I've lived in an empty shell. It wasn't until that I met you that I knew I had something worthwhile to offer the world."

She grabbed his hands and squeezed them. Then, she walked back into the other room to finish packing.

For a long time, he sat at his studio table, stunned. Then, slowly, he accepted the fact that she was leaving. He got up and went into the living room. "Can I help you pack?"

"No, I can manage." She folded a dress and placed it neatly among other clothing in the suitcase.

"You're flying out of Santa Fe?"

"Yes, the plane leaves at noon tomorrow. The broker

## SLOW TANGO IN TAOS

has a rental car, so I'm riding with him."

John walked out onto the front porch. He sat on the edge of the porch resting his feet on the wooden steps made of timbers he had split the previous month. The cold air bit at his cheeks and the smell of piñon filled the air. He wrapped the collar of his coat closer to his neck. He remembered the many good times he had with Maya. He knew he would miss her. He feared this day would mark another turning point in his life, and didn't want to lose the wonderfully carefree and creative days he enjoyed with Maya.

As he sat on the porch, his thoughts flashed to the departure of his wife and daughter that cold Chicago day. He remembered the grief that overwhelmed him when they left, and the loneliness and emptiness that followed. It would not be the same. A loose board creaked as Maya stepped out onto the porch. John didn't want to look at her and betray his distress. He wanted to face her departure with happiness for her good fortune, but he was tormented.

She sat beside him and ran her fingers through his hair. "I'm not deserting you."

He listened to her words, but John knew his world was falling apart once more.

*I can't go through this again.*

"I want to spend some time with you before I leave," Maya said.

"What do we say to each other?" John asked.

"You could tell me that you love me and that you'll

miss me."

"Don't you know?" he asked.

She smiled and nodded. "It makes me sad to know that you're taking it like this."

"How can you ask me if I'm going to miss you. Can't you see that your leaving is tearing me apart?"

"I'm only leaving for a short time," she said.

John took a deep breath. "No, you're leaving me for a lifetime. You'll never come back!"

"John, that isn't true."

"You're going to be successful in New York. All the available men will chase after you, and you'll have your choice of men. The whole male field will be open to you. You'll find younger men attracted to you, and you'll find them talented, attractive and desirable. You won't return, Maya. This is our last hour together. From this point forward both our lives will take different paths."

"Don't John! You're making me sad." She fought to hold back tears.

"You know what I say is true. You've often told me how you liked New York and how you wouldn't mind living there."

"I know I said those things, John, but I didn't mean them."

"Then, why are you going back to New York."

"I've told you, John. We'll never be successful unless we have a showing in a well-known New York Gallery. That's where names are made. Names in the art world are not

## SLOW TANGO IN TAOS

made in Taos. They're made in New York."

"New York isn't where names are made. New York is where artists' lives are broken and their names' bought and sold like commodities," John said.

"John, that isn't so!" She protested.

"Maya," he said. "They'll make you successful. The rich and famous will buy your art, and they'll invite you to their parties, but they won't be interested in Maya, my beautiful Running Bear. They're after the glitter and the name dropping with their friends. Artists rank high on their scale of dinner guests because artists are the creators of the culture they relish. What they're really after is a chance to be near someone who has achieved something that they could never attain."

"That's cynical."

"Yes, but true." He went outside, stood on the porch and looked out at the mountains. A lone deer grazed on the hill and birds chimed in the neighboring trees. Sounds of a fast-moving stream punctuated the stillness. None of this was noticed by John who was steeped in a dark heaviness that permeated his entire body. He returned to his studio and worked until midnight, then joined Maya who had already gone to bed and was fast asleep. He pulled the blankets over the top of himself and listened to Maya's rhythmic breathing. Then, he too fell asleep.

# Phil Cline

# SLOW TANGO IN TAOS

# CHAPTER 25

The next morning, John stood on the porch looking out at the mountains. A light dew covering the land glistened as the sun arose over the horizon. Maya set her suitcase next to him and touched his shoulder.

"Honey, let's go into town," she said.

He picked up her suitcase and placed it into the back of the Jeep, then slid into the driver's seat. Maya opened the passenger's door and got in. They didn't say much to each other on the way into Taos. Sadness seemed to crush him like a great weight with every thought of her leaving. Occasionally, Maya would look over at John and study him as his eyes remained on the roadway ahead.

"John," Maya said when they arrived in Taos. "I don't want to leave you any more than you want me to leave."

John shrugged and pulled into Tina's driveway. Birds

flew from a feeder as they walked across the wooden porch. The morning air was crisp and smelled of piñon from a neighbor's chimney.

"Anyone home?" John shouted.

"Come on in," came Tina's voice from a back room.

When they entered, they found Tina standing in the doorway of the kitchen holding a broom in one hand and a dust pan in the other.

"I'm getting the house cleaned up," she explained. "Socorro went to Mexico to visit her family, so I'm doing the work. Housework makes me energetic."

"We were on our way to the Plaza, and thought we'd drop by," Maya said.

"She's leaving for New York." John said as he stood looking out the window.

"Oh, isn't that wonderful." Tina clapped her hands.

"You must be very proud of her."

Maya glanced at John in anticipation, "Yes," he replied. He turned to Tina. "I'm very proud of her, but I'm going to miss her."

"John thinks I'm leaving him for good," Maya said.

"Oh!" Tina replied with a wave of her hand. "Don't you think that for a moment, John. I've known Maya a long time, and I know she would never leave you." Tina set the broom aside. "How long will you be gone?"

"One month," Maya said.

"Or two," John corrected.

"John, you must come around and visit me more

often while Maya is away. Folks around here have been wondering why you haven't been dropping by."

"John's been busy with his paintings and managing the pottery business," Maya said.

"The shop is doing really well since Maya redesigned some of our pottery," John said. "Tourists are buying more and more. I've left Jose in charge of the shop when I'm not there. That leaves me more time for my art work."

"Does Red come into work?" Tina asked.

"Not often. Since returning to Taos, he's a changed man. He likes receiving a percentage of sales without having to work," John said.

"How's John's artwork coming?" Tina asked.

"Oh, he's becoming a regular Michelangelo," Maya said proudly.

"A Monet," John corrected

"Okay, a Claude Monet. He's becoming an excellent artist." Maya winked.

"I wish I had more talent," Tina said as her chin dipped slightly and she stroked her throat. She paused with a pensive pursing of her lips, then nodded and continued.

"However, being around artists is enough for me."

"You're to artists in Taos what Gertrude Stein was to those in Paris in the nineteen twenties. I don't know what we'd do without you, Tina," Maya replied. "You've done so much for all of us."

"Especially for me," John replied.

"You two sure know how to make an old woman

blush," Tina said.

"You're not old," John replied.

"Thank you, John," Tina smiled. "I'll take that as a compliment."

"By the way, have you heard from George?" John asked.

"He hasn't written, but I always have a premonition about him a few days before he shows up," Tina said. "I was cleaning the back room before you arrived and I was thinking about him. That usually means he's thinking about returning to Taos."

"Like calling ahead," Maya replied laughing.

"It's true," Tina protested.

"I'm not laughing at you," Maya replied affectionately. "It's that George has such a strange influence on people."

Maya glanced at the redwood burl clock hanging on the wall. "It's time," Maya said. "We need to go."

"Have a safe trip and hurry back to Taos. Don't stay in New York," Tina said. "John, we're having a dinner next week. Be sure and come."

"I'll do that," he said.

They drove to the square in downtown Taos and parked in front of the La Fonda. John opened the trunk, removed Maya's suitcase, and carried it into the lobby of the hotel.

"May I take your bag sir?" asked a porter.

"No," John replied. "We're just meeting someone

## SLOW TANGO IN TAOS

here."

The smell of coffee from an adjacent snack bar permeated the air. They waited a few minutes before seeing a short dark-haired man of about sixty coming down an ornate staircase leading from the mezzanine. "I'm glad you're here," the man said as he straightened his blue silk ascot.

"Bradwell's the name." he extended his hand to John.

"Tollifson. John Tollifson," John replied.

"Well, Tollifson, good to meet you." He took Maya by the hand and led her outside.

"By the way, Tollifson. " Bradwell said as he paused in the doorway. "Be a good sport and grab our bags."

Anger flushed through John as he watched Bradwell walk from the lobby. He picked up the suitcases and followed them to the car. His emotions conflated anger and sadness.

*What an ass!* John thought.

"Bring the bags around here, will you sport?" Bradwell said as he opened the trunk. With mounting anger, John set Maya's suitcase inside, and then tossed Bradwell's suitcase into the trunk. Though he wanted to tell Bradwell off, he controlled himself.

"Pay no attention to him," Maya whispered. "I'll miss you."

As Bradwell looked on, John grabbed Maya and gave her a long passionate kiss. "Wow!" She said, reacting to the kiss. "Can't wait to come back to Taos." She got into the car. Bradwell put the car into gear and sped off.

## Phil Cline

## SLOW TANGO IN TAOS

# CHAPTER 26

John's chest felt tight and his limbs limp as he stood in front of the La Fonda. His sadness grew into bitterness and anger as his thoughts flashed over the past few months of his life. How could he live on the ranch without Maya? It seemed pointless. Suddenly, his thoughts shifted to his wife and daughter. He hadn't talked to Jennie for several weeks. He returned to the lobby of La Fonda and asked to use their telephone. He dialed the number and the phone rang several times before someone answered – it was Jennie. They talked and John told her he loved her, and Jennie told him how much she missed him and wanted to stay in touch. They talked a short time before Wilma took the phone from her daughter and hung up. John sighed, returned the phone to the cradle and walked outside.

Native American men, women and children with colorful serapes of reds, yellows and turquoise wrapped

## Phil Cline

around their shoulders awaited in the square for a bus to take them out to the pueblo. In desperation, John mounted the stairs to a restaurant at one end of the plaza. He sat at a table near a window so he could have a view of the Taos plaza. He ordered a coffee and looked out the window as his emotions sunk.

From a nearby table he heard a familiar voice, "Cool man, gotta keep moving, you know how it is." He turned to see Jasper, the man he had met while travelling. He was sitting alone, but was talking to a young man and woman sitting at a nearby table. Jasper appeared to be slightly older than John remembered him. His red bandana, now faded, appeared to be the same one he had worn earlier. Talking to the two between quick sips of coffee, he appeared aged but otherwise little changed. At one point, he turned to face John.

He stopped talking. His forehead crinkled, then a smile broadened his creased face. "I know you, man" Jasper said, pointing to John. "I know you!"

John smiled and gestured. "Join me."

Jasper carried his coffee cup to John's table and sat down.

"Good seeing you, man," Jasper said. "Your name's John, right?" John nodded. "Cool, man. I Remember you say'n you were coming to Taos. Wow, been a long time."

"How have you been?" John asked.

"Been cool, man. Travelling a lot."

"Haven't settled down?" John asked.

## SLOW TANGO IN TAOS

"Tried. Did a stint in a half-way house. Got one out in Berkeley. Got myself cleaned up."

"What happened?"

Jasper took a long sip. John saw deep creases appear in Jasper's forehead as he thought. Then, he set the cup down.

"Got involved with a hippy chick. Pretty young thing. Her friends thought I was an aged relic. They started making fun of me. Got me to thinking. One day, I looked at myself in the mirror -- looked real hard. Man, I saw a disgusting sight. Never looked at myself like that before. Man, I saw a loser. The chick dumped me. Really hurt me, man. Then, my trust fund dried up. After she dumped me, I was sleeping on the streets. I was arrested and thrown into jail. Judge sent me to a half-way house. Few months later, I got me a job at an Oakland dry dock in the inner harbor. I met an old black man there named Tucker. Used to tell me the best way to get ahead is to work hard, keep a job, and live below your means, save money and settle down."

"Did you?"

"Man, I tried. I really tried."

John signaled for the waitress to refresh the cups of coffee. After she poured fresh coffee into the cups, Jasper blew steam from his cup, and took a sip. John studied him. Jasper seemed to be lost in thought. Then he spoke. "You know, man, I used to be a real dude with the chicks. I could go to any campus and get chicks. They thought I was cool. Man, life was easy!" Jasper shook his head as he rubbed his

# Phil Cline

forehead.

"So, what happened?"

"Time happened, man. Age happened. My hair turned grey, my skin wrinkled. Young chicks don't like me no more. Can't say I blame them. Can't be top dog forever."

"So, why are you in Taos?"

"Lost my job at the dry dock – it went bankrupt. Recession shut stuff down. Couldn't find another job in the Bay Area, especially for an old hippy guy like me. Got itchy feet and headed east. This is as far east as I've gotten."

"So, you had a trust fund?"

"Old man left me a little trust fund. Not much, just enough to get by if I crashed on friends' couches. Problem is, people got tired of me crashing in their pads. It's like I woke up one morning and it was twenty years later. Damn!"

John looked out the window, his face contorted. He thought of two of his friends who had received trust funds, and of their tragic ends. He turned to Jasper.

"Trust funds have ruined more people than they've helped. Parents leave kids a small trust fund to help them. Unfortunately, often it produces just enough money to ruin them and keep them in poverty. Well, that's that. So, what do you plan to do now?"

"Man, I don't know. My feet tell me to keep moving. Go east, then go west, like I've been doing. Trouble is, I'm getting old and tired. Travelling ain't no fun no more."

John studied Jasper who stared into his cup of coffee seemingly lost in thought. His demeanor had changed from

# SLOW TANGO IN TAOS

the time they travelled together in Colorado. Jasper lacked the youthful spark that he used to have. Before him was a man who for many years had neglected his health and was steeped in physical decline.

"Would you be interested in working in a pottery factory?" John asked.

"Doing what?"

"Making pottery."

"Don't know nothing about that. What you got in mind?"

"I manage a pottery shop owned by a friend of mine. We could probably give you a job there, but you would have to settle down. No drugs at work."

"Oh, man. I don't know."

"Well, think it over. "I'll take you down and show you where the shop is located. Show up tomorrow morning. Talk to Jose if I'm not there yet and you'll have a job."

"You'd do that for me?"

"I will. Do you have a place to stay?"

Jasper paused and shifted in his chair. "Yeah, man."

"Staying with a friend?"

"No man, I pitched a tent outside of town. That's where I've been living. I like it there."

"Okay. Suit yourself. Let's go, I'll show you the shop," John said.

The next morning, John drove into Taos and arrived at the shop. He looked around, but didn't see Jasper. He walked over to Jose who was turning clay on the wheel.

# Phil Cline

"Did a fellow named Jasper show up this morning? He's supposed to start work today."

"Old hippy guy?"

"That's him. Where is he?"

"Don't know. He showed up, took one look around and said 'no way, man', then he turned to leave. I asked him where he was going and he said 'east, man, east.' Then he left. Don't know where he went. I think he left town."

John shook his head in disbelief. He remembered the words of his father who had a friend who was like Jasper: *Once a drifter, always a drifter. Sometimes people can't stop tripping over themselves.* Then a thought occurred to John that Jasper was a prisoner of his own delusions.

After work that day, he returned to the ranch. He knew it would be lonely and depressing at the ranch without Maya. For several hours, he drove along county roads that wound through the mountains trying to lose his sadness, but grief seemed to cling to him like a mournful moss. Even the trees seemed to weep and every turn in the road came with a sense of loss. It was late evening when he finally parked in front of the ranch house.

He went inside, sat at the desk in his studio, picked up a pencil, and began sketching. At first, he drew a landscape of the mountains that had become so familiar. Then, he set it aside and took out a clean sheet of paper, and began drawing a picture of the firebird that had haunted him. Soon he was lost in his work. For hours he worked until the image looked like it could fly off the paper.

# CHAPTER 27

As the sun appeared over the distant mountains, John stuck kindling and sticks into the wood-fueled stove in the kitchen and lit them. With a fire blazing and the metal plate on the stove sufficiently hot, he placed a skillet on the plate, then threw in an egg and a slice of toast. After breakfast, he carried a pot of hot tea into his studio and sat down at his work station. He found it difficult to keep his thoughts from returning to Maya, and how he missed her.

He knew work was the best medicine for depression, so he set to work. For hours, he painted feverishly on a canvass he had begun a few days earlier, but had been loath to finish. As he mixed tubes of paint on a palette and applied paint to the canvass, he found himself being more and more drawn into his art. It was easier that way. With concentrated effort, his thoughts were less of Maya and more of his craft.

Squeezing black paint from a tube onto a palette, then

mixing it with white paint, he applied the grey paint onto the canvass to create storm clouds gathering over a mountain. He leaned forward to examine his work. Greys seemed to match his mood, but it needed more color. He applied reds, blues and other colors. He worked the paint into angular, then circular patterns. Painting feverishly, he was no longer aware of what he was painting. The brush in his hand seemed to make its own motions as it traversed the open ranges of his subconscious.

Finally, he sat back, exhausted, and examined his opus. Hours of concentrated labor appeared on the canvass in a series of convoluted patterns and haphazard colors. There were streaks of reds and blacks that merged onto a background of blues, greens and purples swirling throughout the painting.

There was no subject matter, nor was there a geometrical configuration which might capture someone's interest. Many thoughts raced through his mind, but nothing existed on the canvass, but a series of random brush strokes. Why had he worked so feverishly for all those hours? He had no answer, but it had served to quell his thoughts of Maya.

In a frustrated rage, he picked up the frame and tossed the canvass across the room. It hit the wall and fell to the floor. Disgusted, he left and went into Maya's studio. He searched through a small cupboard where Maya kept her supplies. There wasn't much light in the room, so he raised the oil lamp so that he could see more clearly. Tubes of paint lined the bottom shelf. Desperately, he searched the cabinet

## SLOW TANGO IN TAOS

looking to fill the void of Maya's absence.

He focused the light on a particular area. Sitting on the upper shelf was a small canvass bag. Maya had taken that bag when she occasionally engaged in spiritual rituals with friends from the Pueblo. Maya had once asked him to join her, but he had refused. Now things were different. What he needed, he didn't know, but he knew he needed something.

He lifted the bag from the shelf and opened it. Inside were several Peyote buttons. He took a ceramic pipe from the shelf, and returned to his studio. Retrieving two peyote buttons from the sack, he held the green disc-shaped buttons in his hand, and looked at them. Then, he crushed them in a mortar and pestle, poured the residue into his pipe, and lit it. He sat on the floor, resting his back against the cool adobe wall as he puffed on the pipe. The slightly pungent smoke stung his tongue but the sensation quickly disappeared as his tongue became numb. He was puzzled that the Peyote had such a limited sensation. After waiting for more than an hour for the drug to take effect, he felt nothing more than a burning sensation in his lungs.

His psychic pain was intense. It was as though his whole existence was a cloud of darkness that enveloped him in sadness. He wanted to escape. In a fit of despair, he placed two buttons into his mouth and began to chew. The bitter taste was almost more than he could stand, but he continued chewing. Then, he took a drink of water and swallowed. For several minutes he waited, but there was no effect. He reached into the sack and popped another button into his

## Phil Cline

mouth and chewed. The button was difficult to swallow and seemed to stick in the back of his throat, so he took drink of water to wash it down. Again, nothing. For long minutes he waited, but nothing. He returned to his studio and began to work. Soon, he was at peace. Everything was blissful until his stomach began to churn. Then, he was no longer tranquil, nor was he at peace. He became violently ill, and more and more nauseous. He ran outside, put one arm against the house, and threw-up. His mouth was putrid with the taste of gall.

He rushed to the stream and washed his face with the cool liquid. He dipped water with his cupped hands, rinsed his mouth, and drank some of the pure mountain water. He tossed cold water on his face. Then, a peaceful bliss overcame him. The world was indeed a wonderful place and his psychic pain was gone. The tranquility was profound. Only the moment was important to him, so powerful was his feeling of peace. The cascading water became as music, and the rustling of the wind through the leaves of the trees were as woodwinds to the symphony of the rushing waters.

Then, he experienced a sense of total contentment. He lifted his head, and saw brilliant colors flowing all around him like streamers of an aurora boréalis. He stared passively at the distant hills, and stretched out his hand to touch the swirling colors. As his hand entered the rainbow, it disappeared, only to reappear with some of the colors clinging to his clenched fist. He brought his hand close to his nose and smelled. The colors had the fresh smell of lemons, and the tangy zest of spices. As he toyed with them, the colors ran out of his clinched fist and flowed over the horizon and down the other side of the mountain.

There appeared in the heavens a multitude of stars which served his increasing sense of introspection and curiosity about the universe. He reached out to grab a star as the thought occurred to him that he must not disturb the symmetry of the universe with his curious hands, least mankind suffers the consequences. In his mirth, he touched the stars with gentleness. He puckered his lips and blew upon the stars with a caring breath of life. Such peace and tranquility he had never known. He felt powerful as he reached out and touched stars in the Milky Way.

A rustling from the stream disrupted his mirth. He turned to see a large phoenix perched on a boulder in the middle of the stream with volant wings of fire radiating an eerie light that cast far and wide. John stared in awe. Its feathers radiated a rainbow of brilliant colors. Each feather a different color. The edge of each feather pulsated in a color of constantly changing intensity. Its outstretched wings were as a banner of fire with flames that shot upward, but never consumed the bird. A spiritual energy radiating from its eyes reached into John's soul. He could not run, nor could he move. His body was under the command of this strange bird.

As he passively watched, a sudden flash of light shot out from the stream and a Great Horned Owl appeared next to the phoenix. The owl's eyes were red as rubies and its feathers pulsated with a rainbow of vibrant colors. It too had an intense stream of energy that flowed deeply into John's soul. Like an immobile child, he sat watching, but unable to move while foreign thoughts danced in his head.

With all his strength, John tried to move his arms, to reach out and shew away the birds, but he was unable. For long moments, a strange soothing warmth flowed from both birds into John. Then, they flapped their wings and ascended into the sky. An iridescent red glow shot across the sky as they disappeared.

Regaining his ability to move, John looked up to see a ball of fire descending from the sky. He raised his hand in front of his face to protect himself from the strange object coming toward him. As it came closer, it took on the form of an old Indian Chief with a headdress of fire. His eyes were as infinite holes into the universe. His face showed the creases of age and wisdom. Around him spun a vortex of pulsating colors and flames of fire. From his palms radiated an energy that shot out toward John.

John's mouth opened, his eyes widened, and his muscles became rigid as he watched in awe. His heart pounded and his breath quickened. The Chief came to rest in the spot where the Fire Bird had perched. The Chief hovered above the water on a base of the purest of light. John shielded his eyes with his hands as brilliant colors swirled around him that seemed to be alive. John feared for his life, so awesome and formidable was the image. He tried to flee, but he was unable to do so because his muscles would not react. It was as if he was in a dream.

# SLOW TANGO IN TAOS

The old Native American held one hand outward as a signal that he meant no harm, then he began a series of conversations with John about life, death and metaphysics. Many profound truths were revealed to John by the great spirit. John was astounded at the simplicity of the truths that had lain fallow throughout his life. He discovered to his amazement that the most profound truths of the universe were the simplest. Simplicity was key to understanding the universe. All his life he had searched to understand complexities, but now he knew the most important thing was to love life itself and all the wonderful world around him.

He remained transfixed, unable to speak, as the spirit revealed more and more, John's thoughts increased in rapidity and profundity. Then, with a sweep of his hand, the Great Spirit displayed a panorama that John understood to be a play of life. Upon the hillside were a group of primitive people who John understood to be his ancestors. Each had thoughts that John could understand. Each had wishes and desires for themselves and their families. Their strongest wishes were for survival for themselves and their offspring. It dawned on John that the people he watched were no different than him. The only difference was the distance of several thousand years.

Then, that scene disappeared as though a page of history was erased. Then, another unfolded. It was of him and his parents at their house in Vermont. As he watched, he could understand the emotions of his parents and even those of himself as a child. It became apparent to John that the desires of his parents were no different from those of the primitives before them. All are part of the human experiment.

Communion with the Great Spirit continued until the first light of day. As the sun threatened to rise over the distant hills, the image gave a wave of his hand, and then arose into the sky. It disappeared with a flash of light and a peal of thunder.

John remained sitting for a long time trying to understand what had just happened. Then he stood and went to the edge of the water. He cupped his hands, dipped them into the stream, and threw water on his face to wake up.

Perhaps, he thought, he had fallen asleep and had dreamed about the old Chief, or had he actually seen a vision that revealed to him so many secrets of the universe? If so, why couldn't he remember the insights he had been given. He couldn't remember anything more than a feeling of love and warmth. What happened to all the profound truths of the universe?

He returned to his studio, and stopped cold in his tracks. A cold chill ran up his back. Lying on the floor where he had earlier tossed the canvass was a painting of the very firebird that had perched upon a boulder in the stream. Its wings were formed of long brush strokes of brilliant red paint. Its eyes were dark and forbidding and seemed to be as holes into eternity itself. John studied the awesome painting. He picked it up and started to place it on the adobe window sill, but as he set it down, the painting suddenly burst into

# SLOW TANGO IN TAOS

flames. Arising from the painting was the firebird. It flew through the open window and into freedom beyond. Streamers of fire appeared behind its wings. A short distance from the window, it spun into a vortex of flames that increased in intensity until it was more brilliant than the morning sun. Then, it disappeared. Stunned, John went to the living room and fell exhausted upon his bed.

# Phil Cline

## CHAPTER 28

In the days that followed, John experienced a powerful surge of creative energies that kept him working in his studio day and night. He seldom ventured into Taos except to obtain needed provisions, or to see if Jose was properly minding the pottery studio. As the days passed, John worked with an increasing furor as though his very existence was dependent upon the act of creation.

One day, while he was ardently working on a painting, he was disturbed by someone entering the house. His concentration disrupted, John turned to the intruder with some anger. In the doorway of his studio stood George Proctor.

"So, this is the way a genius spends his days," George mused as he looked at the scores of paintings lying scattered around the studio floor.

John managed a weak smile and waved him into the studio. "When did you get in?" John put his brushes aside.

# Phil Cline

"Early this morning. I stopped by Tina's. She said I could find you out here. She showed me an article featuring Maya in the New York Arts magazine. I brought it for you to read." He handed the magazine to John who took it, read the article, and then tossed it aside.

"Yeah, she told me she was going to be gone for one month." John's lip curled.

"How long ago was that?" George asked.

John's face contorted. "Nearly two months."

"Have you heard from Maya?"

"I got a letter from her a few days ago. She seems to be doing well in New York. Occasionally, I go down to the La Fonda and use their telephone. I call Maya and we talk. She tells me about things going on at the gallery in New York, and how she has become the subject of articles. Like the one you showed me."

George took a pipe from his pocket, packed it with tobacco, and put it into his mouth. Then he groped around his sport coat pocket searching for a book of matches.

"She got what she was after," John said.

"What's that?"

"Recognition and fame!" John's brow furrowed.

George struck a match, lit the tobacco and exhaled smoke. "She's become somewhat of a celebrity."

"Yeah." John replied. He picked up a paint brush, and then tossed it aside, "Yeah, she is!"

"How are you doing?" George puffed his pipe. "Tina tells me you've become a bit of a recluse, and a puzzle to

## SLOW TANGO IN TAOS

some of your friends."

"They don't understand," John replied. "I'm on the verge of creating something bigger than life. No, wait! It is life that I'm creating. Look!" He walked across to a pile of canvasses, retrieved one and held up the painting of a firebird with an image of the old chief brazened on its breast. The painting contained fine brush strokes that brought out subtle details as though it were a form of photorealism. In the background, the Sangre de Cristo mountains were draped in a purple mist. "Look at this! This is life!" John exclaimed.

"Impressive!" George examined it. "I've never seen a phoenix painted like this. It's as though his wings were actually ablaze with energy, and the eyes…" George examined the painting more closely. "The eyes seem to contain a strange energy that flows out as you look at it. Very impressive! You've come a long way."

George reached into an inside pocket of his coat and took out an envelope. "By the way, the fellow down at the La Fonda Hotel asked me to give this to you." George handed the letter to John.

"What is it?" John asked.

"Don't know. It's a letter from Chicago."

John took the letter and examined it. "It's from the Cyrox Corporation," John said in amazement. A cold foreboding sense of terror swept down his back.

*What did they want? More of my blood? Could I have done something wrong?*

He buried himself into the chair, staring at the

envelope. Then he gently tore the flap on the envelope, and opened it. As he read, several words jumped out at him: *Urgent! Call me at once. Recreated old position. Good chance for you. Congratulations!* Signed M. Newhouse, CEO/Board Chairman. John's jaw dropped, and his mouth remained open as he examined the letter.

"What is it?"

"This is crazy! Marc must have gotten a big promotion. He wants me for an interview!"

"Let me see the letter." George took the message and read it. "Are you going to call them?"

John shook his head. "Why should I?" he replied. Suddenly he turned angrily to George, "Is this some kind of a joke?"

"I should hope not, and, if it is, I can assure you I'm an innocent party. I was told to deliver this letter to you since I was coming out here."

"How did they know I was in Taos?"

"Beats me," George said, then paused. "Wait, some guy from your old company came up to me after a reading I gave in Chicago a while back, and asked about you. He wanted to know where you were. I told him you had gone out to Taos. That's all that was said. Then he left."

"I don't understand," John said. "Why do they want me?"

"Beats me." George puffed on his pipe.

"I'm of a mind to tell them to go to hell after what they put me through."

## SLOW TANGO IN TAOS

"Well, it wouldn't hurt to give them a call and find out the score," George said.

John hesitated, then gave a sigh. "Yeah, I guess you're right. It's signed by Marc. Looks like he's been promoted."

"Do you know him?"

"Not well. We occasionally had lunch together." John said. He thought a moment, then added, "Sorry, I'm rambling on. Would you like something to drink?"

"What do you have?" George asked.

"The alcohol is all gone, but I have tea."

"I could go for tea."

"Good! You can amuse yourself by looking around. Maya's paintings are in the other room."

"I'll heat the pot." John disappeared into the kitchen.

George examined John's paintings with increasing interest. Soon, John reentered with two cups of tea. He set one on his work table, and handed the other to George.

"Are you satisfied with your life out here?" George asked.

John took a sip before answering. "Art gives me a sense of wholeness I've never known before." He furrowed his brow as he reread his letter. "I don't think I can go back to work for a corporation."

"Try this," George said. "Why don't you call them up, and make an appointment. Meet them and talk. Then, you can make up your mind."

"They're a bunch of bastards!"

## Phil Cline

"Look," George said as he set his tea cup down. "If you don't go through an interview, and talk to them, you'll always wonder if you should have gone. Let them fly you to Chicago. It'll be a good trip at their expense. If they make you an offer, you can either accept or reject it, but you should find out."

"I suppose you're right," John replied.

From outside his window came a very loud whoo-whoo-whoooooo. John went to the window. Sitting at the peak of the barn was a Great Horned Owl that sat looking at John. As John watched, it seemed to wink with one of its yellow eyes. Then it flew away. Puzzled, John turned back to George.

"What is it?" George asked.

"An owl," John replied. "I've decided I like struggling. It's something I've never had to do. When I was young, I was an A student without having to study. Then on to grad school. I breezed through. Everything was easy. Sure, there were headaches, but I never struggled. This is the first time I've had to struggle, and where there are no guarantees!"

George wrinkled his brow and studied John, then polished off his tea. He set the cup on a nearby table. "Well, my friend, I told Tina I would borrow her van for about two hours." He looked at his watch before continuing. "… which is right about now. I must return her van."

"Will you be in Taos a few days?" John asked.

"No, I'm leaving the day after tomorrow for New

## SLOW TANGO IN TAOS

York."

"It seems you're always flying somewhere. When do you find time to write?" John asked.

"I write three pages every evening no matter where I happen to be. It keeps the old elbows warn and shiny. You know the way writers fancy those buckskin patches on the elbows of their coats. Makes a writer think he's living up to his calling. If he ever loses his sense of accomplishment, all he needs to do is look at the elbow patches. He knows he's earned them. Come over to Tina's tonight," George said.

"She asked me to invite you for dinner. I'd like to talk with you more. Anyway, thanks for the tea."

Later that day, John parked in front of the La Fonda and went into the lobby. The evening manager, a young man with round-gold rimmed glasses stood behind the counter.

"Could I use your telephone to make a call to Chicago?"

"We're not supposed to let customers make long distance calls," the manager replied.

"I'll pay you for the call." He took his wallet from his pocket and laid a twenty-dollar bill on the counter. The manager looked at the bill then at John and nodded.

"Go ahead and use it, but no more than a few minutes."

"Thank you. I'll make it a brief call."

John picked up the receiver and listened for tone, then dialed the number on the masthead of the letter. It rang twice before a pleasant-sounding secretary answered. "Cyrox

# Phil Cline

Corporation. Board of Directors."

"Hello, this is John Tollifson. I received a letter from--."

"Oh, yes, Mister Tollifson. Mr. Newhouse is expecting your call. Will you hold?"

"Yes," he replied. The phone line went silent for a short while as he waited. Then, a deep husky voice came on.

"John! You got my letter," Marc Newhouse said.

"Yes, I got it today."

"Splendid! Glad to know our postal service is so effective, even in a little town like..." he hesitated. "What's the name of that town out there?"

"Taos," John replied, "Taos, New Mexico."

"Yes, of course, Taos," he replied.

"Congratulations, I see you made Chairman."

"Yep. I told you I was on the short list," Marc said.

"So, tell me about this offer."

"It's about you, and your career, but I don't want to keep you glued to the phone. Would you be interested in coming to Chicago for an interview?"

John hesitated a moment. "Yes," he replied, his throat tightening, "I would like that."

"Good! Good!" he replied, "I knew we could count on you. Been telling the other board members some really good things about you, John. They're looking for a strong contender, potential CEO material. Our former CEO, Mr. Goodman, left for family obligations. Tell you what, I'll have my secretary wire you expense money and arrange a ticket.

## SLOW TANGO IN TAOS

Can you make a flight tomorrow?" he asked.

"Yes, I could do that."

"Great! There's a flight leaving Santa Fe tomorrow morning at 10:30. It arrives in Chicago in the afternoon. I'll have someone meet you at the airport."

"You'll make the reservations?" John asked.

"Oh, yes, we'll take care of all that. All you have to do is arrive at the airport for your flight. Keep all your receipts for the cab, food, limousine etc. We'll pick up your bills. Also, we'll have some spending money awaiting you at the ticket counter in Santa Fe."

"Okay, thanks."

"Great! I'm really looking forward to seeing you in my office. Nice talking to you, John."

"It was nice talking to you as well." John hung up the phone. His legs threatened to give way, his heart pounded, and beads of sweat appeared on his forehead. He sat on a bench in the lobby and took a deep breath. Then, he walked back to the Jeep.

John pulled into Tina's driveway. Lights from her house were warm and inviting. Suddenly, his thoughts flew back many years ago when he was a small boy of 6 years. He remembered riding in an old yellow school bus that rumbled along a rough country road as he held tightly onto a metal bar that extended across the back of the seat in front of him. He looked out the window as cold drops of rain slid down the cold glass. He was happy to be heading home and away from school. Soon, he knew he would see lights from the windows of his parent's house. That always made him happy because he knew he would soon be in a warm house where his parents would welcome him with a cookie and a warm glass of milk. He smiled at the memory and got out of the Jeep. "Anybody home?" he shouted as he opened the front door.

"Come on in stranger!" Tina said.

Tina and George were sitting on the sofa when he entered. A fire in the hearth warmed the room with the occasional pop of an ember. Aromas from the kitchen stoked his hunger.

"So," Tina said. "You're going to Chicago?"

"I'm booked on a flight tomorrow morning."

"It's going to be lonely without you," Tina said,

"We'll miss you."

"I haven't accepted the job," John replied. "At least, not yet."

"How long will you be in Chicago?" George asked.

"Probably a day or two."

"What about your art work? Are you going to give that up?" Tina asked.

"I haven't planned to," he replied.

Tina's face pinched. "They're going to ruin another artist!"

"John's just going for an interview," George replied.

"Don't let them talk you into something you'll be sorry for," she pleaded.

"John's a grown man, Tina," George said.

## SLOW TANGO IN TAOS

Tina's eyes rolled. "It's just that corporations have so much money and influence."

"But, they can't offer me what I have here. Friendship and a sense of who I really am. I found people who offered me selfless friendship. That's more valuable than all the money Cyrox can offer."

"That was a nice thing to say, John," Tina replied, a tear in her eye.

Later, as John was driving to the ranch, he thought about Tina and George. He was fortunate to have such good friends. As he drove up to the house, it looked different as though it somehow had changed. He knew it wasn't the house that had changed, but something had.

A myriad of thoughts bounced around in his head. If he was offered a job, would he turn it down and return to the ranch after the interview, or would he stay in Chicago? His thoughts were a mismatch of confusing thoughts. One moment he was excited at the prospect of again becoming an executive with all the perks, and at another moment he became angry at what had happened.

Later that night, he finished packing, made a pot of tea and went into his studio. A painting he had been working on was on the easel where he had left it that afternoon. He poured himself a warm refreshing cup of Chamomile tea which had recently become a favorite. It somehow helped clear John's mind of confusing thoughts and allowed him to concentrate his energies. He studied the work as he sipped

# Phil Cline

tea, but something was missing. Perhaps the color scheme needed changing. Something essential was lacking. He leaned back in the chair and examined the painting.

Slowly, as John feverishly worked with oils and a brush, a faint outline of a firebird appeared on the canvass. In the background was Taos Mountain. Paint seemed to fly from his brush as the image became more pronounced. For hours he worked. Then, exhausted, he leaned back his chair.

It was finished. The image had come to life and John's oils had finally captured the essence of the firebird's spirit. He admired his work, content that his skills were polished enough to bring to life abstract images floating around in his mind. Being of a late hour, he stored the supplies. Then, he fell exhausted upon his bed and was soon asleep.

# SLOW TANGO IN TAOS

# CHAPTER 29

The alarm went off promptly at five O'clock. John got up, washed, shaved, and dressed. He took one look around, then went out the front door, locked it, and threw his suitcase into the Jeep. The engine turned over several times but didn't start. He sat for a moment.

*Don't fail me now!*

He turned the key again and the engine turned over several times before it finally started. He felt a wave of relief as he pointed the Jeep up the driveway.

Two hours later, he was driving into the parking lot of the airport in Santa Fe. He yawned as he stepped from the car, grabbed his suitcase, and walked into the terminal. When he checked his bag at the ticket counter, the attendant said, "We have an envelope addressed to you."

She handed him the envelope as well as his plane ticket. He opened the envelope to find a Western Union check for eight hundred dollars. John examined the check,

## Phil Cline

and turned to the clerk.

"I'd like to get breakfast before my flight. Do I have time?"

"Yes, Sir," replied the attendant. "Your flight will not leave for another forty-five minutes. There's a restaurant near your gate."

He proceeded to his gate and sat at a table in a nearby restaurant where businessmen and other travelers frequented. It had been a long time since he had flown. Being in an environment with businessmen seemed strange, but at the same time familiar.

"Would you like a menu, sir?" asked a waitress.

"Please," John replied. "Eggs, bacon, toast, and a cup of coffee." The waitress took his order, and later returned with a hot plate of food and a cup of coffee.

As he ate, he became excited about his pending trip to Chicago. The more he thought of getting his old job back, the more his pulse quickened. At last, he would have no more financial worries. After paying for breakfast, he went to the gate and sat in the lounge area. Soon, an announcement was made for his flight to Chicago.

After boarding, he took a seat in first-class next to a window. John watched as passengers filed past. A few stayed in first class, but most continued on to coach. John had spent many hours flying first class while traveling to meetings as a member of the executive staff. He took a deep breath and savored the moment. Being on a plane seemed strange but familiar. Life is full of surprises, he thought, from being

# SLOW TANGO IN TAOS

homeless to flying first class.

John found a magazine tucked in the pouch in front of him, and read about current events, something he hadn't bothered with recently. As he read the articles, he thought it strange that so much had happened in the world. A quick announcement from the pilot and the plane moved away from the terminal. The engines increased in pitch as the plane taxied along the apron and onto the runway in preparation for takeoff.

The plane's brakes squeaked as it momentarily stopped at the end of the field. Then it began moving again and turned onto the runway. The huge engines roared when they were given full throttle and the jet shot forward. John was drawn back into his seat by the thrust. Red and green lights at the edge of the runway flew past as it lifted off. A moment later, the landing gear retracted with a thud. The plane banked and climbed to cruising altitude.

Many thoughts raced through John's mind as white clouds drifted below. It seemed as though he was living in a fantasy. It had been a long time since he worked for Cyrox. He wondered what it would be like going back. So much had happened. From being a corporate executive, assured of success, to a member of the downtrodden. What a change!

He took a deep breath and tried not to think about the interview, but he could not suppress the memory of the last time he was in the Chairman's office. The memory of being told his services are no longer needed cleaved to his soul like a parasitic worm. Once he hated Stevens. Hated him with all his soul. Somehow, all the bitterness and resentment lay in the past. After all, Stevens had retired and was no longer at Cyrox.

He pushed the seat release on the side of his armrest and reclined. No matter how much he tried to keep from thinking about Maya, she remained in his thoughts.

Hours later, as the jet began its descent into O'Hare, the fasten seat belt sign came on. The voice of the pilot came over the public address system announcing the descent and saying the plane should be at the gate in fifteen minutes. The flaps on the wings extended downward, and the leading edges of the wings rolled out and downward as the plane approached the runway.

John watched the distant skyline of Chicago as the plane descended. Soon, the wheels touched down with a screech and a whiff of smoke. As the plane taxied along the runway apron the voice of a stewardess came over the PA system telling everyone to make sure they were taking everything with them, and hoped they enjoyed the flight.

Once at the gate, John waited on the plane until the majority of passengers had disembarked. Then, he walked from the plane. Inside the terminal, he passed many anxious faces of people awaiting the arrival of loved ones. Then, he saw a sign directing passengers to the baggage claim area.

After retrieving his luggage, he turned to see several well-dressed men holding placards with names of people. He found it difficult to tell who was there from Cyrox. No one came up to him, so he took a seat and waited.

## SLOW TANGO IN TAOS

Soon, he heard an announcement: *Will Mr. John Tollifson please go to the ticket counter of Continental Airways.* When he arrived, a tall well-dressed young man with long blonde fashionably-cut hair was waiting. When he saw John, he asked. "Are you Mister Tollifson?"

"Yes," John replied.

"Cliff here," the young man said extending his hand and displaying a quick smile. "Mr. Newhouse sent me to pick you up and take you to your hotel."

"Thank you for picking me up," John said. "By the way, could we stop at a storage unit? I have some things I'd like to pick up." John handed him a business card with the address.

"Sure, no problem," Cliff said, taking the card.

As they drove, a knot formed in John's stomach. His skin was warm and clammy. Memories flooded through his head, with thoughts of his former life with his wife and daughter, his job, his firing and all that had happened.

"Prepayment on the storage unit was all my ex-wife left me after our divorce," John offered, breaking the silence. "She put it on a credit card as long as I needed the unit. I suppose that was nice of her."

"I wouldn't know of such things, I'm not married," Cliff replied.

A light drizzle fell onto the car as they drove along Lake Michigan on Lake Shore Drive. The rhythmic cadence of the windshield wipers moving back and forth reminded him of rainy commutes he had made when he lived on

## Phil Cline

Chicago's North Shore. His thoughts flashed back to the Mercedes he used to drive, the smell of its new leather, and the sleekness of the styling. He thought of the interview he would have at CYROX, and whether he would be offered a job to regain the status he had lost. He would then have a large salary with perks so he could buy another Mercedes and return to his former life style. But, is that what he wanted? His head spun with conflicting thoughts ricocheting around in his head. John struggled to block them out, and enjoy the ride. He took a deep breath, and tried to enjoy being once more in Chicago.

He looked out the window past drops of rain running down the glass. Tall office buildings slipped past like sets in the back lot of a movie studio. Some were made entirely of glass, some metal with patinas of rust, others of older design made of concrete.

Outside, people were getting off of work, and scurrying along the sidewalks. Some had umbrellas, others were hurrying to get out of the rain. In a way, he missed being one of the workers, but in another…He shook his head to remove the thoughts and enjoy the ride.

They sped past several marinas with sail boats moored to floating docks. The boats looked majestic with their main masts extending high into the sky and shifting back and forth in the wind. A few boat owners in foul weather gear braved the weather while they coiled sheeting and tended to their vessels.

Soon the car turned onto narrow streets in an

industrial area somewhere along the wharf. Cliff pulled up to a row of buildings sectioned off into units and stopped in front of an office. John went inside and presented the manager with his ticket for the storage unit. The manager took his ticket, and looked in his files.

"Your name Wilma?" he asked.

"That's my ex-wife," John replied.

"Got an ID?"

John reached for his wallet and handed him his New Mexico driver's license. He examined it and handed it back. Then, he got up from behind his desk and headed for the door.

"I'll show you the unit."

They walked past a series of corrugated metal storage units, each with an overhead door and a padlock. The units seemed to be in good condition. They walked past row after row until the manager stopped in front of one.

"This is unit 344." he said. He removed the padlock, and raised the door. "This is your unit. Take your time, but lock up when you leave, and drop the key back at the office." He handed John the key and departed.

John stood in the door way looking at what was left of his former life. The unit had a slight musty smell, but seemed to have been protected from the rain. He looked around the room. A duffle bag of shoes, a set of golf clubs, a rack of clothing, a light brown leather suitcase with a few scuff marks, framed pictures of him and his family stuck in a cardboard box, and other objects from an earlier life. He opened a leather suitcase and examined the contents. Neatly packed inside were socks, underwear, shirts, two silk ties and a set of black shoes as well as other items. He closed the suitcase.

"Take this," John said, handing the suitcase to Cliff. He carried it to the car, and placed it inside the trunk. John took an expensive suit from the rack that was protected by a plastic cover. He carried it through the rain to the car, and placed it into the trunk. Then, he locked the unit, and got back into the car.

"Everyone has been talking about your coming back," Cliff said. "It's sure going to be swell having you back on board. We missed you."

"Really," John replied. "You weren't even there when I left. How could you miss me?"

"A figure of speech," Cliff replied. "By the way, sir...I know it's none of my business, but why did you leave?"

"You don't know?" John asked.

"No," Cliff replied. "I guess it's the same reason our CEO left. He wanted to become a farmer."

"Wow!" John thought to himself. He shook his head at the naivety of the young man.

Soon, Cliff pulled off East Pearson Street into a circular drive, past a sign with Ritz-Carlton embolden in large letters. A porter came out to meet them. He put the suitcase and other items on a dolly, and took them into the hotel.

## SLOW TANGO IN TAOS

"I'll be back tomorrow morning," Cliff said before driving off.

John picked up the keys from the front desk, and continued to the elevator with the Porter. Once inside his room, John handed the Porter some money who took the money, closed the door, and left.

John hung his suit on a silver rail in the closet, unzipped the cover, then ran his fingers over the fine worsted wool fabric of the dark navy striped suit. It brought back many memories. He tried on the suit jacket. It fit a little looser than he remembered. He looked at himself in a mirror on the bathroom door.

*Is that person really me? I look old and tired.*

He tossed the suitcase onto the bed. Inside was an assortment of clothes. He fingered the silk shirts, and sleek ties. Each touch, each smell, brought back an overwhelming flood of memories. His gaze fell on two small boxes. Inside were a set of gold cufflinks with diamonds in the center. He remembered the day he received them, a gift from the CYROX Corporation for his promotion to department head.

He took a shower, put on the custom-made suit, and examined himself in the mirror. The image of a successful executive reflected from the mirror. The latent pinstripes suggested confidence and command. The modest silk tie and expensive shoes completed the look of success.

John examined himself in the mirror for a long time, as memories of his former life rushed back. Then, he went downstairs to the restaurant. People he passed seemed to give him a subtle but undeniable look of acceptance.

"Good evening, sir," said the desk clerk as John passed. When he walked into the restaurant, he was met with accepting nods from the men and demure smiles from the ladies.

The Maître d'hôtel showed him to a table. "Your menu, sir," he said as he bowed and smiled with deference. In many ways, it seemed to John that he had never left this world. Not much had changed, not the people, not the place, not Chicago, but he had.

Memories of his days on the road and of his time in Taos flooded back. His persona was not that of a corporate executive, but of a hitch hiker on the road with little money and no place to stay. Suddenly, he was ill at ease in this luxurious setting. A streak of burning emotion, hot with embarrassment and uncertainty, shot through him. His face burned with the memories that manifested themselves as a wound in his psychic. Memories that would not let him forget.

After dinner, he returned to his room only to find his self-confidence had left him. He sat shaking uncontrollably on the bed. His hands trembled and beads of cold sweat ran down his forehead. He wished that Maya were with him, or Tina or George, or anyone who might help him through his crises. For a long time, he sat on the bed. Then, he undressed and got into bed. He didn't sleep well that night, but had a fitful night. The next morning, he awoke early, took a shower and dressed.

## SLOW TANGO IN TAOS

Promptly at nine o'clock, the telephone rang with a sound like a knocker banging against a large brass bell. John stared at the phone. After several rings, he picked it up.

"I'll be right down," John said.

The lobby was filled with people, some checking out, others sitting around talking, and others just watching people. John saw Cliff near the reception desk.

"Get a good night of sleep?" Cliff asked with a winning smile.

"Still a little tired," John replied.

"Well, sir," Cliff said. "You look like a different person. That suit must have cost you a lot."

"It did," John replied. "It cost me my life."

"What?"

"Never mind."

They drove down a busy Lake Shore Avenue. Soon the tall multistory Cyrox building came into view with its mirror-like windows. A knot formed in his stomach. He took a deep breath and exhaled, but it seemed so strange to be here again. So much had happened since...a lump formed in John's throat. Cliff pulled into a parking area reserved for executives.

The elevator doors opened on the lower floor, and they entered. John wasn't certain he wanted to see Newhouse. His heartbeat increased as he neared the executive suites. The elevator brought back angry memories of the day he was fired. He clinched his teeth at the thought. His face flushed. A soft bell sounded as the doors slid open, revealing the corporate boardroom. A deep rich burgundy rug lay on the floor with well-crafted maroon colored leather chairs arranged alongside a beautiful rosewood conference table that seemed to extend forever. At the far end of the room was an expensive teak bar. Original Dalis and a Monet hung from the walls, and a crystal chandelier glistened from the ceiling.

"Tollifson! John Tollifson!" shouted a rotund balding man in a dark suit who ambled toward him. "Good to see you again. You look great!"

"Bret Williams. Are you still in finance?" John asked.

"Yep, Still V.P of Finance," he said. "Let me fix you a drink, what would you like?"

"Ah," John replied. "I don't drink hard liquor anymore. Occasionally a beer."

"Well, we certainly have beer, but isn't that déclassé?"

"Déclassé? Yes, I suppose it is," John replied as his thoughts rushed back to his being alone on the road to Taos not so long ago.

"Come on, let me get you something to drink."

"Really, I don't want anything."

*Gotta keep my wits. Don't need alcohol to dull my thinking.*

"Then, I'll fix you some fizz water. Something to hold in your hand. Makes you look more sociable."

"Okay, a club soda with a twist of lime."

"Coming right up." He fixed the drink and handed it

## SLOW TANGO IN TAOS

to John. "Newhouse is really looking forward to seeing you. Said you're the best manager he ever knew. He said, "if there is a job to get done, John Tollifson is the guy."

"I'm glad he holds me in such high esteem."

"He should be here soon." Williams took John by the sleeve and led him aside. "Let me tell you something, John, this corporation is really starting to swing. For a while there it was touch and go. Some of us didn't think we'd make it. The Board discovered that cutting your division was a big mistake. They only did it after painful deliberation."

"Painful?" John gritted his teeth. *How painful was that decision?*

Doors on the elevator opened and other officers drifted into the room. Two of them saw John and walked over to him. "Tollifson! You're looking swell." They said shaking his hand.

"Where's that damn bartender!" Williams shouted. A young man rushed toward them.

"Sorry I'm late, sir. Got held up downstairs."

Soon other executives joined the group and slowly made their way toward John to make small talk as John mingled among them

Suddenly, lights in the room flashed. Everyone turned toward the gold inlaid elevator door trimmed with silver. As it slid open, a tall slender athletic middle-aged man with a warm smile stepped out. When he saw John, he moved toward him.

"Great to see you again, John." Marc Newhouse, the

## Phil Cline

Chairman, extended his hand. "Been too long. I told you I'd let you know if we had an opening."

"Thanks, Marc. I'm glad you did," John said as a knot twisted in his stomach.

Newhouse turned to the group. "If you haven't met John Tollifson, I want each of you to get acquainted with him." Warmth beat its way across John's cheeks. He was uncomfortable being the center of attention.

Most of the people in the room he knew from his previous life, but after socializing with them, he realized they were doing the same jobs, attending the same clubs, going to the same social affairs. Saying the same vapid things.

After more than an hour of socializing, almost as on que, Newhouse clinked his diamond ring against a glass. Everyone stopped talking and left the room. Newhouse indicated toward a large glass-lined office. John followed him. The room contained an assortment of art works. A bronze sculpture of a thinking man sitting on a pedestal by Rodin, and oil paintings by Monet and Pissarro.

"I hope you enjoyed our reception. Please sit."

"Brings back memories," John said. "

"Yes. To start out, I'd like to apologize on behalf of our former board for cutting your job. I never thought it was necessary. I understand we put you through a lot of grief."

John found the words difficult to say. "You'll never know..." His eyes locked on Newhouse. "I can't tell you how...it's hard to understand..." John stopped talking. He felt warm, and his face flushed.

## SLOW TANGO IN TAOS

Newhouse leaned forward in his chair. "You're a rare man. I know I can count on you. I thought it might be good if the fellows spoke with you for a while. That way I could get some feedback. It have been a while since you worked here. But after talking to a few of them, they all gave you a thumbs-up."

John shot Newhouse a penetrating stare. "The reception was a screening device?"

"I wouldn't call it that. Just a friendly get together. It's important that we work as a team. Tell me what you did after leaving us."

A little later, after John relayed the story, his throat was dry, and his muscles were weak. He cleared his throat.

"Here," Newhouse said. He poured water from a crystal pitcher into a glass, and handed it to John.

"That's an interesting story. I'm sorry about your wife and daughter. Divorces can be messy."

"That's all in the past." John took a drink to sooth his irritated throat.

"Frankly, John, something worries me."

"What?"

"I'm wondering if you will be able to come back and work after having had an extended vacation."

John folded his arms. His eyes narrowed. "Vacation?" John asked.

"I've had people take off from work like that," he snapped his fingers. "When they finally come back, they're never the same."

"If that was bothering you, why did you arrange this meeting?"

Newhouse leaned forward. "I'm still impressed with that line you created for us. Hell, I've never seen anyone work with such single-mindedness. We need more people like you on our team."

He stopped and looked directly into John's eyes. "We made a command decision to bring back your old division. You realize," Newhouse continued, "that we would expect you to move into a respectable neighborhood, and join some reputable clubs. We'll pick up the costs. It's good for the company's image."

"I realize that," John replied.

"And we'd expect you to get married, and become an important member of the community."

John nodded.

Stevens paused. "I want to offer you the position of Vice President of our Electronics division. I think you're the person we're looking for. You'll be a strong asset."

John shifted in his chair. He locked eyes with Newhouse.

"You don't have to accept right now," Newhouse said. "Why don't you go back to the hotel, relax, and think about it. Think about what your returning to the corporation would mean to Cyrox…and to you. We'll start you out double what you were making before. It's a good offer with great promotion potential and lots of benefits. Get some rest and think about it. You can stay in Chicago a while, can't

## SLOW TANGO IN TAOS

you?"

"I suppose," John replied.

"Good! Good! I'll send you back to the hotel in our staff car. Been nice talking with you, John. Think it over."

Newhouse indicated to Cliff who was waiting outside the room. "Cliff will take you back to the hotel. Call me early tomorrow morning, and let me know your decision."

Later that day, John stood at the hotel entrance watching the black Mercedes drive away and disappear down the circular drive. He walked into the hotel bar and ordered a gin tonic. The bar smelled of cigarette smoke and alcohol. Casual conversations and the clinking of glasses filled the room along with soft Mozart background music. He nursed his drink while a myriad of thoughts ran through his head. Should he accept or not. He was deep in thought about his life and the course it had taken when the bartender asked, "Like another?"

"Yeah," John replied.

"Coming right up." The bartender refilled his glass and set it back on the counter. "You seemed to have been lost in thought. Problem?"

"Debating taking a new job. Actually, it's the job I had before I was fired."

"What are you doing now?"

"I'm living out in Taos, New Mexico. Trying to be an artist."

"Never been there. Heard it's nice."

"Don't know if I want to leave Taos and come back

## Phil Cline

to Chicago."

The bartender grabbed a cloth and started drying a glass. "I've known a few big shots who used to come in here." he said as he wiped the top of the bar. "They worked themselves to death. Never understood why they did it. Can't take it with you when you die." The barkeeper picked up an empty glass and pushed it against a brush on a basin below the bar, rinsed it, and studied John while he dried it with a cloth.

"No, you can't," John replied.

"Many a time I wish I could walk out from behind this bar, go out through those pretty glass doors at the entrance, and keep on going. That's a dream I've had. But, I've got a wife and kids to support. That's why I'm stuck here. You married?"

"Not anymore," John nursed his drink. "Funny. At one time I thought there wasn't anything more important than getting to the top. Now, I'm wondering if that might not be the least important thing in my life."

"Never aspired to such things myself," the bartender said. "Course, I'm only good at tending bar. Tell you, I've seen executives come and go. I don't think it makes a bit of difference to those companies whether a fellow makes it to the top or not because the worker is just another piece of commodity."

"Commodity, huh?"

"Yep. As an example, there was a fellow who used to come in here every Friday after work. Executive vice

## SLOW TANGO IN TAOS

president, I think he was. One day his company let him go. That day, he came in here, ordered a Jack Daniels, downed his drink and left. See that building over there," he said pointing to an adjacent building visible through the plate glass at the front of the hotel.

"He went up to the fifteenth floor and didn't bother taking the elevator back down. Few seconds later he was back on the ground. Didn't walk away. Never understood why people put so much importance on their jobs. Their jobs don't belong to them, it belongs to the organization. People don't seem to realize that they're only filling a slot, and they can be replaced."

John thought a moment. "If you had a choice of becoming head of a large company, or becoming a moderately successful artist, which would you choose?"

"Well," the bartender said scratching his head, "for me, that's a little like having the choice of being burned at the stake or sitting out on the lake fishing all day. I know the choice I'd make…" he hesitated. "But, I'm not you."

"No, you're not me." John finished his drink and set it on the counter. "Thanks, you've helped me more than you realize." He paid his bill, left the bartender a generous tip, and returned to his room.

That night, he did a lot of thinking. A myriad of thoughts ran through his head. At one moment, he wanted to accept the job, and the next he wanted to return to Taos. He rubbed the back of his neck to counter the painful muscles in his neck.

## Phil Cline

He thought about having a regular job and a steady income. That was enticing. But then he remembered the depression he went through after being fired. Those painful memories were as welcome as a bucket of ice-cold water. His head hurt, and he was weak from emotional exhaustion. At last, he undressed and went to bed. Sleep that night was fitful.

The next morning, he hesitated before picking up the telephone. His thoughts were spinning. Was he about to make a bad decision? He picked up the telephone. Should he accept the job, or should he give up the status and money for a life in Taos? He bit his lower lip, and wrinkled his nose. What to do? He set the receiver back on the base, and took a deep breath. Thoughts raced through his mind like a tempest at sea. Conflicting thoughts bounced around in his head. Then, he thought of Maya and of his life with her. What was worth more, money or love? He took another deep breath, and picked up the phone. When his finger was about to dial the last number, he hesitated. His thoughts were again a bundle of confusion. Money or love, money or love, he thought. He took another deep breath, then completed the call.

The phone rang twice before a voice at the other end answered.

"Cyrox, Board of Directors."

"John Tollifson calling for Marc Newhouse,"

There was a slight pause, then the voice of Newhouse came on the line.

## SLOW TANGO IN TAOS

"Good to hear from you, John. You've decided to come on board, I hope."

"Marc, listen, I really appreciate everything you did for me…"

"That sounds ominous."

"Marc, I can't accept your offer. I'm heading back to Taos."

"Are you sure?"

"Positive."

"Give it some deep thought before turning me down."

"I have."

"Well, if that's your final decision."

"It is. Thanks, again for thinking of me." John replaced the receiver on the base, and took a deep breath. Then, he dialed the airline, and booked a flight back to Santa Fe.

On the return flight, John's thoughts were still conflicted. Had he made the right decision? After a brief stop in Saint Louis, the plane continued its flight. As the plane flew over New Mexico, he looked down at the high desert. He watched the land slowly pass below, as a thought occurred to him that he belongs with this land. Then, calm descended over him, and he relaxed. It was at that moment he realized how much he had changed. He was no longer an upwardly mobile young executive striving for more and more material possessions. Instead, he found something much more valuable. He had discovered the essence of life itself -- he had discovered himself.

After the plane landed, he gathered his bags and returned to the Jeep. That evening when he stepped onto the porch of their ranch house, he paused at the door and took a deep breath of fresh mountain air. As he looked at the hills surrounding the ranch, he felt thrilled. He had a wonderful sense of belonging. After entering the house, he was greeted by the crackling of piña logs burning in the fireplace, and the aroma of beef stew wafting from the kitchen. At that moment, he knew that there was no place in the entire world that he would rather be than right there. A broad smile crossed his face, and a magnificent warmth descended over him. He was home.

"Maya," he called out. "Are you back?"

"John, is that you?" Maya emerged from her studio holding a paintbrush. When she saw John, she dropped the paintbrush, and rushed to him.

"I've missed you so much," Maya said with tears in her eyes as she hugged him.

He gave her a hug and a long warm kiss.

"I'm so glad you're back," she said. "You'll never know how much I missed you."

"I missed you too…I love you." He paused. "I didn't accept the job."

"But…what about your corporate career?"

"That's not important anymore. There's only one career I'm interested in and that's being right here with you."

"Oh John, I love you so much. The Taos Art

## SLOW TANGO IN TAOS

Community will become famous with the two of us working together," she said, her eyes sparkling. "Our love will produce magic in the world of art."

The End

**Author's note:** If you enjoyed reading this book, please go to *Amazon.com/books* and leave a review.
Thank You

# Phil Cline

Made in the USA
Monee, IL
15 March 2022